"THE PROPHET WANTS TO SEE YOU."

Candy felt her heart stutter. Her pulse raced and her insides knotted with apprehension at the prospect of standing in the presence of divinity.

"I hope you understand the extent of the honor bestowed upon you," Sister Penelope said critically. "You are a sinner and not worthy, but you may benefit from his presence."

Candy followed her down the hall, where Sister Penelope rapped on the massive double doors.

"Come in," a deep masculine voice called, muffled by the heavy wood. Candy felt her knees buckle.

"You heard the Prophet," Sister Penelope chided. "Go on in. And try not to disgrace yourself."

Russell W. Martin is also the author of **Rhea:** "The reader hesitates to lay it down... it's enough to chill your spine."
—The Times and Democrat

THE
RESURRECTION
OF
CANDY
STERLING

RUSSELL W. MARTIN

PLAYBOY
PAPERBACKS

CHAPTER 1

A dead gull lay in the surf the night of Candy Sterling's resurrection. She had come to the beach because she wanted to be alone to suck on her melancholy like a sick tooth, and the resolutely monotonous lapping of the waves against the sand seemed appropriate to her mood and to the point life had led her to. And there was the possibility that she would go for a swim, as far as her stamina would take her.

When she had first noticed the gull she thought it was part of an old newspaper that someone had scattered near the surf, but after sitting for a moment she had seen it for what it was. By then some creatures had lurched out of the darkness and begun to feed on the gull, tearing out feathers and nipping off bits of flesh. Candy couldn't see well enough to know whether they were crabs, but she supposed they must be. She thought they were fighting at first, but two of them had merely collided in their enthusiasm over the meal that God had provided. Candy tucked her skirt under her legs, making it a tight tube, to insulate her skin from the snappish breeze that had begun to whip up from the Pacific Ocean. She stared at the savage, quiet spectacle before her, watching the living creatures efficiently strip the dead one. There was little left of the gull by the time she became aware of someone standing beside her, towering above her seated figure. She looked up quickly, apprehensive because she was alone and in an awkward position with her skirt wound so tightly about her thighs.

He was a young man, probably not much older than she, tall and slender with slim, muscular-looking legs that were sprinkled with sparse blond hair. He wore fancy glasses, something like motorcycle patrolman glasses but not dark, and he was to her left. With a surreptitious gesture Candy scooped up a portion of sand in her right hand and looked up at him with a blank, uninviting expression.

"Hi," he said in a light, rather thin voice, and hitched up his plaid Bermuda shorts, smiling in a manner obviously meant to be seductive.

"Fuck off, turkey."

She couldn't remember when she had used such language last, and she fancied that she could taste it rolling across her tongue like wine. The young man stood looking down at her for an instant, apparently stunned by the violence of her outburst. Then he turned and moved down the beach, walking as fast as he could in the deep sand.

Candy allowed the grains to seep from her hand as the savage elation seeped out of her body. Dimly, she heard a feather snap as one of the crabs continued a desultory search for more that was edible. The other less enterprising or less optimistic beasts had moved off in search of new booty. Candy felt something flapping against her clothed thigh and glanced down to see that a page of the newspaper had been blown against her by the persistent sea breeze. She reached down, plucked the paper free, and tossed it away, but the breeze returned it without hesitation. Grasping it, she balled it between her hands and tossed it the other way, but with seemingly deliberate perversity the wind shifted, tossing it back at her. It was then, as she compressed it again between her hands, that Candy noticed the small heading: RESURREC-TION NOW!

The page was from the classified section, the heading a part of the column devoted to "Announcements." Without quite knowing why, Candy smoothed the page and looked more closely at the ad.

RESURRECTION NOW!

For those willing to dedicate themselves totally to the All-Moving Spirit through His eternal and recurring Prophet, the rewards are instantaneous and eternal. Don't wait for spiritual fulfillment after death. It is within your reach at this moment.

There was a telephone number as well as a post office box, both within the Los Angeles area. Candy sat staring at the short advertisement, unsure of what she would do, unsure of the cause for her suddenly heightened emotions, the pounding of her heart and pulse, the tingling of her skin. She had felt like this before, but not for what seemed like ages. With infinite care she tore out the ad and thrust it into the single pocket of her dress. Then, with some difficulty, she pushed herself to her feet, unfurling her long skirt like a banner, feeling it whip and snap against her legs. She walked off, limping slightly at first, toward the row of pay telephones by the sidewalk. The tide had turned, carrying off the feathers and scaled feet of the destroyed gull.

CHAPTER 2

It had been someone's house at one time, a simple white frame edifice, possibly two or three bedrooms, maybe a bath and a half. It had run down in ways that would have been uneconomical to repair, but it was clean, and the lawn in front of it, though sparse, was weed-free and close-cropped. The neighborhood was old and dog-eared, and the offices of the Church of the Prophet of the All-Moving Spirit looked slightly out of place for its neatness as well as for the sign that announced its identity. It was a new sign, and almost professionally cut and lettered and hung. Candy felt her legs tremble slightly, as though her body divined some solemn and awesome turning point in her life, as she walked under the sign and through the open door.

The interior was much like the facade of the house: run-down but clean. Throw rugs had been scattered about the carpet, possibly to conceal bald spots. They looked like the kind of rug one could buy at Thrifty's or Sav-On. She was in what had once been the living room, now furnished with several folding chairs and a scarred desk with a swivel chair and some filing cabinets behind it. A young man, possibly in his early twenties, dressed in cheap wash slacks and a permanent-press pullover shirt, was standing at one of the filing cabinets, his back to Candy. He was filing papers in folders, expending considerable concentration on the task, while a vaguely pretty young woman made notations in similar folders heaped before her on the desk.

As Candy entered, diffident and unsure why it had seemed such a compelling idea to come to this place, the girl looked up. "May I help you?" she asked in a voice that was surprisingly throaty and mature sounding for one so young and slim.

"Well, my name is Candace Sterling," Candy said, embarrassed at the strident nervousness in her own voice.

The girl looked mildly perplexed for a moment, as though trying to call up a reference. Then she broke into a lovely smile. "Of course! You called last night, didn't you? Only you gave your name as Candy."

"That's a nickname, but it's what everyone calls me," Candy explained. The girl's radiant smile had called Candy's attention to her features, and she realized that this young woman was exceptionally beautiful. The impression of vague, bland prettiness had stemmed from the fact that her beauty was subtle and refined, not at all flashy, and also that she did nothing to enhance it. Her face was innocent of makeup, and her soft brown hair was pulled back into a tight bun. The cheap, baggy gray dress she wore did all that could be done to conceal a slender but curvaceous body. She stood like a professional model.

"Well, I'm Sister Claudia," she said, reaching across the desk, "and this is Brother Clifford."

Candy switched the piece of paper she had been carrying, which bore the address of the place, to her left hand and accepted Sister Claudia's hand.

Brother Clifford looked up from his filing, twisting his head about and giving Candy a friendly smile. "Hi," he said.

"Hi." He dived back into his filing. He was a good-looking young man, but now that she had had a better look Candy noticed that his slacks had been mended, and the pullover shirt was faded with age and repeated washings. Still, the place, and these people's clothing, were impeccably clean.

"Come on back to the parlor," Sister Claudia said, gliding off with that special, educated grace. Candy felt a bit reluctant, but there seemed no alternative, unless she chose to walk out of the place. She had been given this kind of glad-hand treatment before, and it had come to nothing. Nothing but betrayal and heartache.

The parlor was smaller than the room she had just left, and connected to it by a hallway that extended back to the rear of the building. It was as tidy as the front room but darker, illuminated only by the light coming through a small window. She had the feeling that it had once been a bedroom. Bookshelves lined the walls, stuffed with paperbacks and pamphlets, and a few hardcover volumes of considerable age. Some old pole lamps stood beside dilapidated easy chairs and a couch, but none of them was lit, and Sister Claudia didn't touch them. Instead she offered Candy a seat on the couch and descended gracefully into a chair that faced it at an angle.

"Now, Candy," she said, "I assume that you are dissatisfied with your life, or you wouldn't be here." Her tone and delivery suggested a memorized recital, as though she had gone through some sort of salesmanship course and committed the sales pitch to memory. "Of course you are not obliged to tell me anything about your past life at this time, but if you should decide to join us, as I hope you will, then it will be necessary for you to file a life résumé. We all had to do it, and of course it must be honest and complete. Don't let that scare you off," she adjured with a professionally reassuring smile. "After all, everyone of us is corrupt except the Prophet, and only he is suited to judge you."

"The newspaper ad said something about resurrection now," Candy said a bit diffidently, unsure of whether she was permitted to ask questions or offer comments.

Sister Claudia smiled to put her at ease. "When we say 'now,' we mean in this life, Candy. Not this instant. We're not selling some patent medicine here, but offering you a new way of life. Actually, your resurrection can begin right now, as soon as you make a commitment to the Prophet of the All-Moving Spirit. How long it will take for you to achieve complete resurrection is determined by many variables, such as your own application to the work of the church, your sincerity of purpose, and the degree of your blood's corruption."

"My blood?" The phrase seemed kooky yet oddly intriguing to Candy.

"Look," Sister Claudia offered, "I'm going to give you some of these pamphlets. They will explain the peripheral mysteries of the All-Moving Spirit better than I can. After you've read them you may join us in our holy work or not. Or you may leave and return when you've thought things over. Fair enough?"

"Of course," Candy said.

Sister Claudia rose and walked to a corner of the room, plucking pamphlets off of stacks. She handed a dozen of them to Candy. "Come on out when you've finished," she said. "I really have to get back to work."

"Thank you," Candy called after the girl as she glided through the doorway. Sister Claudia turned at the waist to toss her a little wave as she vanished down the hall.

Candy's reading skill had never been highly developed, though it had improved during the previous few months during all those Bible meetings she had attended. She opened the first of the pamphlets and began working her way through it.

There were elements of Christianity in the message propounded by the pamphlets, but the differences were far more striking. All human beings were born with corrupt spirits, according to the literature Sister Claudia had given her. This corruption was constantly fed into the spirit by the world and its imperfections and temptations, through the medium of the blood. As the blood grew progressively more corrupt, the likelihood of reversing the process diminished to the vanishing point. Only help from the All-Moving Spirit through its messenger on earth, the Prophet, could resurrect the spirit of a corrupt person. The time it took to purify the blood, and thence the soul, and the nature of the Prophet's methods, depended on the degree to which the corruption had been carried out, which in turn depended on the penitent's age and the degree to which he or she had been steeped in the pollution of sin.

There was more, but some of it was rather arcane, beyond Candy's education. It sounded very deep, though, and impressively logical to the extent that she could make it out. She recognized touches of Eastern philosophy mingled with Christian doctrine, but there were other ideas that seemed foreign to both of them, such as the concept that the coming of the Messiah was not a single event but rather an ongoing state which had begun soon after man's fall from grace. The Messiah was really a physical manifestation of the All-Moving Spirit, the lord and master of the church and the mentor and monarch of all who served.

Candy put down the pamphlets and stared straight ahead for a moment. She had developed a touch of eyestrain from reading in the dimness. Since Sister Claudia hadn't turned on the lights, she had supposed it was forbidden for some reason, so she had moved to a place near the window to make the most of the sunlight that filtered through the hedge growing outside. Her fingertips caressed the topmost pamphlet as it lay on the arm of the couch. She couldn't explain the excitement she felt, but neither could she deny it. For some perverse reason the knowledge that her blood was rife with corruption exhilarated her. One of the pamphlets spoke of the All-Moving Spirit's inspiration, which sometimes took the form of inner serenity and at other times of mild or intense physical excitement.

So this was it. The Spirit had directed her here to this ramshackle house where something had been permitted to happen: something routine to the Spirit, doubtless common-place to the people who worked here, but miraculous to Candy. Lowering her head, Candy wept softly, in gratitude and relief.

CHAPTER 3

While Candy Sterling was undergoing her transfiguration, other forces were being set in motion which would have a potent effect on her life, though at present she was as unaware of them as is the waterborne insect of the pebble whose ripples will drive it into the waiting maw of a fish.

To the north of that scrubby little house in Los Angeles, in a farm county, a young black girl named Victoria McGivern was informed via the chief handmaiden of the Prophet's dwelling that she would no longer be required as handmaiden to the Prophet. She must leave the house in the shortest time possible to take up a dwelling with a husband who would be provided out of the wisdom of the Prophet. Candy Sterling would never meet Vickie McGivern, and would only see her from a distance, across a dusty field, yet it was Victoria's ouster from the Prophet's holy presence that would shortly make room for Candy.

Vickie McGivern was twenty-two years old, the eldest of the Prophet's handmaidens at the moment, with the exception of Sister Penelope, the chief handmaiden, who seemed immune to banishment. Vickie had been in the house for four months and eighteen days, which was a long stay, and during that period the Prophet had seen fit to purify her blood twenty-six times. That experience had been overwhelming to her, its very power attesting to the depth of her need and her wickedness. She knew that only those who had been most effectively steeped in the corruption of the world were brought here to enjoy the direct ministrations of the Prophet, and that the fact that she was being sent out to do his work meant that

15

she had been brought far in a short time, and was ready to yield her place in his direct service to one more in need.

Still, she felt depressed as she went into the servants' quarters for the last time and took off her silk dress. The depression was a complex of emotions that she couldn't untangle, much less interpret. She was disappointed that she would no longer enjoy the direct presence of the Almighty, would not be able to see him, to hear his voice, occasionally to feel his touch. That depressed her, and the knowledge that she was human enough, sinful enough to feel that disappointment, rather than to go forth joyfully to do the Prophet's bidding, depressed her all the more. She had never known, before joining the church, just what a wicked, willful person she was, and now it was becoming more and more apparent to her with each passing day, with each moment.

Vickie hung up her silk dress next to the cot she had occupied these past months, then efficiently stripped the cot and bundled the dress inside the sheets and blankets, as she had been instructed to do when this moment arrived; as she had done twice a week during her stay in the Prophet's abode; as she had seen other girls doing on the day of their expulsion into outside duty. She noticed that she was still wearing the high-heeled pumps which were a part of the servant girls' uniform, so she sat and took them off. They felt light and slender and elegant in her hands, and she put them down quickly before she could think about what all that meant to her.

Someone had placed a crude, serviceable dress on one of the hooks at the head of her cot. Under the dress was a pair of heavy black shoes with thick cotton socks thrust into one of them. Vickie put on the dress. It was made of a synthetic fabric, cheap and strong and, in the heat of the Los Angeles basin, uncomfortable. It was difficult to tell whether the dress was her size or not, so baggy and shapeless was it. That, of course, was good. Outside the dwelling, without the direct protection of the Prophet's aura, it could be disastrous to her soul and those of others to wear clothes that displayed her body, which was dismally alluring. The dress hung nearly to her ankles.

Vickie sat on the edge of the cot once again and put on the socks and then the shoes. She was on her way to deliver her servants' clothing to the laundry when she realized what her wicked nature had nearly led her to do. Only the Prophet's mercy, she was certain, had prevented it. She walked into the servants' bathroom, which was empty at this time of day, and, with a discarded towel plucked from a bin, wiped away the makeup she had applied that morning. When her face was scrubbed clean, displaying an innocence that belied the true, seething evil she knew was inside her, she retrieved the bundle of clothing and bedclothes and walked to the laundry.

Sister Annette was in charge of that duty for the week. She was stuffing dirty linen into a boiling cauldron and stirring them with a heavy stick. Annette was a Chicano girl who had come here after the first quarter of her junior year in high school. She had straight black hair that hung to her waist, and sparkling eyes. The silk dress revealed slender ankles and rounded calves. She was too preoccupied with her chores to notice, at first, that she was not alone. When she did look up, it was with a start. The snappishly black eyes rested on Vickie for a moment before they seemed to focus. Then Vickie saw a touch of fear in them, and knew with iniquitous but unavoidable satisfaction that Annette, who had been in this house longer than any girl except Vickie and Sister Penelope, was thinking with panic that it would soon be her turn to don a baggy dress and quit the direct protection of the Prophet, to take up her place outside, where she would enjoy only the more tenuous connection with him that was the inheritance of all his followers.

"It looks like I've graduated," Vickie said, trying to smile. She handed her bundle to the younger girl.

"Congratulations," Annette said with that faint trace of an accent that was so charming. She seemed to be regaining her composure, possibly taking refuge in a belief that she would not be the next to go. The Prophet didn't always send girls out in the same order in which they had entered the house. Vickie's tenure had bracketed that of two other girls, and Annette herself had lasted long enough to see one newer girl sent away. "May the All-Moving Spirit protect you and look over you."

"I only hope He protects me from my own sinfulness," Vickie said.

"Keep the faith with Him and He will," Annette assured her. "Are you going out of the dwelling wearing jewels?"

For a moment Vickie didn't know what the girl meant. Then she realized that she had neglected to remove the earbobs she had worn at the command of the Prophet. Tears flooded her wide, clear eyes, and she lowered her head, covering her face with her hands. "Oh, God," she wailed. "I'm so evil! I'm hopeless."

Annette laid a rubber-gloved hand on her shoulder, and finally Vickie looked up into the gentle smile of the Chicano girl. "Evil, of course," Annette agreed. "We all are. But how can you be hopeless when the Prophet has taken you under his care?"

With a grateful smile Vickie removed the earbobs from her lobes and handed them to Annette. "Would you return these for me?" she asked, wiping her eyes with a quick swipe, and smiling with embarrassment. "I'm already late getting to my new job."

"Of course," Annette promised. There were no pockets on the dresses, so she held the earbobs tightly in her hand.

Vickie turned and, without a backward glance, left the laundry and the house.

The sun was hot and the air humid, and the moment she left the air-conditioned house Vickie felt perspiration begin to trickle down her body inside the close weave of her dress. The heavy, practical shoes felt foreign and clumsy, as though she had forgotten how to walk and had to learn again. She walked out into the field, a quarter mile from the dwelling, and approached a man in his thirties, who was dressed in old blue jeans and a T-shirt, and who held a clipboard which indicated that he was an overseer. He turned when she was still five yards from him, and his look of impatience prompted Vickie to quicken her pace.

"Sister"—he checked a scrap attached to his clipboard —"Victoria?"

"Yes, Brother," she replied.

"I expected you sooner. We must all move smartly for the glory of the Prophet, eh?"

"Yes, Brother," Vickie repeated contritely, looking at the worn toes of his boots.

"All right. Have you ever picked cabbages before?"

Vickie shook her head mutely, overcome by an inexplicable urge to weep.

"Not much to it. Take one of those burlap sacks and move down a row. Just stay bent at the waist, picking up the cabbages and stuffing them into the bag until it's full. Then trot back for another sack and deposit the full one on that truck there," he said, pointing to a flatbed one-and-a-half-ton Ford. "It may be difficult at first, even painful. But remember, Sister, it's for the Prophet."

"I'll remember, Brother," Vickie said fervently, promising herself more than him.

"Then get at it." She was scarcely two steps away when he called to her. She turned to see him consulting that scrap of paper once again. "By the grace of the Prophet you are wife to Brother Todd. House nineteen."

The grace of the Prophet possessed long tentacles. While Sister Victoria was bending to pick her first cabbage that afternoon, it was early evening in Milbank, South Dakota. Joseph Chambers was tossing some old business records, one by one, into the fireplace, first examining each piece to ascertain that it was of no value. Receipts and canceled checks followed one another into the flames. In the midst of it he discovered a sheaf of U.S. savings bonds, which he extracted from their envelopes and examined. They came to something over six hundred dollars in face value, and contained the names of his wife, Polly, and their eldest daughter, Mary. Joseph called Polly, who entered the parlor in her cotton nightgown and robe, smiling in a vague, desperate fashion.

"You had best sign these," Joseph said in a voice that managed to remain soft and solicitous while brooking no nonsense, "so that we can send them with the other papers."

He returned to his duties, throwing a thick sheaf of advertising brochures into the fire, and then his farm almanac. His wife took the bonds to the desk and seated herself, then picked up the worn plastic pen from its holder, poising it hesitantly over the topmost bond. From the corner of his eye Joseph watched her, pretending not to notice as she looked up at him.

She lowered the pen, then hesitated once again as its tip came into contact with the pasteboard. "Joseph, are you certain—?"

"It's too late to entertain doubts, Polly," he said, striving to keep his voice gentle. He didn't want to quarrel, or to assert himself too strongly, in this, their last night in the house in which his father and grandfather and all his uncles and siblings had been born.

"But— We don't have to send it, do we?"

Joseph stopped and looked at her, astonished at her callous utterance. She recoiled a bit from his gaze.

"What are we to do with it, then?" he inquired. "Keep it for ourselves? Use it to buy luxuries, or a godless education for our children?"

"Well, no, I—"

"Perhaps to purchase another farm?" he asked. "If we wished to continue farming for our own gain, then why didn't we keep this farm, which has been in the family for four generations?"

"Joseph, I didn't mean anything—"

"I know," he said, smiling to soften her guilt. "But you heard the evangelists yourself. You stood right there and listened to Sister Sarah and Brother Morgan. In fact, God—the All-Moving Spirit—inspired you with this idea before me. It was through you that He made His will clear to me. And now you question that will?"

"I'm not questioning His will," Polly explained, setting down the pen. "Are you sure it's His will you're listenin' to, though?"

"He's been speakin' to me clear!" Joseph snapped. He put down the papers he had been checking through and rose, walking to the door. "Don't make things hard for me," he admonished, and walked out of the room. He found his way outside, looking about in the lingering twilight. He wished he could smoke his pipe, but he had given that up when he had decided that God—that the All-Moving Spirit—wanted him and his family to join the church. Tobacco and liquor were forbidden to the faithful, Sister Sarah and Brother Morgan had informed him.

He walked to the field and looked at the sprouting corn. It

would be a good crop this year, and the man who had bought the farm would do well.

Joseph wondered, as he had wondered a multitude of times, why the farm had never meant anything to him. It had been the stuff of life to his father and his father's father. As a youth Joseph had envied his father's love of the soil, had felt an obscure, nagging guilt at not sharing it, as though he had inherited the curse of Cain. Yet farming was all he knew, all he had been privileged to learn. Though it had always been meaningless to him, he had pursued the vocation steadily, ploddingly, and he was a good farmer.

Once he had thought of volunteering for the Peace Corps. Farming skills were in demand, he had been informed. But he could never justify it in his own mind. He had a family to raise, a wife to support. But he had always felt the need of something to lend meaning and significance to the tilling of soil.

Polly had always been a good wife and a commendable mother. At forty-three she was still a pretty woman, a woman who attracted the gaze of most mature men, and who could even gather the attention of some of the younger ones with her figure. She had always worked hard, and had been a faithful mate. But now, when they were on the verge of a great adventure, she had turned into an obstacle. It was all the more galling because the whole notion had been hers in the beginning. Idly, Joseph reached for his pipe, realized he had thrown it away. Turning, he plodded back to the house.

Polly was no longer in the parlor. Joseph found the bonds lying atop the cashier's check for the sale of the farm, all neatly signed and stacked. Joseph picked up the stack and leafed through it. Everything was there: the check Bob Davis had given him for the car, the check the finance company had given him for his equity in the tractor and the pickup, which he had just sold the previous day. And on the bottom was the postal money order he had bought with the remaining cash in the house, including that in the kids' savings banks. In the morning they would find their way into town, withdraw the savings and checking accounts, and convert that money also into a money order. All of it would go into the envelope which was already stamped and addressed to the church.

And then, with nothing in their pockets, they would begin

their trek, walking, hitching rides, working their way across the country to California and their new calling, their new service.

Only a short time past such an idea would have seemed outlandish to Joseph Chambers, outlandish and frightening. But now he knew for certain that, as Sister Sarah and Brother Morgan had told him and Polly, the All-Moving Spirit would lead and guide them just as He had led the Hebrews out of Egypt. Those who truly placed their faith in the All-Moving Spirit needed no money, no cars, no bus or plane tickets. The way to their destination would be provided.

CHAPTER 4

Candy found a job at a taco stand in downtown Los Angeles. The pay was small, but it was the best she could do for the time being. She had had to lie about her age, presenting the fake ID she had carried about with her since before meeting Vernon. She had been tempted to lie about her age on the questionnaire she had filled out for Sister Claudia, too, but she had remembered Sister Claudia's admonition against holding anything back from the Prophet. Nothing had been said about it, and she would turn eighteen in eight months anyway, so it couldn't matter all that much.

After work at the taco stand she would spend some time hunting for another job, either a better one for daytime or a night job to supplement it. She was always dog tired by the time she returned to the house, but even then she wasn't finished. There were chores to do around the place, house-cleaning and the like, after which she had to put in some time on her life résumé, which was due by the end of the first week.

The résumé had turned out to be quite a chore. It had to be so complete, and besides the fact that she wasn't very good at writing, Candy was embarrassed at putting down all the details of her life. But the confession had to be made. It was for her own good, she was informed, because the Prophet knew all about her, as he knew all about everyone and everything. To lie, or to leave out something, would mean instant expulsion and the loss of her chance at resurrection. So before retiring to her cot Candy worked diligently on the résumé.

"I have glorious news for you," Sister Claudia said when Candy arrived at the house on her sixth day.

Candy felt a thrill at the girl's words, though just what she expected the news to be she didn't know.

"The Prophet has granted us the good fortune to find you a night job," Sister Claudia said, and though she seemed outwardly casual, Candy had the feeling that her mentor was watching her closely, gauging her response.

"That's marvelous," Candy said, trying to inject into her voice the proper degree of enthusiasm. She knew it was wicked and unregenerate of her not to feel elated over an opportunity to serve the Prophet with sixteen hours' work a day instead of eight. This meant that two paychecks and two shifts' worth of tips would go into the church treasury in the future. She felt even guiltier for dissembling about her response to the good tidings. "Where is the job?" she asked.

"At Cleo's Coffee Shop," Sister Claudia said. "It's just three blocks from your day job, and there's a half hour time lapse between them, so it will work out perfectly. You'll have Mondays and Tuesdays off."

Since her present job gave her Wednesdays and Thursdays off, there would be four days when she would not have to work the double shift, and of course on those days she would be expected to catch up on her housework. Sloth was a capital sin, a form of disobedience to the Prophet, and one was expected to work during his or her waking hours.

"It sounds perfect," Candy said, smiling tiredly. "Did they mention salary?"

"Two-fifty per hour, and one meal. Plus tips, of course." Sister Claudia's eyes narrowed slightly, and her voice took on a touch of extra weight as she appended this.

Candy fished into her uniform pocket and handed over a fistful of coins and a few bills. "I'm glad you mentioned that," she said. "Here are my tips for today. And now I guess I'd better get to my chores."

"The paperwork was light today," Sister Claudia said, accepting the money and beginning to sort it. "Brother Clifford and I managed to clean the place adequately. You start on your night job tomorrow, dear, so I think you had better finish your résumé now."

As she walked back to the women's sleeping quarters, Candy felt a vague anxiety. She wasn't certain how she felt about working on her résumé. It meant she could get off her feet, of course. (How was she ever going to make it through two shifts standing on her feet?) Still, she felt apprehensive. The more of her life she put on paper, the worse she felt about it. The events of her life, the sins of commission and omission of which she was guilty, all had run together in her memory like the ink on a dampened page. Now she was gathering it all together again, arranging it, bringing it into sharp relief in her own mind, and preparing to hand it over to others, people far purer than she, to study and to judge. The résumé was the worst of it, and she would have taken a third job rather than write it.

But it was the will of the Prophet.

After her shower she put on the thick, shapeless dress that had been handed down to her by the church, thrust her feet into a pair of heavy shoes, and repaired to the parlor with the yellow foolscap tablet and a ballpoint pen. She turned the tablet and read over the last few paragraphs she had written the night before, struggling to make out the childish scrawl. She had harbored a futile hope that her memory had played a trick on her, but now she had to face the fact that she had reached the point in her autobiography at which she had met Vernon. And now she would have to go through it all again, tearing open the wound while it was still fresh and throbbing.

CHAPTER 5

Immanuel Hartford troubled himself to roll over in bed and punch the button set into the wall near his head. Then he lay on his back, staring at himself in the mirrored ceiling and fuming for the five seconds it took the handmaiden to arrive. She was one of the new girls who had replaced Victoria McGivern and Annette Aragon the previous week. He couldn't remember her name or much else about her, but she looked to be about fifteen years old and had black hair that hung almost to the small of her back. Her features, still soft with youth, were fragile looking, but she had a generously cut mouth and huge, innocent eyes. Below the short red dress her legs were startlingly shapely. He remembered that she had been brought to the colony just a day before he had quartered her in the house, and that her parents were out in the fields picking cabbages or something. Now she stood next to his bed, dipped a bit at the knees to show obeisance to the Prophet and smiling with extreme nervousness.

Hartford pointed with an arched finger at the thermostat across the room. "It's broiling in here. My sheets are damp!"

"I'm sorry, Lord," she said in a quaking voice.

The first time she had been subjected to crossness from the Prophet, no doubt, though he wasn't certain of it. At least Hartford couldn't remember ever having chewed her out before.

"Well, *do* something about it!" he grumbled in a Vesuvian tone, and with another knee dip she scurried to the thermostat and turned it down. She looked back over her shoulder.

"How low—?"

"When you address your Lord and Savior, *face* him!"

Hartford roared. She actually jumped, and for a moment he could see signs of faintness in her. But she turned to face him, and he noted her breasts, surprisingly full and lush for a girl her age.

"Forgive me, Lord," she pleaded in a shaky voice. "I just wanted to ask what temperature—"

"Seventy-two, now that I'll be getting up soon," he said. "But at night it should be kept at sixty-eight in here, *always*! Do you understand?"

"Yes, Lord." She turned with alacrity and adjusted the tiny lever, apparently unconscious of what the swift motion did to her skirt. Hartford caught a glimpse of tight, round buttocks. "Will that be all, Lord?" she asked, facing him punctiliously.

"Come here, girl." He softened his tone a bit, but kept it edged enough to maintain her tension. Even as she walked to him he could see a tic in her throat, and it excited him. She stopped a bare three inches from the side of the bed, swaying slightly on rubbery legs and stilt heels. "Recite your name, girl," he commanded.

"Kathryn, sir."

"Well, Kathryn, aren't you aware that laxness in the service of the Prophet is a sin?" She nodded, too choked to speak, and kept her gaze lowered. Her black lashes looked lush and graceful against her cheeks. "And yet you neglect simple duties," he said, reproving her in a gentle voice, designed to stimulate and maximize her guilt. She was actually trembling with emotion by then, and Hartford felt a stirring in his genitals under the silk sheet. "Be truthful," he commanded. "Is this the first such negligent transgression since you entered my service? Remember, my dear, you can fool yourself, but you cannot fool your Lord."

His quiveringly admonitory tone brought on a fresh rush of trembling. It was almost as though she were suffering a malarial seizure. Hartford could see a sheen of cold perspiration on her arms. "Answer me," he demanded, his voice still soft, but his tone a bit more abrasive. Of a sudden the girl dropped to her knees, burying her face in his body, just above the abdomen. Through the sheet he could feel the contours of it, nudging, soft.

"Forgive me, Lord, please!" she sobbed. "I can always work harder. There is always more I could do! But I get tired!"

"You grow slothful," he amended. "If you were properly devoted your fatigue wouldn't stop you. I would lend you the strength to see you through. But you prefer to be slack." She was nodding against his belly, nodding with furious energy, as though astonished by his insights into her character. As usual in these sessions, Hartford was enjoying himself. He ran his fingers through her thick black hair, luxuriating in the clean silkiness of it.

"Do you see why I brought you here into my direct presence?" he asked gently. "Do you see how corrupt you are? How iniquitous? Do you realize how sinful you would be if I cast you out on your own devices?"

She froze for an instant, then raised her head to look at him in stunned horror. "But you wouldn't! You are too merciful to —"

"Don't worry, child," he assured her in a chiding tone. "You can be salvaged yet. You can be made pure and strong against sin. Is anything too hard for the Lord?" He grasped her arm and pulled her toward him. "Tell me, child, have I purified your blood as yet?"

She nodded, smiling shyly. "Once, Lord." Her face was shiny clean from the tears, tight looking and somehow even more attractive than before.

"Well, for as scurrilous a sinner as you that is clearly not enough. You will need frequent treatments until your blood and spirit are clean." His hand slipped behind her, pulling down the zipper of her dress. She lay against him, her body limp and yielding, her breasts plush against his bare chest. Casually, Hartford finished undressing her, and then purified her blood, taking his time and thoroughly enjoying himself.

When his passion was spent he lay there, the girl beside him, limp after the exertions of her own pleasure. This, Hartford told himself for the hundredth time, was the best of all scams. He had never had it so good, and he had never heard of anyone who had had it so good.

"Go draw my bath," he ordered the girl, whose name he had forgotten. And as she scampered into the bathroom, still naked, he drifted into a luxurious doze.

CHAPTER 6

He lacked even the excuse of a harsh or deprived childhood. His father was a hot-tempered but basically decent construction worker who led the nomadic existence of such people. Immanuel's mother was very different from her husband, though just as admirable. She was an inveterate reader and dreamer, intrigued by matters of the mind, though her own was not deep or quick enough to qualify her as an intellectual. She read magazines and mystery stories, and often best sellers.

Immanuel's earliest memories centered around her late-night readings. He would be allowed to sit up late because her own nocturnal habits, conflicting with her husband's more conventional hours, left her lonely. Immanuel's attitude toward reading developed from this, and it was as complex and paradoxical as the rest of his personality. He envied his mother the ability to decipher those cryptic squiggles, since she appeared to gain considerable satisfaction from it. And he enjoyed being allowed to stay up late, though he only dimly comprehended the connection that his mother's reading bore to that. But he resented the attention the magazines and the flimsy paperbacks elicited from his mother, attention he would have preferred to be directed at him.

When he started to school, his performance was mixed: He was invariably one of the best readers and the best speller in his class, but he was never particularly good at anything else, a fact that aroused his parents' frustration and resentment, thus kindling resentment in Immanuel himself and worsening his scholastic performance as he withdrew into a world of daydreams.

His social skills, like his studies, were variable. He never totally lacked friends, but neither was he widely popular. His keen intellect and esoteric interests repelled most children his age, and he often displayed a preference for the company of adults. And he was never popular with girls, between himself and whom there abided a mutual apprehensiveness.

Still, he was normal enough so that as he grew into young manhood he yearned for the admiration and desire of attractive young ladies. Since it never happened, he dreamed of it, and by that very act shoved it inexorably deeper into the world of fantasy, divorcing it in his own mind from reality and possibility. When, in his early teens, he learned of the solitary charms of masturbation, his fantasies took on a different, less wholesome hue. The lovely creatures who peopled his daydreams gradually ceased to love and admire him. More and more frequently, and finally exclusively, he dreamed of girls he desired as being helplessly under his control. There was a brief period when his sexual fantasies took on an overtly sadistic aspect, involving the infliction of pain and the commission of murder. But as he grew in sophistication the tortures of which he dreamed moved from the physical to the psychic.

His standard sexual fantasy included one or more of the popular girls in school. The girls didn't like him in the dreams any more than they did in reality, though they were certainly more acutely aware of his existence; but through some fortuitous circumstance they were incapable of denying him whatever bizarre or unsanitary delight he demanded. One of the girls who peopled these fantasies was Peggy Boling, head cheerleader and student body vice-president. It was through Peggy that Immanuel Hartford was to learn for the first time that occasionally, if one is diligent enough, and ruthless enough, dreams can come true.

Peggy Boling was two years older than Immanuel, and for that reason as well as others seemed the personification of unattainable glamour. A long-legged (fully two inches taller than he) blonde, she was busty and trim, and possessed of a face that managed to combine innocence (which was strictly an appearance) and sultry sensuality (which was genuine). In addition to possessing these attributes she was an excellent student, and was admired by everyone for her thoughtfulness and friendliness. It was entirely appropriate that she was the steady of Bob Hoyt, the most popular boy in the high school. They were engaged to be engaged, and planned to attend the same medical school after graduation.

It was just before midterm examinations that Immanuel enjoyed his incredible stroke of good fortune. Peggy was teaching assistant to Mr. Carstairs, the chemistry teacher, and it was in Mr. Carstairs's classroom that Immanuel encountered her after school hours. He had gone there to talk to Mr. Carstairs about the possibility of doing some extra work to get a passing grade. Peggy had gone there to misuse her position of trust by copying down the questions that would appear on the midterm examination.

She was bent over the desk, her miniskirt raised to reveal the exciting swell of her thighs, when Immanuel walked in behind her. His first thought was to stand and look, to drink in this sight, which might add some authenticity to his onanistic fantasies that night. There was no one else in the room. Suddenly Peggy glanced over her shoulder, saw him, and nearly leaped over the desk.

"Oh, hi," she said, and he knew that she was searching through her memory for his name. "You—you startled me," she explained, brushing back her thick, silky blond hair. There was something odd about her behavior, something that suggested to Immanuel that she was concerned about other matters than his unheralded appearance. She leaned back over the desk, as though to conceal something there.

"Sorry," Immanuel said. "Is Mr. Carstairs around?"

"No. He won't be back for at least a half hour, he told me."

"Okay. I guess I'll wait." There was an air in the way she had stated Mr. Carstairs's estimated time of return that aroused further suspicions in him, as though she were bolstering her own hopes.

"All right." She turned suddenly, picking up two sheafs of papers from the desk. A glimpse told Immanuel that one sheaf was notebook filler and the other blank scratch paper. "I have to go out for a moment anyway." She folded the filler paper and thrust it into her textbook, then placed the scratch paper in Mr. Carstairs's desk drawer. She was careful about that operation, as though placing it exactly where she had found it.

Then, leaving her textbook atop the desk, she walked out of the room.

Immanuel sat there for a while, staring at the book and the folded sheets tucked inside it. She had naturally assumed that he would refrain from looking through someone else's property, and normally he would never have considered doing such a thing. But he felt a strange and potent excitement now, though he wasn't certain why. His legs trembled under him as he rose and walked to the desk. His hands shook as he opened the book and removed the sheaf of filler paper.

He knew instantly what it was. In her hand, which was as distinctive and lovely as her face, Peggy Boling had duplicated the first twenty-three questions of Mr. Carstairs's midterm exam. The top of the filler sheet on top, which had apparently been intended originally for some more legitimate purpose, even displayed her signature and the date.

The excitement in him had reached Vesuvian proportions. He had a fierce erection, so stiff it was painful. He wasn't even certain why he did what he did, but without stopping to think about it he placed the copied exam questions in his own binder and left the room with swift, long strides.

CHAPTER 7

She was working Harbor Boulevard the night she met Vernon. She had moved down to Orange County because things were getting hot in Hollywood, and the competition was pretty stiff, too. She had been told that a lot of the girls, the free-lancers, were drifting to Anaheim, but that the cops hadn't reacted as yet. The pickings had turned out to be slim, but that was nothing new. At seventeen Candy had already accepted that as a way of life.

She was standing around in front of a coffee shop across from Disneyland, a mile or so from the Civic Center, when the light blue Chevy pulled in and she saw a tall, slender man emerge. It was getting late, past eleven o'clock, and she had had nothing to eat since the previous evening, and hadn't arranged for a place to stay the night. There were two other girls there, but they had had something to eat, and so were comparatively sleek and slow-footed. Candy beat them to the tall young man as he was approaching the entrance to the coffee shop.

"Hi," she said, smiling and looking pathetic at the same time. She was dressed in worn blue jeans, tight around the ass and crotch, and shower clogs. A checkered shirt completed the ensemble. Her hair, none too clean, hung straight past her shoulders. The young man stopped and smiled back at her. "Can you spare a couple of dollars for a hungry girl?" she asked, taking in his dark slacks and short-sleeved white shirt. Middle-class stuff; not expensive, but not cheap either.

He looked her up and down too. "Are you really hungry?" he asked.

"I haven't eaten since yesterday morning," she replied,

stretching it a little. He looked straight into her eyes in a way that made her nervous, and Candy wished for a moment that she hadn't approached him. But she was weak and headachy from hunger, and had to bull it through. Out of the corner of her eye she could see the other girls watching with the intentness of predators.

"I'm going in to have dinner," the man said. "Why don't you join me?"

Candy felt a little thrill, because just maybe she had found a place to spend the night. "That's great," she said, sparing the other girls a little smirk.

The waitress had seen Candy panhandling, but there was nothing she could do without offending a customer, so she led Candy and the stranger to a booth in a far corner, where Candy's grubby clothes and dirty fingernails wouldn't be too conspicuous. She handed them menus with the bare minimum of cordiality and went off to scoop up a tip from a nearby table.

"Gee, what shall I have?" Candy mused, looking over the menu. She hid behind it, waiting for her benefactor to give her some notion of the extent of his generosity.

"I'm going to have a porterhouse steak," he replied, studying the menu. "Why don't you have the same?"

So. She had found a real live one.

Forty-five minutes later, when she had put away her steak and baked potato, and a little bit of his steak as well, and was just digging into a slice of berry pie, Vernon, as she had learned to call him, took out a thin roll of bills and laid a twenty on the check the waitress had brought. He put another twenty on the table.

Candy looked at it, trying to seem casual, though her heart was pounding with excitement. "What does a person have to do to get one of those?" she asked around a cheekful of pie.

He shrugged. "How much of your time do you figure that's worth?" he asked.

Candy shrugged. "My time is pretty reasonable, Vernon. I guess that's worth the rest of the night, anyway."

"You've got yourself a deal."

He took her to a neatly kept two-bedroom apartment in Garden Grove. It was a cheap place with an unenclosed kitchen, but to Candy it was the height of luxury.

"You live here all alone?" she asked.

"At the moment." He smiled. "My roommate is away for a couple of weeks."

"That's convenient." She moved close to him, inviting him to start something. Instead, he started up the stairs. She followed.

"Why don't you take a shower?" he invited. She might have guessed he'd be a clean freak from the look of the place. He was already pulling a towel and a washcloth from a built-in cabinet, so she shrugged.

While she was in the shower Candy heard the bathroom door open. For a moment she thought he was going to get in with her, but his shadow withdrew and the door closed.

When she emerged from the shower her clothes were gone and in their place, neatly folded atop the toilet cover, was a man's robe, neatly striped in red, yellow, and blue. She pulled its folds around her and knotted the sash. She found a hair dryer in a cabinet and ran it over her hair a few times to take out the greater part of the wetness, then walked downstairs.

He was in the living room, leafing through a book as he sprawled on the couch. He had turned on a stereo radio, filling the room with the strains of soft rock music. As she entered, he grinned up at her and put his book aside. "Something to eat?" he asked.

Candy hesitated. She had learned never to turn down food, whether she was hungry or not, since she didn't know when the next opportunity would present itself. But she still felt bloated from the heavy meal in the coffee shop. She shook her head reluctantly. "Maybe in an hour or so, all right?" She tried to say it casually, but there was a little catch in her voice, born of nervousness. She still wasn't certain he was going to keep her for the night, and she sought reassurance that she wouldn't be turned out. He smiled and nodded. Candy returned the smile, using the shy look she had come to know turned on most men. With elaborate nonchalance she walked to the couch and sat as close to him as his position would allow. She had begun to wonder whether he was so square that he actually didn't know what she was there for. It seemed incredible, but she had heard that there were men like that, and this guy seemed pretty straight. Then, abruptly, he sat up, and she thought, *Thank God*, and slid close to him, allowing their hips to touch.

"Where you from, Candy?" he asked.

Maybe he's nervous, she thought. *Maybe he has to get to know me a little bit.*

"Washington," she replied. In a way it was nice to have a man talk to her instead of pawing her right away.

"D.C. or state?"

"State. I used to live in a little town called Battle Ground."

"How long you been in California?"

"A few months, I don't know." She laid a hand on his knee, trying to get things started. Maybe the guy had decided that she didn't turn him on or something. She grew a little fidgety at the thought.

"How old are you?"

"Eighteen." She said it quickly, and looked straight at him, but he didn't buy it. She could tell that from his expression, and a dubious tilt of his head. So she shrugged. "Seventeen," she amended. She wouldn't be for another two months, but that was close enough, and she didn't want to scare him off, since she had begun to hope he might like her enough to make this a semiregular occasion.

"Are your parents still in Washington?"

"What the fuck is this?" she demanded, suddenly openly annoyed and suspicious.

"If I get too personal, just tell me so."

She came close to doing just that but decided to go along with him for a while.

"My father died five years ago. My mother lives in Washington with my stepfather. I left because the son of a bitch tried to rape me." That was the way she always described it on the rare occasions that she talked about the incident at all. She didn't like to articulate, even in her own mind, the fact that he had in fact raped her three times on two separate occasions. "And I'd kill anyone who tried to make me go back. Now it's my turn to ask a question." She was beginning to form a suspicion about this guy. "When you picked me up tonight, where were you coming from?"

"Melodyland."

He said it casually enough, without a hint of challenge, but he sounded a bit smug, she thought.

"Just my luck. A Jesus freak! And you brought me here to save my soul, right?"

"I can't save souls," he said with that unctuous modesty she had encountered in the tribe before. "It's already saved. All you have to do is accept the gift."

"I need this," Candy said, looking at the books on the shelf against the opposite wall. "I really need this. Jesus H. Christ! If my clothes were only here."

"Well, you'll have to wait till they're washed and dried," Vernon reminded her. "Besides, we made a deal. You're mine for the rest of the night."

CHAPTER 8

The trial period was three months, and it was that long before
Candy Sterling would be entitled to be called Sister Candace
by the other members of the movement. It was during this
period that the majority of the slackers, those who were not
serious, dropped out. Though the trials were severe, it never
occurred to Candy to leave. She hadn't come to the church
expecting anything but a chance to add meaning to her life, and
it had been made clear to her, through the literature she had
been permitted to read and through the talks she had shared, on
rare and brief occasions, with Sister Claudia, that she had no
right to expect earthly happiness. The person who achieved
earthly happiness had already received his reward and could
expect none in the afterlife. She knew that she was being
resurrected, brought back to life in the sight of the All-Moving
Spirit, and that was sufficient satisfaction.

After a month Sister Claudia found her a third job, working
on two of her days off, and so she was at the house less
frequently than ever. It meant more money to bring into the
Prophet's coffers, more effort on her part to advance his work.
The very fact that this knowledge did nothing to lift her spirits
warned Candy that she was more corrupt than she had
suspected.

Four hundred miles north of Candy, the Prophet was
considering the extent of her corruption. It was his policy to
require that all converts to the movement be photographed, and
that the photographs be sent to his quarters, and while
browsing through the current crop he came upon a Polaroid
shot of Candy Sterling, stapled to her application for admission
to the movement. The photograph stopped him, holding his

attention. She was a pretty girl, though not exceptionally so by the standards he had been able to maintain of late. There was something else about her, a softness to her mouth, a depth and sparkle in her eyes that managed to show up even in this little photograph, that interested and managed, through his jaded senses, to excite him. She looked sensuous and vulnerable at once. He read her application, put the papers aside, and decided, as he helped himself to his morning glass of wine, that Candy Sterling definitely was a girl who needed her blood purified. The thought of it stimulated him, and when his current chambermaid entered to pick up his dishes, he slid his hand under her skirt. As the dusky Latin girl slipped onto the bed next to him, he had to chuckle to himself. He had always known there was a better way to start the morning than by getting up.

To Candy, in Los Angeles, getting up was the beginning of a very long day. She bathed quickly, made up her cot after dressing in one of her waitress's uniforms, and then, with another uniform in a bag, left the house at seven in the morning. Her shift began at eight, and she would have to walk twelve blocks to get to work. To be late would not only endanger her job, it might also deprive the Prophet of tips she could have made during her unauthorized absence. It was far better to arrive early so that, if the place was busy, the manager might ask her to start work immediately.

She went through the day like a zombie, scarcely aware of her surroundings, tired before she started, and exhausted by ten o'clock in the morning, with another fourteen hours ahead of her. The only part of it that impinged on her consciousness was the tips she made, which she counted carefully and kept in her head as a running tally. She took no breaks and only the shortest lunchtime, getting back on the floor early to scoop up extra dimes and quarters, smiling vaguely at the male customers because she had learned that this frequently increased their generosity.

Then, at four P.M., she departed for her second job, just three blocks away. Now at least she was on the downhill pull, the second eight of her sixteen hours' work. By the time she reached the coffee shop her legs were as numb as her feet had been since noon, and she was in a kind of trance, too tired to be drowsy, moving through her job with a strange, heightened awareness, as though she had been popping pills.

A bit past midnight her relief arrived, and she knew that in less than half an hour she could make her departure, walk back to the house, wash her hair, and fall into bed after saying her prayers to the Prophet.

But then a surge of business materialized. Two busloads of people, evidently returning from some sort of outing, entered the shop. Candy saw a few of them seated at her tables, and so she snagged some menus and approached them, forcing herself to move smartly and to smile as though she were fresh from her bed and shower. She was intercepted by Jan McCullough, the night manager.

Jan grabbed her menus from under her arm. "Go on home, Candy. It's time."

"Oh, I don't mind," Candy said, smiling and trying to look bright and perky. "It looks like it's going to be—"

"We can handle it."

"But I don't mind, Jan, really. I'm not all that tired."

"You're about to collapse. Now get out of here."

"But—" Candy had trouble functioning. For some reason, her mind wouldn't clear. She supposed it was because she was tired, but with the help of the Prophet she could overcome that.

"Look, Jan, I don't mind a little extra work," she said in carefully measured, deliberately precise tones. "You don't have to put it on the time sheet. I want to help out. And frankly, I can use the extra tips."

"So can the rest of the girls."

"Oh. Well, I didn't mean—"

"Listen, kid." Jan placed a hand on Candy's arm in a friendly, gentle gesture. "I don't know what's drivin' you, but you're washed out and hung up to dry. Now go home and get some sleep."

"I—"

"Night, Candy." Jan turned and walked away to deposit the menus on the tables. Candy stood for a moment, looking after the older woman, feeling vaguely disoriented. She wanted to cry, and she didn't know for sure just why. Finally she turned and picked up her purse from behind the counter on her way out.

The cold night air made her skin tingle. She needed a sweater or something. Perhaps there was one at the house that she might use. The movement collected discarded clothing to pass out among its followers. Candy walked down the street toward home, feeling a vague anxiety creep through her and wondering why. She had tried to work the extra time. She had really done her best to talk Jan into letting her stay.

Why was she kidding herself? She had been glad when her request had been denied. She had felt like kissing the hem of Jan's skirt in gratitude for her refusal, and her strength. Perhaps that was why she had been refused. The Prophet was showing her in his own way how unworthy she was to serve him. She had tried to work that extra time. But she really hadn't wanted to do it.

" 'Scuse me. You got the time?"

She was too exhausted and preoccupied even to be startled. It took a few seconds for the voice to sink in. She stopped and stared at the man before her. He was tall, perhaps a foot taller than her own five-four, with a slender body and narrow shoulders but muscular, competent-looking arms. His black skin gleamed in the light from the street lamp. He wore a huge, exaggerated Afro.

"What?" She wasn't sufficiently recovered to feel fear yet, though the first seepings of apprehension ran through her. "What? Oh, no, I'm sorry." She started to walk around him, but he stepped in her path again. Candy looked at him more closely. There was a nervousness to him, a look of fretful disquiet that, belatedly, rang a bell, or sounded an alarm, somewhere in the back of her mind. A second later she had identified her reaction.

He's strung out, she thought, and prepared to run. There was no one else around. She had walked two blocks from the coffee shop, and the street was deserted except for her and this junkie. She backed away a step, glanced to the side and saw that an entrance to a parking lot was just a step away. Without giving any sign of her intent she spun to her left and darted through. It was an incredibly stupid thing to do, especially for someone as street wise as she was supposed to be, but in that instant she panicked, thinking only of opening up distance between herself and the potential threat.

He was right behind her, overhauling her with his long powerful legs, and when his hand grasped her shoulder she realized how foolish she had been because now she was really alone, removed from any potential help. Spinning her about to face him, he slapped her across the face, hard enough to twist her head to the side. Candy stared up at him, stunned and terrified.

"Now don't go givin' me no bullshit, honky bitch," he cautioned, holding up a stiff, thick finger in an admonitory fashion. His eyes were wide and white, seeming to fill the upper portion of his face. "I got no designs on your lily-white body," he said. "I just want your money, and then I'll be on my way."

"Money? I don't have any money!" But her protective gesture, hugging her purse to her side, belied her words.

"Don't be tellin' me that, bitch," he warned. "You're wearin' a waitress's uniform, an' you just come off work, an' you got to have some tips. Now give me what I come for, or I'm gonna rearrange that pretty white face."

"I tell you, I don't have—" It was obvious that he wouldn't believe her. She hugged the purse tighter, wrapping the carrying strap around her wrist. "It's not mine," she said. "Please, it isn't mine to give you."

"Well then, it *sure* ain't worth takin' no beatin' for, is it?" He reached for the purse. Candy turned, pulling it out of his reach, and looked for somewhere to run. But he stood between her and the opening in the cinder-block wall through which she had entered the lot. She would have had to cover an expanse of at least two hundred feet to reach the nearest clear exit, and he could easily overtake her in that distance.

"I can't give you any money," she told him. "Really. I would if I could!" Again she stepped back, but he matched her step, maintaining the same distance between them, heading back to the sidewalk. He grabbed her arm, wrenching it in a powerful grip and yanking her close against him. She could feel his hard, muscular body, smell the tang of his perspiration.

"*Gimme* that fuckin' purse, goddam it!" He grasped for the bag, missed it as she twisted away, then caught it and yanked. The strap, looped about Candy's wrist, held, eliciting another curse from him. He pulled harder, yanking her arm out of joint. She cried out but managed to wrap her fingers around the strap, clutching it tightly. "Goddam crazy bitch!" he yelled, suddenly driving his fist into the pit of her stomach. Candy hadn't realized anything could hurt that much. Her vision fuzzed over and she felt a violent nausea as the wind was driven from her, but she could only think of the Prophet's money, entrusted to her. It would be wicked and sinful to let it go.

As though that first punch had released some sort of torrent, Candy's assailant struck her again and again, his fist pummeling her back and arms and neck as she fought, with feminine instinct, to protect her face. Once she felt consciousness slipping away from her, but she brought it back by a force of will, bending her body over the hand that held the purse, using every muscle to keep him from taking it.

"Hey!" The voice was masculine, originating from some distance away, but for a moment those facts didn't mean anything to Candy. She was intent only on holding onto the money as long as she could. Heavy footsteps approached. Someone running. "Hey, you!" There was anger, outrage in the tone.

"Shit!" Candy's attacker muttered. He made one more try at pulling the purse away from her, then ran. Candy wasn't aware of falling until she felt the rough asphalt against her bare legs. She ached all over, and her contact with reality was tenuous, but she knew she had saved the money, that for once she hadn't failed.

CHAPTER 9

Immanuel Hartford walked home from school that day because he wanted to be alone to think about what he had done, and the possible consequences of it. He didn't want to put up with the chatter and horseplay that took place on the school bus, nor did he trust himself to maintain a cool demeanor so soon after having stolen Peggy Boling's crib notes. Arriving home a little after three o'clock, he went straight to his room. After placing the stolen sheets of paper inside one of the books in his bookcase, where they were unlikely to be found, he took off his clothes and stretched out on his bed.

Potent fantasies assailed him, thoughts of Peggy Boling pleading for the return of her papers, and himself dangling before her the likelihood of her ruin unless she did as he ordered. His hand slipped down to his genitals as he allowed his imagination full bridle, relishing the fantasy as he had previously enjoyed other fantasies about Peggy Boling. In the middle of things, there was a tap at his door. He pulled away his hands guiltily, sat up on the bed.

"Yes?" he asked, after taking a moment to assure himself that his voice would be steady.

"Manny? I wasn't sure you were home." His mother's voice was muffled by the door.

"Just a minute, Mom, okay?" His mother was a firm believer in the principle that everyone, including minors, was entitled to privacy. She never entered his room without knocking. Immanuel came to his feet and began putting on his clothes.

"There's a phone call, dear," his mother said through the door. "Some girl asking for you." There was a touch of wonder in her tone. Immanuel had never previously received a phone call from a girl. The significance of her announcement took a moment to occur to him. Then his heart leaped and pounded. He felt prickly warmth all over his body, and his mouth went dry.

"A—all right, Mom," he said chokingly. "I'll be right out."

He forced himself to walk to the hall telephone in a leisurely manner. He paused a moment before picking up the receiver, taking control of his breathing. Then he lifted the receiver, held it a moment, and placed the earpiece to his ear.

"Hello?" He heard his mother hang up the kitchen phone as soon as he had spoken.

"Manny?" It was Peggy Boling's voice. He was certain.

"That's right," he said. His voice was all quavery, which annoyed him. It was never like this in his fantasy world. There he was always supremely confident, taking his insuperable advantage quite for granted.

"This is Peggy Boling," she said. Manny made no reply, and after a few moments she said, "You have something of mine."

"Have I?" It was all he could trust himself to say, his breathing was so ragged. There was an odd note in her voice, as though she couldn't decide whether to accuse or placate him.

"I want it back," she said, and still her voice couldn't decide between firm demand and winsome entreaty. At least his breath was in control now. Almost.

"Are you sure I have it?" he asked, and then paused a moment, taking a deep draft of air. "Maybe you ought to go ask lost and found. Or your chemistry teacher. Maybe he has it." There was a whole chunk of silence after that, and he began to feel guilty, because in his fantasies the girls were just phantoms, but now, for the first time, he was aware that he was dealing with a human being, someone who could be hurt. It was all the more puzzling, therefore, that he was so *excited*. His fantasies had never brought him to this pitch of feeling.

"Stop this nonsense, Manny! You know very well what I'm talking about, and I want you to give it back to me!" Her display of anger was a tactical error, hardening rather than intimidating him.

"You want me to hang up?" he demanded. The raggedness

in his voice was acceptable now, because it could be taken for rage.

"No! Please! Manny, it was wrong of you to take that!"

"It was wrong of you to have it," he reminded her, beginning to enjoy the verbal play. "I guess the honest thing to do would be to give it to the person it belongs to. I mean, it's kind of a civic duty in a way, exposing a thief and cheat. Somebody who wants to be a doctor and who cheats on chemistry exams could be really dangerous." He could hear her crying, and that made him ashamed, and the shame brought increased, defensive anger.

"Manny, why are you doing this to me? I've never hurt you." Apparently it had never occurred to her that she could hurt through indifference.

"Doing what?" he asked innocently. "I only said maybe. I'm just exploring my options." There was a tang of extra meaning in his tone, and it brought a momentary silence to the line.

"Do you want money?" she asked finally. "I have a little saved up. About a hundred dollars." A hundred dollars was far from a little bit to Manny. It was more than he had ever had in his life, but he wasn't ready to sell out his ascendant position yet. Besides, the fact that she could call such a sum 'a little' brought home to him how pampered she was, how accustomed to things that he had only imagined having. It wouldn't hurt Peggy Boling to crawl a bit, he decided.

"I'll tell you, Peggy, I really don't think it would be right to sell out my principles for money. Anyway, I can't stand here talking about it on the phone. B'bye."

"Wait! Don't hang up!"

He still had the receiver planted firmly against his ear. Her urgency, the pleading tone of her voice, thrilled Manny. He had never felt power before, and it was a delicious experience. For the first time he began to wonder if he might be able to get her to do what he really wanted. He doubted it, but it might be worth a try. He could always settle for the money later, if she refused. "Okay, but make it quick," he said, hoping he sounded bored.

"Can I see you?"

Manny had never been asked that by a girl, and certainly not in such imploring tones. He was already getting over his first qualms of remorse and beginning to enjoy himself. "I don't know. When?"

"Well—tonight?"

He started to tell her that was out of the question, just to let her stew overnight, but decided that he would like to see her, to feel her nearness. "I guess so. After dinner sometime."

"Where shall we meet?"

He was about to suggest a spot when a better idea occurred to him. "You've got a car, haven't you?"

"Yes."

"Pick me up here." She was silent for a long moment, and there was a seething air to the silence, but by this time Manny knew that she was going to assent. He had her by the nipples.

"All right. Seven o'clock all right?"

"Seven-fifteen." If she had suggested seven-fifteen he'd have specified seven-thirty, or seven o'clock. It was important, he thought, to strike the proper tone in their relationship right away.

"All right, Manny. I'll be outside your door at seven-fifteen." He thought of insisting that she come to the door but decided against it. The less his parents knew about her, the better.

CHAPTER 10

Candy felt guilty for lying on her back in the clean hospital sheets, and guiltier for being glad that she couldn't go back to her jobs for the time being. Of course she had tried. She had begged the doctor, a young intern who had been friendly but intractable.

"I'll tell you when you can get up," he had said. "In the meantime, just relax and get some rest. I'm not going to release you until I'm certain there are no internal injuries."

"How long will that take?" Candy asked, injecting impatience into her voice, and hoping guiltily that he would give her a long sentence.

He looked at her for a moment before replying. "Two or three days," he said finally, entering something on her chart and hanging it on the end of the bed. "Unless, of course, we come up with something. Then you could be here for a while."

"Don't worry, honey," the middle-aged patient with the dyed red hair advised Candy after the physician's departure. "He'll be there when you get back. Just think of it as a vacation."

Candy turned her face away, uncertain whether she was choking back sobs or laughter. A little later, she fell into an exhausted sleep.

She was never certain of just how long after that she woke in the darkened ward, tense and clammy without knowing the reason. Then she became aware of the huge form that hovered over her bed.

"What?" she whispered, her chest and belly tight, her knees aching from tension. "What is it?" The form didn't reply.

Could it possibly be a nurse that large? An orderly? But why didn't he answer her?

With apelike quickness a giant hand clamped her mouth. The grip was powerful, scrubbing the insides of her cheeks against her teeth, twisting her lower jaw out of joint painfully. Her first inclination was to grab the hand, to try to wrest free of it. But she stayed her hands halfway, realizing the futility of that impulse. Her breath wheezed noisily through her nostrils as she gazed into the opacity of darkness, her eyes uselessly wide and large. The form hunched down, crouching beside the bed. She caught sight of a huge head, improbably large. Then she realized that what she saw was an Afro haircut, and she was more terrified than ever.

"I ain't gonna hurt ya," the black giant whispered. "You dig me? I ain't gonna hurt you unless you make noise. You get where I'm comin' from, girl? No noise, no hurt. Do you get it?" He shook her head for emphasis. Candy nodded as well as she could. Tentatively, the grip loosened. She made no attempt to pull free or to cry out. The hand left her mouth, hovering an inch away.

"Plea—please," she begged in a stammering whisper. "I didn't— I told the cops I—"

"I ain't worried about that," the black man whispered. "I looked you up to ask you somethin'."

"Ask?" It was such a stupefyingly outlandish statement that she could think of no other reply.

"Why'd you do that tonight? Was that true what you said? The bread wasn't yours?"

"Yes." She was gradually regaining control of her voice. But her body was still rigid with terror.

"Then why'd you do that? I coulda killed you." She didn't know how to answer in terms he would understand. The silence lengthened between them. "Where'd you get the money?" he asked surprisingly.

"I earned it. Waiting tables." Once again the silence was extended.

"Then how come it wasn't yours?" he asked, his whisper giving way to a vocalized grunt. The redhead in the next bed stirred and sighed, and the black man's body poised for flight.

Candy considered screaming but decided against it for the

moment. "Everything I have belongs to someone else," she whispered. "To—to the Prophet of the All-Moving Spirit."

This time he was silent for so long she wondered whether he had heard her. He stirred briefly, drew back a bit. His hand moved away from her mouth. Then he leaned close again. "That the bunch over near Figueroa?"

"That's right."

"You were ready to die for a few lousy dollars 'cause of them?"

"You—I can't explain it."

"Well, you gotta be nuts," he said, and withdrew his arm from the grill the nurse had raised on her bed to keep her from falling out. "You gotta be plain crazy."

"I'm sorry." She didn't know what she meant by that, but he might not have heard it anyway. He was standing again, staring down at her in the darkness, as though by looking hard enough he might penetrate the gloom, and her skull, and see just what it was that had made her do such a foolish, inexplicable thing. Then he moved back, so quietly that it took her minutes to be certain she was alone except for the other women sleeping around her.

CHAPTER 11

After that first meeting with Vernon, Candy went back to his apartment once a week, telling herself that sitting and listening to him talk about Jesus was just another way of being screwed. He paid her twenty dollars each time, and put her up for the night. On other nights, when she couldn't find other accommodations, she occasionally used his place as a crash pad. He never objected, nor did his roommate, who was usually asleep anyway. Sometimes Vernon too was asleep when she arrived, but he would genially descend the stairs and let her in, fix her something to eat, talk soothingly to her for a while, and let her crash on his fold-out couch.

She kept waiting for the payoff, but he never touched her. The thing that made it tough to figure out was that he wanted to. If he had proved immune to her attractions, Candy would have concluded that he was queer and let it go at that, but she had been around enough to feel it when a man found her desirable. She took to prodding him with deliberately provocative acts, showering and leaving the door open, wearing his robe loosely so that her breasts' cleavage was exposed, leaning across in front of him as they shared the couch. He never responded in any overt manner.

Candy was astonished by her own response to his restraint. She would have thought it would frustrate her, but each instance of his strength made her flush with pleasure. She was confused because she had never known anyone like him before, and because his purity excited her in ways she had not known possible.

And then she found that some of the things he was telling her, things she had shut out of her mind in the beginning, made sense. There was an internal logic to it that appealed to her. And if it had produced a man like him, if it actually had lent him the strength to resist her blatant overtures, then it must be potent stuff.

On the fifth visit she asked him for a Bible, which he gladly provided. When he took it out of a drawer she noticed that the drawer was stuffed full of copies. It was a paperback edition in modern language, which was fortunate. She had never been able to hack through that jungle of "thous" and "hasts" in the King James Version she had glanced through in motel rooms.

The next morning she woke to find him dressed and sipping a cup of steaming coffee at the little bar separating the kitchen area from the living room. His roommate was just going out the door. Candy lay in the makeshift bed, nude except for the covers. She noticed for the first time, looking at Vernon in his neat three-piece suit, how attractive he was. It had been a long time since she had thought of a man as attractive. Sex had become a commodity, or a service, to her, and the sudden surge in her loins took her by surprise, startling her in a pleasant way.

He turned, as though he had felt her eyes on him, and smiled. "Morning," he said.

"Hi." She sat up, hugging the covers to her neck, not only for his benefit, but because suddenly she was aware of her nakedness as something other than a bargaining point.

"I have to leave pretty soon," he said.

"You want me out of here?"

"Not until you want to go. There's plenty of food in the fridge, if you'd like some breakfast."

"Thanks." She was pleased by his willingness to leave her alone in the place.

"How are you fixed for money?" he asked.

"Oh, I'm fine."

"Sure?" He put down his coffee and started toward her, reaching for his wallet.

She shook her head vigorously. "Please," she said. "I don't want you to give me any money." It was half true, and for some reason she desperately wanted him to believe it.

"Okay," he said gently. He was smiling, and she felt closer to him than she had previously.

"I just realized I don't even know what you do," she said. Suddenly, surprising her, he sat on the edge of the bed. She flushed slightly, like a virgin finding herself in a daring situation.

"I work for a Christian group," he explained. "We're trying to raise the money to start a radio station."

"Oh." She was so intensely aware of his proximity that she hardly heard his statement.

He looked at his watch. "Wow, I'd better get going." Rising, he looked down at her, and she saw something dart across behind his eyes, and knew that in that moment at least he had been very much aware of her nakedness, her availability. Then he picked up the Bible she had laid next to the bed the night before and extended it. "Why don't you read this?" he offered. "Take a ball pen to it. Circle anything you want to ask me about. I'm no Bible scholar—"

"Oh, I'll bet you are," she said, suddenly feeling little-girl coy. "I'll bet you're good at anything you try."

"Well, anyway, I'll try to answer any questions you have." He flushed pleasantly at her compliment. "Right now I really have to run."

She wanted to kiss him, but it was impossible without rising up and dropping the covers that hid her nudity, so she just smiled.

When she was alone Candy rose and padded to the little kitchen. She fixed herself some scrambled eggs and sausage patties. When she had eaten she carefully washed the dishes, including the cup Vernon had used for his coffee. Then, because she wanted to do something to show him her appreciation, she gave the entire apartment a good cleaning. She felt good doing it, like a wife or girl friend. She did the laundry, too, using her own money for the machines, and when that was finished found that she had used up half the day. It was noon, so she made a bite of lunch and, eating it, began to read the Bible he had given her. Before she was through the first page she went looking for a pen, circled a passage, and continued reading. Suddenly it was absorbing, though she had never found religion the least bit interesting before.

By the time Vernon arrived at six that evening, she had struggled through the whole book, and had circled something on nearly every page.

CHAPTER 12

"You realize this is blackmail," Peggy Boling said.

Manny sat looking at her for a moment, concealing the guilt-fed anger her words aroused in him. She was so beautiful, so pampered, and this was probably her first encounter with frustration, with someone who wasn't so smitten by her that he would do anything, give up any advantage, just to keep from contemplating the horror of her disapproval. He had been tempted to do just that ever since she had picked him up in her two-year-old Mustang, looking so lush in her short skirt and tight sweater, with her gold hair brushed down around her shoulders and the cloud of perfume that hung about her like a benign spirit. He might have caved in, and his subsequent life taken a far different turn, if not for the underlying tone of haughty disapproval in her manner. That had been just enough to keep him on the course he had set.

"When I talked to you on the telephone tonight, you offered me money," he reminded her. "That would have been blackmail. This is just a convenient way of handling the matter." She looked chock full of bottled up outrage, her lips tight and thin, her eyes smoldering with resentment. But there was nothing she could do about it, and she knew it. The war that had been raging in Manny between enjoyment of his dominant position and nagging guilt shifted once more in favor of the former. He knew that the moment he returned the crib notes to her she would cease to be aware of his existence, but at the moment he was the most important person in her world.

"All right," she said, acknowledging his preeminence. "When?"

"Next Saturday, I guess."

"I already have a date next Saturday."

"Break it." She just stared at him, her eyes narrowed, her arms resting on the table of their booth and crossed in front of her, as though to block him off from her breasts. He felt that if she could kill him and get away with it, she probably would. The thought was a little scary. He had never elicited such emotion in a human being before. But it was exhilarating too.

"You think you're such a smart little shit," she hissed. "You're really enjoying this, aren't you?"

"Or don't break it," Manny said, allowing a trace of anger into his own voice. The choice of words on her part had stung, possibly more than she had intended. "But make up your mind right now, because I'm not going to stick around while you ponder the matter." He drank the remainder of his Coke and looked at her with the air of one whose departure is imminent and significant.

"All right," she said. "We've got a date. But you'd better come across." He smiled at her turn of phrase and she reddened, refusing to be stared down. "What time shall I pick you up?" she asked finally. "Assuming you want *me* to pick *you* up?"

"Seven," Manny said, after pausing to consider the question, and to relish the moment. "Seven sharp."

And sharp she was, arriving at exactly seven o'clock Saturday evening. Instead of the Mustang, she was driving one of her parents' cars, a Chrysler New Yorker. That was the first surprise. The second came when Manny slipped in beside her. She was dressed in blue jeans and a man's checkered shirt with the sleeves rolled up past her elbows. A bandana held her hair in place. She noticed him looking at her as she slipped the car into drive and pulled into traffic.

"I didn't think it would matter how I dressed for this sort of date," she said with vindictive tautness.

So, Manny thought, she was going to be like that. "Where are we going?" he asked.

"I know a place." Her eyes remained fixed on the road as she replied. After that she was silent, studiously ignoring him. Manny, who had been nervous, grew angrier with each silent minute, angry at her attempt to ruin his moment of triumph, to snatch victory from the jaws of defeat by making this night as unpleasant and perfunctory as possible. When they were a half hour out of town the hum of the engine dropped in pitch. Manny looked around, lifted from his reverie by the change in the car's speed. Peggy braked almost to a stop and pulled the car off onto a side road. It pitched and bounced on the dirt path, and the trees seemed to envelop them, cutting off the view of the highway. Finally, staring into the gloom, she slowed even further and turned off the path into a clear spot not much larger than the car. Switching off the engine, she cranked the shift lever into park with an impatient gesture and set the emergency brake.

"All right," she said, looking at him for the first time since he had entered the car. "Let's get it done." She was already unbuttoning the shirt, revealing a substantial white cotton bra. Manny watched in silence as she shrugged out of the shirt and then unhooked the bra deftly and dropped it to the floorboard. She stopped and looked at him impatiently. "Well, are you going to fuck me or not?" Her tone was artificially blasé, her expression agate hard, but Manny saw through the guise she had adopted, saw that in addition to making his triumph less palatable, she had undertaken this means of discouraging him from going through with it.

"You're goddam right I am," he said in a tone that matched hers for coldness.

Minutes later, in the back seat of Peggy Boling's father's Chrysler, Immanuel Hartford was introduced to the ultimate pleasure. It was quickly accomplished. If Peggy had hoped that her gelid manner would render her tormentor impotent she was disappointed. He was diamond hard by the time she was half undressed, and stayed that way as he got into the back seat with her. It was all new to him, thoroughly different from his phantom dreams. Peggy Boling's body was real and substantial, yet so soft, so fragile-seeming. The feel of her stretched out under him, the attendant smells and sounds, the sight of her face so close to his as he prepared to duck into the thick gold jungle of her hair, were fresh experiences, novel delights even in the crushed conditions under which he was operating.

The ride home was a replay of the journey to their trysting place. She pulled up in front of his house and looked at him as though he were a stranger making out a check.

"I'll have those papers now," she said. Manny was about to excuse himself and get the papers, but her manner suddenly brought back all of it, the way she had treated him, the deliberate contempt she had used as a weapon to rob his victory of all its wonder.

"No you won't," he said, surprised at the steadiness of his voice.

It seemed to take her several seconds to absorb his reply. "What?"

"You haven't earned them," he explained.

Her hands twisted into claws and moved toward his face, checked halfway. "What the hell are you talking about? Didn't earn them? You son of a bitch, do you think I *enjoyed* what you did to me?"

"How much do you think *I* enjoyed it?" Manny demanded. "You've still got to earn your way out of this one, you little tramp, and you're not going to do it in the back seat of your old man's car, and you're not going to do it by treating me like some panhandler receiving a handout!" He yanked savagely on the door handle.

"Manny, you give me those papers right now or I swear I'll charge you with rape." He looked at her, trying to seem unconcerned. Apparently he did a better job than he thought, because she grew even more agitated. "You did rape me, you know. Sexual blackmail is rape, legally. I looked it up."

"Is that a fact? So you cribbed on this exam, too, huh?" That brought a deep, violent flush to her face, but she continued to stare at him threateningly. "Well, you go ahead and charge me," he advised. "I'll tell the same story as you, but with variations. Like I found those papers and decided to turn them in, but you begged me not to, and said you wanted to explain. So you drove me out in the country in your old man's Chrysler, and then you seduced me, and afterwards, when I still wouldn't agree not to expose you, you said you were going to get me into worse trouble than you were in yourself. That sounds pretty good, doesn't it?" Manny stared at her, gloating as she flushed even more deeply. "Pretty close to the way it happened, isn't it? And I think a lot of people will believe my version. A lot of the guys who've struck out with you will want to believe it. And either way, you're going to be exposed, right? A cheat. You won't even graduate." He opened the door, sat looking at her. "You've got till Monday morning to make up your mind and get in touch with me. Then, if you've come to your senses, *maybe* I can be talked out of giving that stuff to the principal. But you're not going to buy me off with one quick stab in the back seat of a car."

He was sliding out when her hand grabbed his arm, desperate and clinging. "Manny, I'm sorry," she said. "I'm sorry if I hurt your feelings tonight. I just didn't know how to handle things. I wish I could undo what I've done, honestly. But I can't go through this again. Can't you see that? I just can't!" She was crying, huge thick tears running down her face.

The twinge of guilt he felt only angered Manny further. "You really can't?" he asked with mock softness. "Then you better save the bullshit for the principal!"

CHAPTER 13

The farm was larger than Candy had anticipated. For some reason she had pictured a few acres, with an unpretentious dwelling housing the Prophet and his people. Instead it was so large that it took the better portion of an hour to drive from the periphery to the center. A young man named Walter picked her up at the bus station and drove her out in a battered pickup that jounced along the unpaved road.

Her first glimpse of the house really shook her. It resembled a mansion, or a palace. Towering over the surrounding grounds, three stories tall, enshrined by trees and neatly clipped shrubbery, it dominated the scene to such an extent that she didn't notice, until the pickup had pulled to a jolting halt, the tar-paper shacks that stood close to the fields, a respectful distance from the Prophet's dwelling. Scores of people, industriously tending the crops of cabbages, either ignored the pickup's arrival or barely glanced at it before returning to their chores. They were dressed in sturdy clothes, well worn and practical, reminiscent of those worn by the people at the chapter house in L.A. It comforted Candy to see them after hours of embarrassment on the Greyhound, when she had huddled in the rear seat to avoid curious glances at her own hand-me-downs.

Walter walked up beside her, careful to remain at a chaste distance. "I'll take you to the house," he said, phrasing the order as an offer. "I've got permission to approach," he continued with an unseemly touch of pride.

Candy assumed that he meant he was allowed to approach the mansion, something not vouchsafed to everyone. She followed him up the scrubbed concrete steps to the spacious porch and stood by while he rang the bell. Barely five seconds later the door opened and a beautiful young girl in a red minidress peered out at them. She was exquisitely coiffed and made up, with wavy black hair lying across her left shoulder. The dress, almost paper thin, appeared to be made of real silk, and was cut to reveal her figure. Her feet were enclosed in spike-heeled shoes which seemed only to accentuate her diminutive height.

"This here is Sister Candace," Walter said to the girl.

"Come in, Sister," the girl invited and, a moment later, with Candy inside, closed the door without acknowledging Walter's existence.

The interior of the house was, if anything, more imposing than the outside. The furnishings were massive and dark, the carpeting luxuriously thick. The most impressive point of all was the temperature, which was at least thirty degrees lower than the outside and stunningly refreshing. Candy was suddenly aware of the caked sweat and dirt that covered her, the dusty old clothes she wore. Next to this ravishing creature she must seem a hag. But the girl seemed unaware of the difference in their appearance. Without a word she gestured to Candy to follow her and led the way through a maze of lavishly appointed hallways and rooms to a more Spartan portion of the house, a basement room at least twenty feet square crammed with folding army cots. Each cot had at its head a gray metal locker, though none of the lockers boasted a lock.

"I'm Sister Juliet," the girl said. These were the first words she had spoken since Candy had entered the house. She asked Candy's dress and shoe sizes, then pointed to a doorway at the far side of the room. "That's the handmaidens' shower room," she said. "Place your clothes in one of the bags. When you've showered and shampooed you'll find some clothes here on your cot. Put them on and wait."

The bathroom was as simply functional as the dorm. Three metal toilets, without lids, jutted from one wall, while perpendicular to them ran a stainless steel wall covering bearing a half dozen shower nozzles, with soap dishes next to the taps. A pile of neatly folded laundry bags rested on a built-in bench opposite the toilets. The entire room was scrubbed as clean as a naval vessel.

Candy stuffed her clothes in one of the bags, as Sister Juliet had instructed her, then showered, thoroughly enjoying the experience. A pair of plastic bottles stood on the floor, lined up as precisely as soldiers on parade. One contained shampoo, and its mate, cream rinse.

There were no towels, so she padded back into the dormitory still shiny wet, her sopping hair hanging down her back in a tangle. Someone, probably Sister Juliet, had laid out one of the red dresses on a cot, and next to it lay a thick white terry-cloth towel. When she had toweled herself to a ruddy pink, Candy hung the towel on the foot of the cot and put on the red dress. It was the first time since she could remember that she had worn pretty clothes, unless one considered the waitress uniforms pretty. She sat on the edge of the cot and strapped her feet into the spike-heeled shoes. They were black patent leather, and increased her height by three inches.

"Sister Candace?" a mature feminine voice asked.

Candy started, jarred from her reverie. She turned to see a middle-aged woman in a long red dress regarding her from the doorway. "Yes," she replied. "I—"

"Come with me, please." The woman turned and strode out of the room. Candy followed as well as she could, teetering on the stilt heels. The woman led her into a nearby room. It was lined with mirrors along two walls, each mirror accommodating a vanity crammed with makeup and perfumes. A beautician's chair stood in a corner. The woman indicated that Candy was to sit in it, which she did. The vinyl was cold, alien to her bare legs. "Pay attention to what I do," the woman advised. "Because you'll have to see to yourself for the most part. I can help out, but I can't see to the grooming of all the hand maidens."

"Yes, ma'am."

"My name is Sister Fay," the woman said, and studied Candy's face like an architect inspecting a site. "Your features are perfect," she said.

"Thank you."

"Nice thick lashes, too. But I think a bit of eye makeup to set off those eyes." She turned to the nearest vanity and selected a blue makeup. Then, as an afterthought, "We'd better do something with that hair." She rolled a dryer behind the chair and adjusted it over Candy's head before turning it on. The blast of hot air made Candy's neck prickle. Sister Fay immediately set to work, applying the eye makeup with impressive skill. Next she selected a bottle of deep red nail polish, which she applied expertly. While that was drying Sister Fay applied lipstick, also deep red, to Candy's lips. Then she removed the hair dryer, switched it off, and began to brush out Candy's long blond hair.

"I think you'll do now," Sister Fay said, granting Candy a businesslike smile of approval. "Take a look at yourself."

Stiffly, Candy rose from the chair and examined herself in one of the mirrors. She had never looked so good. Sister Fay was obviously a real artist. Why she was here, why the handmaidens dressed and made themselves up so differently from the other women, Candy couldn't guess, but it wasn't her place to question or to speculate, she thought with a touch of complacent comfort. "It's wonderful," she said, turning to face the older woman.

Sister Fay smiled briefly and then, as though remembering that pride was a sin, assumed the flat, expressionless look she had shown before. "I think you'd better go on upstairs now," she said. "Find Sister Penelope. The Prophet wants to see you."

Candy felt her heart stutter. Her pulse raced and she could feel sudden dampness in the creases of her knees and elbows. She had supposed, when Sister Claudia had told her she was to come here, that she would eventually see the Prophet, but probably only at a distance, perhaps as he walked by during her work. But to be ushered into his presence! And so soon! Her insides were knotted with apprehension at the prospect of standing in the presence of divinity. She wanted to run from the house.

Sister Fay, apparently sensing her feelings, favored her with another brief smile. "Go on, now," she said. "You wouldn't want to keep him waiting."

Sister Penelope, a tall girl with a peachy complexion and long red hair, looked Candy over critically. She was the only girl Candy had seen wearing anything other than a red silk minidress. (Sister Fay didn't seem to count, somehow.) Her dress was of silk, and was as brief as the others, considering her height, but it was blue, which Candy took to be some sort of badge of rank.

"I hope you understand the extent of the honor that is bestowed upon you," she said a trifle archly.

"Oh, yes, Sister."

"To serve in the Prophet's house is an opportunity to amass a considerable amount of his grace. You can never be worthy of it, and if you were worthier, you wouldn't even be here, since the prophet selects the worst sinners, who may best profit from his presence."

"I know that, Sister."

"I'm told that your dedication has been adequate," Sister Penelope said, moving down the hall.

Candy followed, trying to match her superior stride.

"But here we work twice as hard. Sixteen hours a day, and we don't take breaks. We keep this house immaculate, and see to it that anything the Prophet desires is right at hand. It's enough that he is here to save mankind, without having to wonder why there are no handkerchiefs in his bureau drawer, or when his breakfast will be ready." She stopped in front of a massive double door. "There is no time for socializing here," Sister Penelope concluded. "So we maintain a strict rule of silence, speaking only in the line of duty."

"I understand."

Sister Penelope rapped on the door.

"Come in," a deep masculine voice called, muffled by the heavy wood.

Candy felt her knees buckle under her. She was able to remain standing only through a supreme force of will.

"You heard the Prophet," Sister Penelope chided. "Go on in. And try not to disgrace yourself."

CHAPTER 14

Peggy Boling beat the deadline with plenty to spare. It was Sunday morning when she called. Manny's mother was clearing the breakfast table, so it was he who answered the phone. Fortunately, he was in the hall, away from his parents' hearing.

"Manny?" Her voice was much more controlled than when he had last heard it, but no less desperate. The desperation was wrapped in a soft, conciliatory tissue.

"That's right." He kept his own voice flat, as though he didn't care why she had called, or that she had called at all.

"Are you alone? I mean can you talk?"

"For a minute."

"I've found a place for us."

He let that one lie for a moment, absorbing not only what she had said, but the way she had phrased it.

"Did you hear me, honey?" she asked.

Manny was getting an erection. "Sure I heard you," he replied indifferently.

"Well, will you be free next Saturday night?"

"I guess so."

"I thought maybe you could tell your parents you were staying with a friend. That wouldn't really be a lie, would it?"

Manny felt a sheen of perspiration on his forehead. He suspected that she was suggesting that they spend the night together, but didn't want to ask and give away his Joe Cool act. "Yeah, I might be able to do that," he said. "Only you better not pick me up here in that case. I'll meet you around the corner, on Loara."

"Okay. What time?"

71

"Seven sharp."

"Right. I'll be there."

When he had hung up Manny went into his room to ponder the call. There had been something in Peggy's voice that seemed out of place. It wasn't just that she was sweet-talking him. He supposed she had learned her lesson, and knew that she was going to have to be really nice to him if she wanted to salvage her dreams. Right now he supposed she was biting her lip and pounding her shapely thigh because she had had to yield so much. His fantasy world was beginning to merge with his conception of reality, so that the pleasure of domination was taking on the same air as it had when he had fantasized it in the past. The embarrassment and fear he had felt in the beginning, which he had overcome only through the anger Peggy Boling's reaction had engendered in him, were beginning to give way to the joy of power, which was, if anything, more captivating than he had imagined. But there had been that something in Peggy's voice, something he still had not identified.

It came to him in a blinding flash. The undercurrent of her tone had been one of excitement. The same sort of excitement he himself had felt, and felt at this moment. It had sounded as though she were also living out some cherished fantasy, some daydream in which she had indulged during masturbation or perhaps lovemaking.

Manny sat bolt upright on his bed, his heart tripping with the thrill of this fresh insight. If Peggy Boling, the soul of normality, the sweetheart of Chesterton High, the pampered little all-American girl, could display a streak of masochism powerful enough to respond to blackmail of this type, then what of other people? There must be many of them.

Could the way Peggy had treated him during their tryst have been the consequence of a desire to punish herself as much as him? Had she been hoping, in some preconscious cranny of her mind, that he would take offense and force her to do it all again, establishing his dominance over her in the process? Had she left the crib notes lying around in the first place because, on some level, she had wanted him to take them, either to expose her or to hold them over her head?

It was a dazzling vision. It could mark the turning point in his young life. If there really were people in the world who wanted nothing except to be punished and tormented, then such people would richly reward someone who would not only serve their desires but justify them.

Though Manny didn't know it, his new insight, and his response to it, marked another turning point. He had looked upon the temporary dominance he enjoyed over Peggy Boling as a fortuitous accident, a lapse of the odds, something that could never, in a single lifetime, repeat itself. An opportunity to live out one's fantasies, with the object of those fantasies, was clearly a freak accident. But now, for the first time, he saw it as something that had had to happen, if not now with Peggy Boling, then eventually with someone like her. His fantasy world had merged with reality. It was possible, he now believed, to make fantasies come true. You only had to be in control, to recognize people for what they were and act accordingly, and any fantasy could be brought to realization.

People who are crazy enough to believe that such things are possible often find that they are. Such people can be very dangerous.

CHAPTER 15

The Chambers family had arrived at the farm a few days prior to the appearance of Candy Sterling. They were unaware of her existence at that time, and thus oblivious to the fateful link that was being forged between their presence and hers.

At the moment of their arrival they were exhausted, having begged and stolen rides across half of the United States, walking for days at a time when rides were simply not to be had. Joseph Chambers had weathered the ordeal quite well for a man of his age. Working hard all his life on the farm had kept him hardy. His three youngsters—Mary, Henry, and Virginia —had plodded along with their parents, complaining remarkably little. Polly, his wife, had had the worst of it. Never a hardy woman, she had begun, on this trek, to show signs of a pernicious frailty that would ultimately wear her down.

They had hitched a ride from town to the edge of the farm, arriving early in the morning, and thence had walked to the location of the house. All of them stood awed at the sight of this edifice. The children, who ranged from thirteen years to sixteen, were mutely impressed. Polly looked upon it as though it were a cathedral. Joseph felt a stirring of something inside, something he quelled with a conscious effort. Then he approached the house, his family trailing close behind.

A young man who had been tending the shrubbery intercepted them. " 'Scuse me," he said, smiling a bit diffidently. "My name is Brother Walter. I—"

"I am Joseph Chambers," Joseph informed him. "This is my wife, Polly, and these are my children."

"Do you have business here, Mr. Chambers?"

"We've come to—to serve the Prophet," Joseph said,

grasping for the term he had heard the evangelists use. "I think we're expected."

"Well, I have authority to approach the house of the Prophet," Brother Walter explained. "If you don't mind waiting here for a moment?" Joseph nodded, feeling that stirring again in the pit of his stomach. The younger man mounted the stately porch of the house and rang the bell. A moment later the door opened a crack. Someone inside, someone Joseph couldn't see clearly, exchanged words with Brother Walter, then closed the door. Brother Walter smiled at the Chambers family and returned to his chores. Joseph was about to approach him and ask what was going on when, ten minutes after the brief meeting on the porch, the door opened more widely and a young girl in an astonishingly short red dress leaned out and motioned them to approach.

She led them through a sumptuously furnished, air-conditioned house, speaking not a word. Joseph Chambers felt that thing in his gut again, and once more quelled it by a force of will. It was simply intolerable to think that he had made a mistake in bringing himself and his family to this place. He had come expecting a godly atmosphere, but this house for some reason seemed to him more likely to belong to Satan than to Jehovah. The girl knocked on one of a pair of thick oaken doors. Instantly a masculine voice from the other side invited them to enter. The girl opened the door, seeming, in Joseph's opinion, more than a little nervous. She ducked a bit at the knees the moment they were in the room.

"The Chambers family, Lord."

The use of the reverent title gave Joseph a mild shock, though it shouldn't have. He had been told that the Prophet of the All-Moving Spirit was divine. He had accepted that, or thought he had, before starting on this journey. He had clung to that belief when his wife had been assailed by doubts. Indeed, only his determination had brought about their ultimate arrival. But what he saw before him, in the middle of this commodious house, was a young man in his late twenties sporting a close-clipped, pointed beard and wearing what seemed a very expensive three-piece suit in conservative gray. The man was no more than five and a half feet tall, and far from the most imposing figure Joseph had ever seen. His hair had begun to gray at the temples, which added a touch of distinction to his appearance, but all in all he looked like an overdressed store clerk to Joseph.

"Leave us," the young man ordered, and the girl fled as though the command had rumbled from the center of a burning bush. The Prophet, for such Joseph assumed he must be, rose from the leather couch on which he had been sprawled and, hooking his thumbs in his vest pockets, approached the Chamberses.

"I can see to the core of your wretched souls," he cautioned them. "It would be rash and futile to try to deceive the Prophet." From this closer vantage Joseph could see something different in the man, something that had not been apparent from across the large room. There was an air to his bearing, and a ring to his voice, and most significantly a fierce sparkle deep in his eyes, that were intimidating and somehow comforting at the same time. As he fastened his gaze on each of them in turn, Joseph could feel the effect on his wife and children. Mary, who had recently turned sixteen, stirred as though something deep inside her had just awakened. Thirteen-year-old Henry tried to meet the man's gaze but faltered and lowered his eyes. Virginia, almost fifteen, gasped aloud as though the expression in those eyes had actually struck her with physical force. But the most marked response came from Joseph's wife. Polly Chambers seemed to revive under that gaze as though a stimulant had been injected into her bloodstream. She stared into the Prophet's eyes with a fascination that astounded her husband.

Joseph himself was far from immune to the effect of the Prophet's gaze. His family's response, too, had its effect upon him, overriding his scepticism. Joseph lowered his gaze as the Prophet looked at him.

"Why have you come here?" the Prophet demanded sternly, still looking at Joseph.

Joseph stirred, trying to frame a reply.

"If you have come seeking happiness, you have made a grievous mistake," the Prophet warned. "The All-Moving Spirit offers no earthly joys to those who serve Him. Happiness in the next life, yes. But here, only tears and travail. Those who are happy in this life have had their reward. Can they expect more in the hereafter?" He looked up and down the line, as though reading answers in their souls.

No one spoke, though the three females stirred with nervous excitement. Joseph felt his veins contract, his pulse labor. He was ashamed of himself for the doubts he had entertained. He supposed he had come to this place looking for some transitory earthly happiness. That had been his mistake, his sin. "We have come to serve, Lord."

"Yes, Lord," Polly murmured.

The Prophet showed no sign of having heard them, or of caring. But then he turned his gaze upon Joseph again. "Opportunity to serve I can promise you," he assured. "And I shall grant you the grace and strength to do it. Whether you will meet the test depends on yourselves. Not on your strength, for all strength comes from the All-Moving Spirit, through His Prophet. Success or failure, resurrection or spiritual death, depends on your sincerity, on the degree of your honest dedication. If you are not dedicated I shall not have to cast you out. You will cast yourselves out. And those who have once rejected the grace of the All-Moving Spirit have no hope."

The Chambers family stirred, fidgeting a bit, anxious and disturbed at this prophecy of their damnation. Joseph felt his throat go dry, and for one insane moment he knew an urge to fall at the Prophet's feet and swear that he would never reject the grace of the All-Moving Spirit.

When the Prophet spoke again his voice was less stentorian, more perfunctory. "You and you," he said, indicating Joseph and Henry, "go outside, and do not approach this place or my person again without invitation. Jobs will be provided. Work to your full capacity and remain in a state of grace. I shall speak further to the women."

It never occurred to Joseph to question the Prophet's intentions. He even found himself bowing at the waist slightly as he and his son backed toward the double oaken doors. It would be days before the spell would wear off sufficiently for him to question the feelings that had pervaded all in the Prophet's presence, before he would begin to suspect that he had been in the control of an expert spellbinder. For the moment, he was relieved to quit the oppressive atmosphere of the man's library.

Ten minutes later, oblivious to the weariness of his journey, he was picking cabbages, trying vainly to keep up with those who had been there before him.

CHAPTER 16

Candy had known Vernon for three months when she finally seduced him; that is, it had started out as a seduction, but what it was by then she couldn't have said with any degree of certainty. In the beginning she had approached the task as a challenge and a test. To Candy, sex had always been a means of livelihood and a weapon, one which she used against herself as much as the men with whom she lay, though she was unaware of that. Sex as an expression of love or affection, or even healthy lust, was something she had heard about but thought existed only in fairy tales and movies. It was something men wanted, rather indiscriminately, and therefore something that could be bartered for money or favors. It also lowered the men because they had to make concessions out of need for something that meant nothing to her.

Vernon was the first man to remain in intimate contact with her for very long without trying for a score. What made it even harder to comprehend was the fact that she could sense his attraction to her. She had learned early that obviousness wouldn't work with him, but she was certain that all that held him back was some angle of his own, and that he wanted what all the others had wanted. At first she set out to prove this with a zest for the challenge. After the first few weeks, when the sense of frustration had worn off and she had begun to feel something new and different for this man, had learned something of his beliefs and come to share them, she found that her sympathies were enlisted on the other side. She still tried to seduce him, but found herself hoping that he would not succumb to her blandishments. She had begun to suspect that what he seemed to be was genuine. She had to know that for

81

certain, which was why she continued to test him at every opportunity; but now she wanted desperately to fail in her attempted conquest.

Halfway through the third month of their acquaintance she began to shift again, to hope that he would prove susceptible to her advances. But this time her motivation was different. For the first time in her young life, Candy Sterling felt the pangs of desire. She wasn't certain of when the desire to conquer Vernon had metamorphosed into a deeper, more genuine need, but somewhere along the line, probably earlier than she realized, she had begun to want this man, to feel affection and need for him, need which she translated into sexual desire.

Candy had been prey to conflicting emotions and desires all her life, though she had never been quite so acutely aware of them before. She feared that Vernon would succumb to her and prove himself no different from any other man, and she feared that the unfamiliar passion that flared in her would remain frustrated. The two fears seemed irreconcilable.

She had left the streets for some time, living partly off Vernon and partly from the little money she could earn at part-time jobs. She had taken up waiting tables, since it was something she could do with no education or training. In the beginning she simulated a new moral sense, putting it on like a long, baggy dress, in order to fool Vernon and keep his support and aid. Then, as her feeling for him grew, she did it to make herself worthy of him, the kind of girl he would be likely to want. And then an even stranger thing happened: She began to make sense of all that stuff he had her reading.

She had branched out from the Bible to books and pamphlets interpreting the things she had read, and explaining them. Within a week she found that she had become a devoted believer. And then came the night when she finally seduced Vernon. Only she didn't do it by herself. She had a lot of help.

They were alone in his apartment, his roommate being away on another of his skiing weekends. Candy and Vernon lay on the floor, surrounded by books and papers. He had been explaining some particularly abstruse point to her, relating it to her own experience, the experience he kept insisting she would enjoy once she had accepted Jesus Christ as her personal savior and lord.

"But I told you, I *have* accepted Him," she said wearily. They had been at it since early evening, and it was now in the wee hours of the morning. Candy didn't want to end things, tired as she was, because she was enjoying Vernon's company. He merely smiled at her assertion. As much as she loved him, Candy was sometimes infuriated by Vernon's superior manner. "Damn—darn it, Vernon, how do you know whether I've done it or not?" she flared.

"Because," he explained, "when it does happen, you and I will both know it. I've seen it happen too many times, Candy," he said over her burgeoning objection. "It's like a volcanic eruption: Once you've seen one, you can recognize it every time. And you'll always know a fake."

"I am *not* a fake!" she gasped, staring at him through eyes suddenly filled with tears. From him such an accusation was intolerable.

"I didn't say you were," he explained. "I just said that your acceptance of the Lord is a fake. It's counterfeit, honey, and you don't know it because you've lived with counterfeit experiences all your life."

Candy stared at him, the tears still in her eyes, but her mouth curling into a smile. He looked bewildered by her response. It was the first time Candy had seen him thrown off balance. "That's the first time you've ever called me honey," she said, her voice charged with quiet, proud joy.

"Oh. Well, it's just—"

"It's just a term," she finished. "I know." Her smile broadened. "Like 'darling' or 'sweetheart.' "

"Candy, stop it!" he ordered with such sudden vehemence that Candy drew back, startled. They had been lying on their stomachs as they poured over the tracts and books. Now he slid away from her and sat up, hugging his knees in a protective, prenatal position. His face creased in a frown and he refused to look at her. "I'm only human, you know," he said in a tone that combined moroseness with entreaty.

"Are you?" Candy said, a note of humor sneaking into her voice despite herself. "I was beginning to think you were more than that."

"You don't know how much I've prayed for the strength to resist you." Suddenly he looked directly at her in an accusatory manner. "Did you think I was unaware of what you were doing, or trying to do?" Suddenly Candy felt a wave of shame, or embarrassment, as though she had been discovered doing something unwholesome. Before she could speak Vernon continued, looking away from her once again. "I didn't bring you here to make love to you."

"I know that," Candy said softly. "I wish you had. I wish you would."

"Candy, we are not man and wife," he said intensely, his gaze skittering past hers.

Candy felt a chill run through her, a complex emotion she couldn't disentangle. The thought of marriage had never entered her mind on a conscious level, but now she was certain that it was what she had wanted from the first night, that time they had met in front of the coffee shop. To be his wife. The idea pulsed through her like something alive and distinct from her own personality, something that had entered her to possess her. But at the same time she felt this other thing, this sudden terror, this intense melancholy.

"You look down on me, don't you?" she asked in a dead voice. He looked at her in surprise. "Because I've screwed around so much. Because I've been a whore." Suddenly he came toward her. She drew back a bit, suddenly fearful of his touch. His hands closed about her slender arms and he looked down into her eyes. He was kneeling and she was sitting on one hip.

"No, Candy, no, I don't look down on you. How could I? Don't you know better than that now? Haven't I told you? Haven't you learned? We're all miserable sinners, darling, all corrupt to the core of our being. Our only chance is through Jesus Christ. That's the only difference between you and me: His help and support. I'd have done things just as bad as the things you've done, maybe worse, if not for His aid. That's why I'm trying to help you. I want you to know His help, too. I want the Holy Spirit to enter you as He has entered me."

It wasn't so much the things he was saying as the stunning difference in his manner that captivated Candy in that moment. She had heard most of this before, but always in a flat, pedagogic manner, as though he were a teacher and she a pupil. She had had no notion that he could be overtaken by this sort of intensity. It communicated itself to her, filled her with an excitement she had never known. Her breathing went all ragged, and warmth spread from her loins up into her breasts and down into her thighs. Her eyes watered from the force of this sudden emotion. The room wavered in and out of focus and seemed to rock under her. Strange, strangled noises erupted from her throat, frightening her. She thought she was undergoing some sort of attack, a brain dysfunction. Dimly, she heard Vernon's voice, as though from a great distance, and muffled by multiple layers of insulating material.

"Don't fight it, Candy, go with it," he was saying. "Let it happen, honey."

It was hard, doing as he asked, but she tried, stifling her own impulse to resist this thing that was happening to her.

And then it was as though it had all exploded inside of her, something hot and strong and strangely joyous.

When she came out of it she was lying on her back, staring up at the ceiling, feeling weak and purged. On the edge of her vision she saw Vernon smiling happily, and she knew what it had been, what had happened to her. She smiled back at him.

"It happened, didn't it?" she asked in a soft, furry voice. "He came into me." Vernon nodded enthusiastically, too happy to answer in words. She closed her eyes and let her head roll slowly from side to side. "How could I have thought I had —? I didn't know, Vernon. I didn't know what it was like, how it was."

"I know. Nobody ever knows until it happens. You've just been born again, Candy. You're a new person now."

"I love you," she said so suddenly she surprised herself. Vernon's eyes blazed with a sudden pleasure, and she knew that her feeling for him was reciprocated. Involuntarily, he moved toward her, stopping himself just within reach. Candy reached up and grasped his neck, lacing her fingers behind it. She felt the tiniest bit of resistance on his part, but pulled his face down to her own. Their first kiss began as a chaste, almost symbolic touching of lips. Candy felt a resurgence of the emotion that had wrung her out a few moments before, and she pushed her tongue into his mouth hungrily. She had never felt genuine desire before, though she had learned to simulate it. The power of this need was something new to her, something astounding. It felt almost exactly as the experience of being born again had felt. Vernon resisted weakly, making a listless attempt to disengage himself from her. Candy broke off the kiss and pressed her cheek against his.

"It's all right, Vernon," she whispered. "It's all right, darling. He wants us to love each other. I know He does. I know . . ."

CHAPTER 17

On the occasion of her first meeting with the Prophet, Candy had her blood purified. She had stood in the middle of his den, awed and terrified in the knowledge that she was in the presence of divinity, more convinced of that fact than ever before now that she had been subjected to the hypnotic gaze and manner of the Prophet. She felt as though flame hovered about her while she stood before him, flame that desired to consume her and was held in check only by his sufferance. Her legs felt weak and elastic under her. Her insides churned convulsively. It was not altogether an unpleasant sensation: There was a potent physical stimulation mixed in with the rest, an excitement that made her skin tingle and her bowels tighten. She had felt it before, just prior to sexual relations with Vernon. But she believed that she had never felt it this strongly, and certainly not from just being in the presence of a man. To Candy that seemed proof, if proof had been needed, that he was indeed the Prophet of the All-Moving Spirit.

He stood several feet from her and allowed his eyes to move over her from top to bottom to top. There was contempt in his expression, as though he found her body not just repulsive but somehow reprehensible, as though he blamed her for its lushness. "You are filth." His voice was low and toneless, with a tom-tom rhythm. He almost chanted. "Offal," he said, elaborating on his opening statement. "Refuse." His words took her by surprise, widening her large, curved eyes. She took no offense at any of it because she knew in every cell of her corrupt body that his statements represented a truth which he, of all people, had every right to express. "You are an insult to the majestic and benign creation of the All-Moving Spirit," he continued. "Your existence is an affront to all that is good."

Candy felt an overwhelming urge to lower her eyes but knew somehow that she must not, that it was part of her chastisement to stand in the full heat of the Prophet's gaze as he castigated her.

"You have allowed your spirit to mingle with your body," he continued in the same violently monotonous manner. "Your spirit, which the All-Moving Spirit created in perfection, you have sullied. Your body is a collection of filthy juices, blood that is tainted, and it has washed away the cleanliness in which your soul was born. The All-Moving Spirit looks upon you with greater loathing than you would feel toward a spider, or the moist droppings in a privy. Your stink fills His nostrils, as the voluptuous sinfulness of your body fills His eyes."

He paused, looking her over again with that same indolent contempt, sending fresh waves of shameful excitement through her. Then, slowly, he walked to her, standing at last only inches away. She could feel the warmth of his body, his breath on her face. For some reason her nipples stood erect under the thin dress she wore. He looked at them meaningfully, as though she had just proved the validity of his accusations. She willed them to soften, to stop advertising the very corruption he had seen in her so clearly. They merely grew harder, bigger, and she trembled, barely able to maintain her erect posture.

Reaching out with elaborate casualness he pulled her dress off her shoulders, revealing her breasts. Candy started, looking directly into his eyes. She could see no excitement in his gaze, no attraction. He looked at her breasts with chill revulsion.

"You are not only evil," he observed. "You are brazen. The worst parts of you rule your spirit and advertise their ascendancy. Your blood is as corrupt as any I have encountered." The dress, no longer supported by her shoulders and breasts, began to slip past her hips, and she grabbed at it. The Prophet slapped her hands aside, allowing the dress to drop into a puddle about her feet. Candy wavered, very nearly falling, but he seemed not to notice. "The unclean juices of your body are flowing," he said.

And it was true! Candy wanted to weep, to beg his

forgiveness for her wickedness, but her throat was constricted, her voice locked inside her.

"Your blood must be purified," he warned her in flat, perfunctory tones. "Merely serving will not save you. Without purification you are lost."

Lost . . .

The word seemed to echo all around her, as though she were already falling through some deep, dark cavern into a bottomless, eternal pit. She recognized that cavern and that pit. She had begun that fall once already, and the thought of falling into it for all time frightened her beyond her own power to conceive of fear.

"Please . . ." Candy's voice came out finally, a soft, croaking sound that was foreign to her, with a huskiness that spoke of excitement. She had forgotten the excitement. But it was still there, its edges hovering about like a dark curtain, ready to enfold her.

"You have indulged in lewd and sensuous acts," he said, not so much accusing as stating an obvious fact. "You are no longer virginal."

"No. I . . ."

"I can restore your virginity. I can make you pure again, and pleasing in the gaze of the All-Moving Spirit. Do you want me to purify you?" Candy dropped suddenly to her knees, no longer able to balance her own weight, and embraced his knees, laying her face against the soft texture of his trousers.

"Oh, please," she moaned in a tortured wail. "Oh, yes, please, Lord, please save me!"

Somehow she found herself on the huge couch, the leather cool and comforting against her skin. Then his weight was pressing her into it, and he was inside of her. She had never felt anything so intense, so powerful and overwhelming. Something seemed to explode in her, searing her veins and intestines. It was cathartic, wringing her clean of all the corruption in her system.

Later, as she went about her unfamiliar chores, doubts assailed her. They were sinful doubts, and she tried hard to suppress them, finally succeeding. She had been told, and had read in the movement's pamphlets, that all sexual activity was sinful and corrupt, and that the Prophet was incapable of sin.

Had a sexual act really taken place between them, or had she only imagined that part of it? Had it just seemed, as she was being reborn, that he had been wreaking these feelings in a way she could understand? For a while she decided that that was indeed the explanation: Incapable of encompassing what had been happening to her, she had simply translated it into mundane terms.

But there was another possibility. It was just possible that the Prophet, to test her faith and credulity, had chosen to use his body as a vessel and work his miraculous will in a manner that would have been degrading and corrupt if done by any other man.

She didn't know which alternative was true. Quite possibly she would never know. The only thing she knew for certain was that she was indeed the disgusting and profane creature the Prophet had perceived and described.

CHAPTER 18

Immanuel Hartford's growing suspicion that he could indeed bring his fantasies to life and have anything he wanted was given a large boost a few days after his second and more satisfying assignation with Peggy Boling.

On that occasion she truly capitulated, making herself as ingratiating as she possibly could, doing anything he demanded, and initiating the things which he, in his inexperience, could not have conceived. She waited on him as though he were a pasha and behaved as though he were an irresistible god of masculinity. With stunning feminine insight she anticipated his desires and catered to them before he was fully aware of their nature.

She was cordial and cheery to the end, even as she drove him home. Manny sat on the far side of the car, tired with all the unaccustomed screwing and slightly depressed because his golden weekend was over. Peggy parked her Mustang a half block from his house. It was twelve minutes to nine Sunday night.

"Well, did I earn my freedom this time?" she asked.

He had been thinking about that, wondering whether he dared to refuse her the blackmail papers this time, and had decided there was no way he could do so. It wasn't any consideration for justice that deterred him but the simple fear that she might react insanely, bringing it all out and wrecking them both.

"Just a minute," he said. "I'll be right back." He went to the house and retrieved the crib notes from where he had stashed them. Crumpling the papers slightly in one fist he took them outside and back to the waiting car. The engine purred softly.

He tarried along the way, reluctant to return the papers to Peggy. The papers, and the threat they implied against her, were certainly worth more than a single weekend. He wished that he had insisted at the outset on several such trysts. But it was too late now to think of such things. To shock her with additional demands might prove disastrous. He approached the car and leaning in, thrust the papers at her.

"Here," he said. "From now on, maybe you'll be more careful what you leave lying around."

"You bet I will," she said, her eyes snapping. Grabbing the sheets from his hand she put the car into drive and pulled away from the curb, barely giving him time to extricate himself from the rolled-down window. He stood looking after the car, wondering for the first time whether his brilliant flash of insight on the day she had called and offered him this weekend had been valid. A wave of melancholy swept over him as he watched the little car accelerate, the exhaust leaving a trail of smoke that seemed to evanesce in the same manner as his dreams.

The next morning he passed her in school. They were moving from one class to another, and she walked by him as though she could see through him, as though he were a stranger rather than a boy who, less than twenty-four hours before, had held her delicious tit in his hand, feeling it quiver with delicate responsiveness.

It was the day after that that she called him. Less than an hour after school the telephone jangled, and since he was standing next to it, and there was no one else at home at the moment, he grabbed the instrument off the cradle, feeling a sudden heart acceleration.

"Manny?" she asked, when he had spoken. There was a soft, conciliatory tone to her voice, as though she had regressed to that day when she had called to invite him to the cabin.

"Yeah," he said cautiously. He suspected some sort of vindictive trap.

"This is Peggy," she said, as though he didn't know it. "I want to talk to you."

"So talk."

"No, not like this," she said. "Can we meet? I thought maybe I could buy you a Coke or something."

They met half an hour later at a coffee shop where the high school kids didn't normally hang out. It was a crowded place where, if she had arranged to have some bruiser get him, he could take refuge in the presence of other people. She showed up in her cheerleader outfit, causing most of the men in the shop to swivel their heads with greater or lesser degrees of subtlety. Manny recalled that there was some sort of athletic event scheduled for that evening. There was no reason for her to dress for it so early. She looked stunningly sexy in the short skirt, with her hair hanging loose and free down her back. Sliding into the booth he already occupied, she smiled at him shyly.

"Manny," she said after ordering the Cokes, "I want you to swear something to me." She wasn't looking at him, but at her slender white hands, lying atop the table.

"What is it?"

"I want you to assure me that"—suddenly she looked straight into his eyes, captivating him with her own wide blue ones—"that you didn't make any copies of that . . . thing you gave back to me the other night." There was a pleading air to her, as one would expect, but it had a cryptic quality to it that told Manny this might be a good moment to play for time. Fortunately, the waitress showed up promptly with their Cokes, setting them on little paper coasters.

"Will there be anything else?" she asked perfunctorily.

"No, that will be all," Peggy said softly. The waitress tore off their check and laid it on neutral ground, halfway between them. "Well?" Peggy asked when they enjoyed a measure of privacy.

"Would I do a thing like that?" Manny smiled smugly, allowing her to lend her own interpretation to the question.

"I don't know," she began, and then looked straight at him again, trying to appear challenging and not quite making it. "Don't play games with me, hon— Don't play games, Manny. I *have* to *know*!" Manny took a sip of his Coke and sat back, sprawling in the booth with an elegantly loutish manner.

"When you think of it, a Xerox copy of those papers would be just about as damning as the original, wouldn't it? And a dozen or, say, fifteen copies would be even better. I could send them to the teacher, the principal, your boyfriend, your parents, even the school paper and that medical school you were—I mean you are—planning to attend next fall."

"Manny?" Her voice was soft, confidential, but she was beginning to cry.

Manny wasn't certain of just how far he could push this one, but he intended to find out. "Of course, there'd be no reason for me to do that if you and I were . . ." He let it trail off.

"How many times?" she demanded, her manner a mixture of anger, outrage, and despair. "How many times do I have to do it before you'll let me go?" She had apparently convinced herself that he had engineered this meeting, that it was all his idea. Manny had no intention of challenging that fantasy. She had been home free, but maybe, on some level of which she was unaware, she didn't want to be free.

"How many times do you have to do what?" he asked, deliberately, insolently cruel.

"You know what!" Her voice had crept up a decibel, and she brought it down quickly, looking about her at the people, who seemed unaware of her existence. The coffee shop was filled with the hum of conversation. "You know," she almost whispered.

"I want to hear you say it."

"How many times do I have to put out for you?" This time her sublimated feelings made it close enough to the surface to produce a little smile, just at the corners of her mouth, that luscious mouth that could do such wondrous things.

"I didn't say you had to put out for me." Manny took a large swig of his Coke. "I was just remarking that a lot of people would find those Xerox copies very interesting, were I to send them out."

"But what good would that do?" she asked in a desperate voice, looking at him with an intense expression in her eyes.

"It's a question of duty, Peggy. If a guy refrains from doing what he knows is right, it has to be for the sake of someone who is very close to him." Manny took a huge swallow of his Coke, almost draining the glass. He took a sensual delight in it, looking at those lush breasts under her sweater, and then at the thick blond hair that hung luxuriously down her back. She couldn't hold his gaze but sat staring into her own Coke as though it were a crystal ball holding the black secrets of her future.

"Are you free Saturday night?" she asked in a miserable but vibrant voice.

"Sure. And Friday night, too. And Sunday."

"I guess we're going steady now, aren't we?" she asked despondently. But those breasts were heaving with a strange excitement.

"We might, if you ask me nicely. Thanks for the Coke."

He whistled all the way home from the coffee shop.

CHAPTER 19

Some were less susceptible than others to the Prophet's charisma. Virginia Chambers was not unmoved by the hypnotic quality of his personality on that first meeting. She had fallen under his spell to nearly the same degree as her parents and siblings. But even from the first moment, she entertained doubts about him. There was something overly dramatic in his delivery, something that looked like a role he had played a bit too often, like a tired actor after a long run. It reminded her a bit of the barkers she had seen at the fairs back in South Dakota, or an old movie with John Barrymore that she had once watched on TV. She had felt the power of his personality, but at the same time had felt a conflicting urge to giggle at his performance. She hadn't felt much like laughing after he had sent her father and brother out of the room and confronted Virginia, her mother, and her sister.

He fixed that gaze on each of them in turn. Virginia could see her sister flex and ripple as the Prophet's eyes moved over her, and when her own turn came Virginia felt like crossing her arms in front of her body. She had the feeling that he could see right through her clothes, and was appraising her body.

Then he moved away a couple of steps, leaned back against his desk, and began to tell them how horrible they all were. He seemed to concentrate on the young girls, mentioning in a kind of aside that their mother was a rotten sinner but not nearly as bad as her daughters, who were very nearly beyond redemption, and had come to the farm and the movement just in time to save their mortal souls, or some such thing. It made Virginia mad, though she had to fight at moments to keep from buying into it. She had never considered herself rotten, consciously, and had certainly never thought of Mama that way.

What really shocked her was that she could sense Mama accepting everything the Prophet was saying, and her older sister seemed to be going along with it too, unless she was just going along with Mama. Both of them hung their heads as though he had caught them at something, as though they had always known of their own iniquity and had been hiding it shamefully. Mama! And Mary! It was more than she could have believed if she hadn't been there to see it for herself. Finally, having fed enough of his message into them, the Prophet approached Mama, looking directly into her eyes. He wasn't much taller than she but seemed to have mastered some trick that allowed him to tower over people regardless of their height.

"Woman," he said directly into Mama's twitching, tear-stained face, "you can benefit from my service by working in the fields. I shall permit you to return to your husband. But remember," he remonstrated, raising a stiff finger something like the villain in an old melodrama, "that here marriage is a spiritual bond, and an aid to efficiency. You will live with your husband purely, like a sister. You will be his helpmate. Mark my words well! If you fall from grace, I shall know it, as the All-Moving Spirit will know it, and you will be barred from salvation, lost, destined irretrievably for the pit, the flame that burns but consumes not!"

Mama just stood there, trembling in terror, and Virginia wanted to kick this man in the shin for scaring her like that, when she was in bad health, tired, and such a good, well-meaning soul anyway. But she knew that if she stood up to him Mama would be shocked.

"Do you hear me, woman?" the Prophet demanded in a loud, officious tone.

Mama gulped audibly and nodded so fast she seemed to be trying to shake something loose from her hair. "Yes, sir," she stammered.

"Address me properly," the Prophet commanded. "Address me as Lord, for I am your lord in all matters."

"Yes, Lord," Mama amended. Virginia could tell she was about to pass out and needed to get out of that room right away. But the Prophet wasn't quite finished with them. He fixed his gaze on Virginia for a moment, and then on Mary.

"Your daughters are another matter," he announced. "In time they too will be allowed to take their places in the fields, and I shall assign them husbands to live with in purity. But for now they are not ready. They are too evil, too besmirched by wickedness. Only the foulest sinners among my followers are brought into this house to serve. Those who most need my presence to sanctify them. It is fortunate that in such matters my power is infinite, for they are indeed corrupt. Their blood is polluted with sin, and the ways of the world, and their souls have been awash in their blood. Do you want your daughters to spend eternity expiating their wickedness?"

"No, Lord, no!" Mama gasped, her knees going all rubbery so that she nearly fell. She had to thrust out one arm for balance.

"Then they must be totally entrusted to me," he said. "You must forget them for now, and think not of them, for only by dissolving the parental bond can you help them. They will work in this house, where they will serve their Lord as handmaidens. By being in my holy presence they shall be saved. The progressive corruption of their blood will be slowed, halted, eventually reversed. Only in this manner can they be afforded a chance of redemption. Do you understand me, woman?"

"Y—yes, Lord." She was unable to look at him.

Virginia could see that there was something other than fear in Mama's trembling. She seemed excited in some strange way that she herself was probably unaware of.

"And do you believe?"

"Yes. Yes, I believe, Lord."

When she said that, there was a moaning, almost ecstatic sound in Mama's voice, something which Virginia couldn't even understand. It was as though she liked being told what to do by this awful man. It was as though it—turned her on.

"Now go," said the Prophet. "Go out in the fields and work for my glory, and the advancement of the movement. You must work night and day to retrieve yourself from the bog of evil in which you have wallowed these many years. *Go!*"

Without a word Mama backed away a few steps and then turned and bolted out those heavy double doors. Virginia and

Mary stood there, the empty space between them seeming still to contain the echo of Mama's sadness.

"And now for you," the Prophet said to Mary. "And you," he added, glancing toward Virginia. "You disgusting creatures are to serve here, to work as my servants for my welfare, to relieve me of the cares and petty considerations of life. In return for this small duty you shall enjoy the healing, sanctifying quality of my holy presence. Do you understand?"

"Yes, Lord," Mary replied quickly.

Virginia felt herself still smoldering from the horrid thing he had done to Mama. But she knew there was no sense making trouble with him at this point. Not until Mama and Papa came to their senses. So she nodded, averting her gaze from him so he wouldn't see the expression of contempt in her eyes.

"Yes, Lord," she murmured, and it seemed to satisfy him. As a farm girl she was no stranger to hard work, and she would clean this man's house if that would keep him off her back and satisfy Mama and Papa. For a while anyway, it wouldn't hurt her.

But why did she feel this formless horror whenever he looked at her, or at her sister? Why did she feel that she could see the future in him, a future that was ugly and short? And why did she feel like hiding, or covering herself, when his eyes passed over her body like a rancid caress?

CHAPTER 20

Candy Sterling was putting in more hours even than she had at her three jobs in Los Angeles. She was exhausted all the time, even when she awoke at four in the morning to begin her day of eighteen or twenty hours' duration.

There were more sessions with the Prophet, either in his den or in his bedroom. These had taken on a dreamlike quality, like something she had imagined, or lived in a previous life. There were intense emotions and sensations involved, but later she could barely remember any of it. She knew that the Prophet, through his infinite mercy and power, had cleansed her. The fiery emotions, the potent sensations of a sexual intensity were proof of that. The exact way in which he had done it was a mystery. Her recollections had the quality of a movie scene so badly out of focus that one could barely tell where the human forms were, leaving only a vague awareness of motion and form, with the colors and sound the only parts that remained vivid.

She had been there for a couple of weeks when Benjamin Disraeli Butler showed up at the farm. By a freak coincidence Candy was one of the first of the disciples to see him. She was cleaning windows at the time. The Prophet was very rigorous about the windows, as he was about the house as a whole. With her own ears Candy had heard him threaten to damn a girl for her laxity in leaving a window streaked. It was difficult because they had no glass-cleaning components of any sort. The cleaning supplies as a whole were of the most primitive kind. "Elbow grease," as the Prophet liked to remind them, was all the cleaning substance that was really needed.

Candy was standing at the window, scrubbing away with a

piece of newspaper, searching meticulously for streaks on the glass, when she saw the tall black figure trudging down the path toward the house.

There was something in the shape of him, the way he held himself and moved, that arrested her attention at once. She felt her heart begin to pound with an emotion she could not immediately identify. Standing there, her hand pressing the scrap of newsprint to the glass, she stared at the advancing figure, her eyes widening, her skin prickling with an embryonic recognition. It wasn't until he was within fifty feet of the house that she realized finally who he was.

She moved away from the window in a sudden, convulsive reaction, pressing her back to the wall and listening to her own ragged breathing. She knew, in some corner of her mind, that she was perspiring, a sheen of cold sweat covering her legs and her back, and oozing from her joints.

The Prophet will protect *me*, she told herself, articulating the words in her mind. I cannot be harmed while I labor in his service.

Ben didn't recognize Candy. As he plodded down the dusty road leading to the center of the giant farm he became aware of a very sexy white girl standing in one of the windows. She would have been noticeable anywhere, but the capper was the way she was dressed, in a bright red dress that barely touched a point five inches above her knees. He had seen other women since entering the property, many of them young and pretty, but all had been dressed in ragged, shapeless dresses that hung nearly to their ankles. This, despite the oppressive heat of the place. They looked dirty, too, their hair matted, their skin streaked. But the girl in the window, from what he had seen, was immaculate, freshly made up, her hair so clean it sparkled even in the comparative dimness of the house.

Ben had been impressed by the loyalty this Prophet commanded in people, first in the girl who had refused to give up money she thought belonged to him, and later in the little house in Los Angeles where he had met Sister Claudia and her husband. He had been impressed by all that but had decided to see more of these people before deciding what he would do himself. He wanted to see just what it was that decided them to live a life that would make a monk blanch.

As Ben neared the house a young man approached him. The man was dressed in worn overalls and clublike shoes with the heels worn down. He smiled at Ben speculatively. "Can I help you, sir?" he asked.

"My name is Ben Butler," Ben said. "Sister Claudia sent me here from L.A." He felt a stab of guilt at the lie. He couldn't understand why he should feel penitent about lying to these people. He had never worried about such matters before.

"Have you come to join the movement?" the young man asked.

"Well, I—" Ben had been about to say that he was thinking about it, but something in the man's face and bearing warned him that an expression of doubt would likely doom his chances of learning more about the place. He had never seen such devotion in people, such a sense of duty, and he was more than intrigued by it: He was attracted to the novel experience.

"I already joined it in my heart," he explained, once again feeling that tug of guilt at using bullshit on these people. Ever since the night he had tried to mug the girl named Candy Sterling, about whom he had learned at the movement's Los Angeles house, he had been prey to these odd sensations of guilt and apprehension. He couldn't understand it for a moment, and though he had been an atheist for most of his twenty-eight years he was beginning to believe that the feeling came from some power outside himself.

"I have come to learn more about it, and to join it in body as I have in spirit," Ben finished, surprised that he felt more and more comfortable with these tales. As though they had gained truth with the telling. Surely it meant something that he hadn't had a jolt of any sort since that night, the night he had come to think of as the night of Candy Sterling. Before that he hadn't gone a whole day without a fix of some sort since he was fifteen years old.

"Joining our movement isn't difficult," the young man said, looking very slightly less wary. "It isn't complicated, I should say. All it requires is total dedication to the Prophet of the All-Moving Spirit. You must work for his glory and the advancement of his cause. Nothing else matters."

"How do I do that?" Ben asked. "Working in the fields like these other folks?"

"Our tasks are assigned to us by the Prophet," the young man said. "He has assigned overseers to do it, too. But Sister Claudia should not have sent you here unless you had already served your trial period."

"Well, she didn't really send me in that sense," Ben said, looking intently ingenuous. "She just mentioned the place, and I come here to join on my own."

"I don't know what to do about you," the young man mused. "We don't recruit people here." Ben was about to apologize and to point out that he was there, whatever the usual procedure might be. But at that moment a door opened in the house and a young girl emerged. She was tall, leggy, in a blue dress like the scarlet one he had seen through the window. Her hair was auburn, smoothly brushed and hanging down her back almost to her fanny. She strode across the uneven ground, doing remarkably well considering the high-heeled shoes she wore, and addressed the young man from a distance of several feet. Benjamin had the feeling that she maintained the distance as a matter of decorum.

"The Prophet would like this man to report to him," she announced in the peremptory tones of a favored servant. The young man didn't even reply. The young girl turned to Ben, who had been looking at her admiringly. She seemed totally unaware of him as a sexual entity, as though she had forgotten that there were such things as men and women. "Will you please follow me?" she asked without a trace of cordiality.

Ben felt a bit cowed despite himself. Not long ago he would have knocked such a woman on her butt, or if that weren't feasible, would have read her off. Now he followed her up the steps and into the house.

The feeling of reverence which the people and the place had impressed on him was enhanced by the interior of the house. From the outside it had been impressively large and well tended, but the inside—with its dimness, its almost shocking coolness, the burnished taste of its expensive furnishings, and the young girls who floated about tending their chores with the pious silence of acolytes—lent the house the air of something between a palace and a cathedral. Ben found himself wishing he had a hat to doff. Fresh flowers stood in delicate vases. The girls, other than the one leading him, all wore little red dresses, and the only sign that they were aware of his presence was the studious manner in which they ignored him.

The girl in the blue dress led him to a wide staircase and up to the top floor, then out onto a kind of veranda. A man, short and rather plump from easy living, sat in a padded chair before a glass-topped brass table. He wore a robe that was either nylon or silk, probably the latter, and a pair of slippers. Under the robe Ben could see the fringes of expensive-looking pajamas. On the table were the remnants of a substantial breakfast. Egg stains marked the fine china, which supported the skeletons of three large pork chops. The man sipped richly creamed coffee from a delicate-looking cup. Beside the cup stood a silver coffee service. Beside the man stood a girl in one of those short red dresses, and she was Candy Sterling, looking at Ben in a nervously defiant manner. Ben didn't know just how to respond to the girl, so he remained impassive.

"This is the man you wished to speak to, Lord," said the girl in the blue dress.

The man at the table looked up at Ben with a mixture of wariness and amusement. "Take that with you," he said to the girl, indicating his dirty dish and silverware.

"Yes, Lord." The woman picked up the articles, bobbed once at the knees, and departed, moving with swift grace.

The man at the table sat back in his chair, looking Ben up and down as he drew a long brown cigar from the breast pocket of his robe. Absently, he handed the plastic-wrapped cigar to the girl next to him, who unwrapped it hurriedly, fumbling in her nervousness, then clipped the end with a silver cutter lying atop the table and returned it to her lord. The Prophet, for Ben supposed this man to be he, fingered the cigar for a few moments, drawing it under his nostrils with casual elegance. The act was so sensual that Ben could hardly keep from smiling. Candy Sterling was already snatching up a silver lighter from the table, ready to ignite the cigar at the proper time.

"Have you come here to rob us?" the Prophet asked with a mixture of accusation and droll humor.

"No, sir," Ben replied. There was something about the man that commanded a certain degree of respect, though after seeing the house and the way he lived, Ben was half convinced that the Prophet was nothing more than a super scam artist. Even so, he deserved some recognition because he was way out in front of any other con man Ben had encountered.

"My handmaiden informs me that that is what you do," the Prophet announced. "Rob people, I mean."

"With all due respect, sir," Ben replied, "that is what I used to do."

"Mmmmm," the Prophet replied, puffing on the cigar as Candy lit it for him. Since his arrival she hadn't looked at Ben, though she was obviously aware of his presence, perhaps painfully so. There was an extra flush to her cheeks. Ben hadn't noticed, that other night, just how beautiful she was. He felt ashamed for having beaten her up, and that was another first.

"And now," the Prophet said, plucking the cigar from his mouth and regarding the glowing tip with judicious attention, "you are a reformed man. Is that right?"

"I honestly don't know," Ben replied. He was tired and wished that the man would offer him a seat. But he supposed that to allow a mortal to sit in his presence would impair the dignity of a divine being. "I come here 'cause I saw how your people were devoted to you, and I wanted to see what it was that made it that way."

"My people are devoted to me," the Prophet replied, "because I am their salvation. And because, benighted as they may be, they understand that the way to redemption is through absolute service. Now, does that satisfy you?" The cigar had gone cold. The Prophet knocked off the ash, allowing it to drop to the floor of the veranda, and reinserted it in his mouth. Candy Sterling lit it again.

"Well, it tells me what I wanted to know, sir," Ben replied. "Only it don't really satisfy me."

"And just what would satisfy you?"

"I want to join your movement, sir."

If the Prophet was surprised by that one, he didn't show it. He regarded the tip of his resurrected cigar. "Why?"

"Because I want to be saved too."

"You don't understand. This isn't something you can join lightly and leave when you choose. Those who join my movement are dedicated to my service for life."

"I understand, Lord," Ben said.

"It will mean a life of unremitting hard work, and no reward in this life," the Prophet informed him. Ben didn't reply. "Very well," he said finally. "Go down to the field and find Brother Philip. Tell him that the Prophet said you are inducted into the movement, and that you are assigned to his work force. He will assign you to work, and will see to it that you have everything you need." He looked away, indicating that the interview, if that was what it was, had ended.

"Yes, Lord," Ben said respectfully and, with a quick glance at Candy, left the holy presence.

On the way to the field Ben thought it all over. He could still turn and walk off this place if that was what he wanted. But he could do that anytime. Whatever the Prophet might say about committing yourself to this place for life, there was no legal way he could keep a person here against his will. Just why he wanted to stay around, Ben wasn't certain, except that he had never seen quite this good a scam operation, and he thought he might be able to get in on it in some way.

And there was Candy Sterling to think about. Would a girl like her devote herself so completely, risk her life even, for something that was totally phony? It was hard to believe.

Ben asked someone where he could find Brother Philip, and then walked up to the man, a huge, slightly stooped fellow in worn Levi's and an old flannel shirt with holes at the elbows.

"Brother Philip?" he asked. "I'm Brother Benjamin."

CHAPTER 21

It was well past noon, and the workers in the field had slowed in their tasks from the exhaustion of having worked, at that point, for some seven hours without respite, when Virginia Chambers burst out of the Prophet's quarters and down the steps, nearly tripping in her impossibly high heels. She stood in the middle of the well-manicured lawn for a moment, looking about like an animal caught in a spotlight, already feeling the oppressive heat of the sun after days in the artificially generated comfort of the house. Then she ran toward the fields, still clumsy in the high-heeled shoes.

No one pursued her, but she ran as though there were killer dogs on her trail. People glanced up for a moment, nervously curious at the sight of this scantily clad youngster with her cosmetics and her earrings, and then guiltily returned to their appointed chores, grateful that this matter was none of their concern. Virginia stopped, looking at the people near her, considering for a moment grabbing at an arm to gain attention and then realizing that these people had become zombies through their devotion to the Prophet, and through the stunting effect of their labors. She had to find Mama or Papa.

And so she ran some more, teetering on her spiked shoes as she covered the rough ground, until she saw a woman in a dirty, patched dress, bent double to pick cabbages with painful determination. The woman was forty yards distant, and turned partially away from Virginia, but the girl thought she recognized her mother and ran toward the figure, dodging other workers and their partially filled sacks. When she was within ten yards she was certain, and she cried out, her voice thin and tormented, like that of a wounded creature, "*Mama*! Mama, *help* me!"

The woman didn't look up at once. It was as though her senses, or perhaps her powers of recognition and response, had been dulled. Then her head swiveled slowly and she straightened her back with a visible effort. Virginia threw herself at her mother, embracing her, holding to her as she had done when she was an infant.

"Child, what is it?" Instinctively, Mrs. Chambers put her arms around her daughter, feeling the incredibly thin silk of the dress over the girl's soft, supple body. "What's the matter?"

"He— Oh, Mama, he tried to—" She couldn't say it, couldn't articulate the thought. She began to sob, as though this comforting, dependable presence had released something in her, had allowed her the luxury of weeping.

"Virginia, tell me what happened," Mrs. Chambers said in a voice that mixed tenderness with a touch of firmness. It was an inflection with which Virginia was totally familiar, and it soothed her as it had in the past.

"Mama, he wanted to have sex with me! And he told me it was my duty, it was for my own good! Oh, Mama, he's evil!"

"Who? Who you talkin' about?" Mrs. Chambers demanded. She seemed dazed, her mind numbed by the heat and fatigue.

"Him! That man in there. In the house!"

Though her daughter couldn't see it, Mrs. Chambers's face suddenly drained of the little color it had held. She grasped Virginia's shoulders and thrust her away with surprising strength. "Virginia, what wicked thing are you telling me? What—?"

"Virginia, are—" It was Papa's voice, originating from behind her, and Virginia turned, pulling free of her mother's grasp to run to the hulking, comfortably substantial figure of the man, burying her face in his broad chest. She sobbed out her accusation again. Papa put his arms around her, but she could tell from the rigidity of his body, the feel of his arms, that he was confused and dubious.

"You're a sinful little liar!" her mother snapped from behind her. There was such venom in the voice that Virginia let go of her father and turned, astonished at this uncharacteristic attack.

"Mama, I—"

"You get back into that house, young lady, and stop spreading lies about the Prophet!" Mama's eyes glittered with something malign, almost sadistic.

Virginia just stood, hang-jawed, staring at the distorted face of her mother. It was as though the very ground had failed to support her.

Papa's hand grasped her shoulder in a diffident protectiveness. "Polly, maybe we should listen to—"

Her mother suddenly shifted her attention to Papa, turning her white, withered face upon him. "Don't you listen to this filth, Joseph!" she commanded. "This girl is attacking our Lord! What's the matter with you, crediting this ungrateful whelp?"

"Well, it's just that we don't know—" He was reticent, apparently taken aback by his wife's new demeanor, a strength she had never shown before.

"Know! We better know not to listen to such vile lies. At least I do, and you should. Have you lost your faith already? Or did you ever have it?" The power of her attack, the acrimony in her voice and manner, seemed to rise from some deep well in her, something long buried, perhaps long unsatisfied.

"Mama," Virginia said, approaching her mother a step. "I'm not lying. Why should I lie? I swear—" She was stopped by the resolutely cold, intractable face of her mother.

"If you want to damn yourself by saying these things, I certainly don't have to go to hell with you for listening," she said. "Don't you think he knows everything that happens? He was right when he said that you were even more corrupt than me. At least I know I'm a sinner!" She turned her back on Virginia, bending to pick up her sack.

Virginia, distracted and confused, reached out, touching her mother's back. With a stunning suddenness the older woman spun about, lashing out with a slap that jarred Virginia, knocking her off balance for a moment and dazing her. By the time Virginia had regained her senses, Sister Polly was back at her chores, bent at the waist, picking cabbages and stuffing them into the gunny sack with fierce, violent energy. Virginia turned back to Papa, but he was standing there as though lost, his eyes a study in irresolution. He raised a hand slightly, as though to comfort his daughter, but the gesture died for want of certainty. Virginia looked at him, feeling the tears refreshed in her eyes. It was as though she had seen a loved one die.

She started back toward the house, plodding now, barely able to maintain her balance on the furrowed ground. Her father took a faltering step toward her, mumbled a sound, something less than a word, a formless, tormented grunt.

"It's all right, Papa," she murmured without looking at him.

She went back to the house. There was nowhere else to go. She had thought about leaving, just walking off the grounds and not coming back. But a fifteen-year-old girl, dressed as she was, could come to worse, hiking down a country road, than was likely even under the ministrations of the Prophet. She might be picked up by the police, and then she would be returned to her parents, unless she told the story. And even now, with her mother's complicity and her father's ambivalence about the Prophet's intended violation of her, she didn't want to make trouble for them. She would just have to get through it, make it from day to day until Mama and Papa came to their senses.

The coolness of the house chilled the sweat on her body. There were stains in the armpits of her dress, so she went to the handmaidens' dormitory in the basement and removed the garment, dropping it in the hamper. She sat on the edge of her bed, careful not to disturb the tightly arranged blankets, and unhooked the ankle straps of her shoes, lining them neatly under the bed.

The shower felt good, washing away the sweat and the dust of the field. She lingered under it, letting the warmth numb her, leaning her forehead against the shower nozzle as the water pelted her and ran between her breasts. Finally she twisted the tap closed and turned from the nozzle.

Her reaction was almost comical. She could see that, even through the shock of finding him there, leaning languidly against the side of the entranceway, watching her with apparent relish. For a moment she didn't see him at all, as though her senses, dulled by the afternoon's events, could not absorb the concept of a man here, in this place. Awareness came over a span of several seconds, her eyes widening, her body pulling back reflexively, her hands moving to cover her breasts and genitals.

"They wouldn't believe your story, would they, Virginia? Of course not. Did you expect them to, really?" His voice was mockingly gentle. "Your parents are wicked and sinful, Virginia, but not corrupt enough to lend credence to your lies and calumnies."

"I didn't lie!" she half squealed, half hissed. She had never felt such panicky embarrassment before. She was naked! Why didn't he leave her alone? "I told them the truth, what you tried —" There were towels stacked against the wall, but she would have to pass close to him to come within reach of them. She wasn't certain of the wisest course of action—to stay where she was and cover herself as best she could with her hands, or to try a dash past him to retrieve a towel and a semblance of modesty.

"You are so befouled with sinfulness that you don't know what I tried to do," the Prophet informed her, still looking slightly amused at her reaction to his presence. "It was a holy act, an attempt to cleanse you, to redeem you. You see, like nearly all people, you are so corrupted by evil that your blood is rife with impurities. In order to cleanse your soul, I must cleanse your blood."

"And you're going to do that by—?" She broke off, flushing more deeply than before.

"It wasn't like that, dear. It was the impairment of your senses, occasioned by your sinfulness, that caused you to see it as a lewd sexual act. You see evil as good and good as evil. Only I, as Prophet of the All-Moving Spirit, possess the power to redress that. Someday, Virginia, you'll see. Someday you'll beg my forgiveness for your slander. You'll be embarrassed by it even more strongly than you are embarrassed now. Do you think it really matters that I come here and look at you? Don't you know that the Prophet can see anything? I have seen your naked body before. Even before you came here."

"Oh, stop it!" she hissed, nearly forgetting her embarrassment for the time being. "I don't believe any of this stuff, so don't waste it on me. You've fooled a lot of people, but I know what you're doing, and I'm not going to let you get away with it. Not in my case, anyway."

"Some day you'll regret having said that," the Prophet reminded her. "You'll be pitifully grateful, then, that I cared enough to purify your blood."

Virginia stood looking at him for a moment. Then she lowered her hands defiantly and walked past him, mutely daring him to touch her. He stood with his arms crossed, smiling, watching her as she padded past. Virginia picked up one of the terry-cloth towels and, turning to face him, began to dry herself, holding the towel so that it draped down in front of her body.

"Listen to me," she said, nailing him with her gaze. "I'll stay here, because I don't have any choice. And I'll work, because that's what's expected of me. But don't you ever try to put your hands on me again. Remember, I'm underage," she said with a touch of relish. "Just for trying something like that I could have you locked up." That seemed to jolt him a bit, but only temporarily. His eyes narrowed, and he drew himself up, taking on that fierce expression that cowed everyone. Even now it affected Virginia, making her want to stare into his eyes, making her feel a bit detached from her surroundings, and from reality.

"I don't think I'd try something like that if I were you, Virginia," he said crisply. "Remember, I have over a hundred followers right here on this farm, who would give any testimony I ordered, and give it righteously. They would tell a jury just what a vicious little tramp you are, and how saintly their Lord is."

"I think nowadays people might doubt that kind of testimony," Virginia said, flinging down her towel with deliberate casualness and brushing past him to move to her bunk and locker, where she removed a fresh dress and pulled it on over her head. She felt better with something on, more secure, so she faced him with a defiant smile.

"Maybe, and maybe not," the Prophet said, shrugging. He had turned around but had not followed her. He still stood in the entranceway to the bathroom. "But my followers are very steadfast, you know. Consider your parents' reaction just now. How do you think my people would react to someone who tried deliberately to bring evil to their Lord? Someone who tried to have him removed from them? To destroy this holy community? It might be most unpleasant, Virginia." He walked toward her, covering the distance at a casual pace. "It might even be terminal," he said softly. Then he smiled in a way that gave her gooseflesh because it looked like such a normal, friendly smile. A moment later he was gone from the dormitory, from the place she had foolishly considered a kind of sanctuary. Something of him seemed to linger, as though he had left a tactile echo, a damp hollowness in the air.

Virginia sat on the edge of her cot, glad that she hadn't yet put on her makeup. Because she was going to cry again, maybe for a long time.

CHAPTER 22

The girl's threats were a sobering experience to the Prophet. He wasn't a superstitious man, but something of this sort, happening for the first time, had the feel of an omen, and it made him think about moving on. He had known from the first, from that day back at the old church, that this life was temporary, and that it was his indicated procedure to enjoy things while they lasted and to make certain that he had enough money to live an easy life when it was time to split.

The takeover, back in the church, had come as almost as much a surprise to him as to those around him. It was right after he had left Peggy. He had intended for some time to enter some sort of religious group and see if he could make something good of it. It had made sense to him to seek, in such a group, the people he needed. His experience with Peggy had been salutary, educational. But he had grown tired of her. And when she had started to blow up with her pregnancy, he had seen no reason to hang around. One night, while she slept a troubled slumber beside him, Manny rose, dressed, and took a ready-packed bag he had stashed away. It contained three changes of clothing and one extra pair of shoes, as well as all the money they owned. Hefting the bag in his right hand, he left without looking back at his wife or the apartment they had shared for six months.

He took a Greyhound bus, going north because that was the first bus he could get that was moving more than a hundred miles nonstop. In the Capay Valley he disembarked and found a motel cabin to stay in until he decided exactly what he would do next. That was when he found the church.

It was the next morning, actually, while he was taking a

stroll to orient himself in this new place. It was a shabby little building, once a house, with a sign in front of it that said, "Church of the All-Moving Spirit." Manny stood looking at it for a moment, wondering what he was going to do, wondering why his heart was tripping a bit more quickly than it usually did. There was no one around the place. It looked deserted, as though it had been put there precisely so that he could occupy it. Finally, he walked to a hot dog stand across the narrow street and sat munching on a breakfast of two hot dogs and a cup of coffee while he continued to stare at the unremarkable edifice. The more he looked at it the more convinced he became that it had something to do with his destiny. Finally he rose and walked across the street, climbing the steps and entering.

The interior smelled of mold and varnish. It looked rather like a conventional Protestant church except for the pictures that lined the walls, which included not only Christ but Mohammed and Buddha, as well as some other personages Manny didn't recognize. He sat in a pew in back of the building for a while, then moved to the front row. He couldn't imagine why it was, but he felt as though he owned the place.

"Can I help you, Brother?"

The voice was deep and mellow, aged and ambivalent. It seemed to combine a tentative welcome with a stern caution. Manny froze for a moment, glad that he had refrained from showing any degree of startlement, at least any that would be detectable from behind. Finally, he donned a beatific smile and turned to face the storklike man behind him.

He was tall and thin and dressed in a black suit with a vest and a string tie; a cliché right out of some B western.

Manny rose respectfully. "I am a stranger here, friend. I saw your church and entered to rest a while. I should like to learn more about your faith."

And that was the beginning. It was astonishing how easily he had taken in the old man. The Reverend Bartholomew Henry, he called himself, though Manny always suspected that he had made up at least part of the name. He was the founder of the church, and its only functionary. He lived in the basement, cooking his meals over a two-burner hot plate. He lived off the voluntary contributions of the congregation. Pickings were slim, but the Reverend Henry seemed satisfied.

Manny hung around long enough to check out the congregation and found them to his liking. There was something about each one of them, whatever the age or sex, that reminded him of his wife. A quivering, subliminal uncertainty; a formless, directionless hunger. They came and listened to the Reverend Henry on Tuesdays, which, for some reason, he had named the holy day. He didn't speak very well, but Manny, sitting in the church on each of those Tuesdays, used his sermons to gauge these people. He noted that when the Reverend Henry spoke of sin, of their innate evil and lack of grace, they seemed interested. But when he spoke of their good qualities, as though to leaven the loaf, they drifted into a sort of reverie. There were only a few of them, but a couple were farmers with pretty sizable spreads. They came in with their wives and children, in some cases nubile daughters who seemed as convinced of their depravity as their parents. Manny found the daughters interesting, the landowning parents intriguing. After four weeks he laid his plan.

"I should like to become your assistant here, Reverend Henry," he told the elegiac old man one Monday. "I could relieve you of some of the routine work, perhaps speak on occasion when you don't feel up to it." Henry was in ill health, and deteriorating almost daily. That helped to convince Manny that this was meant to be, that the situation had been arranged for him.

"There is little enough sustenance here for one," Henry reminded him.

"I expect no payment, sir," Manny replied. "I have a bit of money left with which to support myself, and when it is gone I can find work. I only seek to serve the Almighty through His chosen spokesman."

Henry nodded with sage satisfaction. The next day he introduced Manny, who stood before the congregation. The people eyed him with unconscious speculation. He kept his eyes blank, having already eyed them exhaustively. Two weeks later, while Henry languished on a sickbed, Manny delivered his first sermon. He dwelt on the vicissitudes of the congregation, their sins and their worthlessness, to the exclusion of any other topic. He read from the Bible, since he knew it better than the Koran or any of the other books through which the Reverend Henry wandered aimlessly. He had gone through it the night before, assiduously underlining passages that spoke of man's ultimate depravity, and the deliciously horrendous punishments that awaited him.

"A most rewarding sermon, Reverend," one of the farmers said as the congregation filed out of the door. He seemed almost exalted by the experience of being told how evil he was. His teenage daughter, standing next to him, fidgeted and looked at Manny from under her long black lashes. Manny thanked the man in stern, cold tones and turned away.

The next week the congregation was larger than it had been on previous Tuesdays. The people seemed disappointed when the Reverend Henry stood up to speak. The following week the crowd had shrunk a bit but was still larger than usual. It was Manny's opportunity to speak once again, perhaps because the old man had noticed that the contributions had been unprecedentedly generous on the occasion of his previous ministry.

Manny continued in this manner, building up his following for the next several weeks. The Reverend Henry played into his hands, yielding more and more to his age and infirmity, allowing this new assistant whom Providence had entrusted to him to take over the work. Within a three-month period Manny had built up a sizable following, some of them hippies from San Francisco, and even a few who had been attracted by his waxing fame from as far away as southern California.

On the first Tuesday of the fourth month Manny decided to make his move.

He got halfway through his sermon, holding before him a limp-bound Bible, flaying his listeners with a thorough recounting of their shortcomings, when suddenly, certain that he had them in his grasp, he raised the Bible aloft, holding it over his head for a long moment.

"You people are paying too damned much attention to this," he roared. They sat staring, his words gradually soaking into their consciousness. "And not enough to me!" And he hurled the Bible on the floor. It lay there, its India paper pages splayed, the bookmarks dangling across the worn carpet like thin trails of blood. The people stared at him, apparently stunned, obviously frightened. Perhaps they thought he had gone mad in that moment. Perhaps they expected lightning to strike him, or a biblical flood to erupt from the earth and swallow him up. The fact that nothing of the sort occurred seemed to do nothing to slake their horror and apprehension.

Manny turned on his heel and strode to the bookshelf on which Henry had stacked his other holy books. "You've been paying too much attention to all this drivel," he warned them, yanking books off the shelf and tossing them onto the floor. Then, turning to face them, he glowered. "If you must read your goddam Bible, then turn to John, chapter one, verse ten." One young girl with thick glasses and stringy hair actually began leafing through her Bible, looking for that part. The others sat staring at Manny, and he could see a touch of excitement mixed with their fright. Still, Manny began to fear that he had made his play too soon, that they weren't ready yet, that he had blown it and would have to find another lot of patsies. But there was no way out now except to play it through.

"I come to you," he shouted, "and you don't know me. You have never known me. These past months I have stood in your midst, ministered to you, spoken the word to you, and you have taken me for a mere mortal, for one like you, stained with sin and sullied by transgressions!"

The girl with the stringy hair had apparently found John 1:10, because she dropped her paperback Bible to the floor and sat staring at Manny. Her eyes were almost as wide as her glasses. He had never seen awe even approaching hers in a human face. It made him want to giggle with mirth and relief. He had an ally now, a convert. He fixed the girl with a steely look until her eyes dropped.

"There is one among you," he said finally, in tones so soft they had to strain to hear him. "One who now recognizes me. Only one of so many. I shall take this miserable sinner with me when I leave you. When I go to find more disciples. You think that because you come here to this church one day a week, and leave a few coins from your purses, that you are saved. You believe that the All-Moving Spirit is satisfied with your insulting sacrifices, that He will cleanse away the corruption of the soul." Manny laughed with genuine contempt. "You will all die in sin," he shouted. "As you were conceived in it. And when you come before the All-Moving Spirit, *you will be condemned to everlasting torment!*"

"I recognize you, Lord." The girl with the stringy hair was rising, pushing herself free of the pew with difficulty. Her arms and legs seemed all rubbery, but she was determined, and finally got to her feet and into the aisle, shouting, "I recognize you, Lord!" over and over again.

Some of the others had begun fidgeting, as though they couldn't decide whether to go or stay, but when they saw the girl running up toward Manny, her face awash with sweat and tears, her body wavering atop her spindly, weak legs, they sat freshly riveted. Then the girl was at Manny's feet, on her belly, writhing and grasping at his ankles in a paroxysm of orgasmic anguish. Impatiently, Manny yanked his feet away, out of her reach.

"Save me, Lord!" she squealed, as piteous as a wounded animal. "Save me, tell me what to do!"

"I have not seen such faith since coming among you," Manny intoned. The others sat, still stunned, looking at him with guiltily shifting eyes. He was beginning to believe that he had them. The girl's outburst had swung things in his direction, and now he was almost certain he could pull it off. "At least this vile creature knows her savior when she sees him. At least she recognizes him belatedly. There is hope for her, but for the rest of you, when I have left this place, there will be *no hope!*"

And then they came forward, almost every one of them, weeping and moaning, pitifully grateful for the long-awaited opportunity to lay their fears on one who was strong enough to support them.

It was the most lovely sight Immanuel Hartford had ever seen.

CHAPTER 23

In the end, the Prophet decided that it was not yet time to cut and run. All little Virginia needed was to be screwed royally, and he was determined to help her out in that department. She was the first girl who had been so intransigent in a long time, and the challenge was something of an aphrodisiac to him.

In the meantime he needed some new girls. There were always some nubile and promising creatures around. New converts came from all over the country. It was amazing how soon a man could tire of a girl when they came so quickly and so easily. That very afternoon he rummaged through the records and selected three new girls to take their places as handmaidens of the Prophet. It meant he would have to get rid of some of those who had already been filling that exalted position, and for the time being he chose to dispense with Candy Sterling. There was something about her that disturbed him, though he couldn't identify it.

An hour after the Prophet's ruminations three new girls entered his house, still dressed in their rag-tag working clothes, looking upset and apprehensive at being in the very presence of divinity. Sister Penelope approached Candy, who was scrubbing out the bathroom appended to the handmaidens' dormitory, with a satisfied expression on her face. Her long legs looked strong and competent below the short blue dress as she stood in front of Candy, staring down from her superior height.

"The Prophet has determined that you have been sanctified enough so that you no longer require his holy presence," Sister Penelope announced crisply. "You are to take your place in the fields."

Candy had known this was coming. She had expected it to

happen at any time, dreaded it, known that she would enjoy only a short stay in the Prophet's house. She had known what Sister Penelope was going to say before she had uttered a word, when she was still approaching from the other end of the dormitory. She had always failed tests, and she considered this another in the string. She didn't want to leave the house, hated the thought of being deprived of the Prophet's direct presence, his personal ministrations. It was a wicked, selfish sentiment. Only the Prophet could judge when it was time for a girl to take her place in the fields or other external duty, and it was wicked of her to question his impeccable judgment. It was further proof of her corruption. To hide her failings from Sister Penelope, she managed a smile.

"Yes, thank you, Sister Penelope," she said. "Am I to leave at once?"

"Of course," Sister Penelope replied with a touch of archness. "What would be the sense of delaying it? Your clothes have been laid out for you."

"I'll change at once, Sister," Candy said submissively.

Sister Penelope, with a slight smile of satisfaction, turned and strode away, those long, strong legs flexing seductively with each step.

Disconsolately, the artificial smile slipping from her lips and eyes, Candy walked to the barrel supplied for the purpose and tossed in the two damp rags she had been using for her cleaning chores. Then she walked out into the dormitory. Laid across her cot (no longer hers in any sense, she reflected) was a long, baggy dress, mended and patched, which Sister Penelope had dropped there. The hem was ragged, but the dress was clean and serviceable. Under the cot stood a pair of clublike shoes, the kind one might expect to see on a member of the Yokum family, with thick socks stuffed inside them. The socks were worn but still good. One of them was white and the other gray.

Candy stripped off her silk dress and laid it across the bed, then sat down and unstrapped her high-heeled shoes. She lined them up carefully under the cot from habit, then pulled on the socks and thrust her feet into the shoes. Even with the heavy socks the shoes were a bit large for her, so she laced them up as tightly as she could before standing. The dress was rough against her skin after the thin silk she had been wearing. She put her earrings on the bed and went and looked at herself in the mirror in the bathroom. She wanted to cry, because she had grown accustomed to being pretty, and because she hated herself for caring about such earthly and inconsequential matters. It seemed that the Prophet's presence had really had its beneficial effect on her, because she had at least grown capable of seeing how thoroughly iniquitous she was. Since entering this house she had had it brought home to her afresh with each day.

Returning to the dormitory she picked up the earrings, dress, and pumps, placed them carefully on the next cot, and then stripped her cot of its bedding, folding the blankets at the foot of the bed and bunching up the sheets and pillowcase for the laundry room.

It was all as unceremonious as receiving a dismissal notice from a dime-store job. Ten minutes after changing into her new attire Candy had turned in her handmaiden's dress and shoes and her bedding, and stood outside the house, sweating under her heavy dress in the oppressive heat. She couldn't help feeling embarrassed, for some obscure reason, so she didn't look at anyone as she walked to the field, but kept her gaze fastened straight ahead. She walked awkwardly because she had grown accustomed to the spike-heeled light pumps, and the cumbrous clod busters would require a period of adjustment.

Once she reached the field she had to speak to someone, because she didn't know where to go or how to start on her newly appointed task. She was told by a heavyset man with a midwestern accent that she should seek out Brother Philip, whom he was kind enough to point out.

"Yes, I've been informed," Brother Philip said, consulting a list on a clipboard. "You're which one, Sister Catherine or Sister Candace?"

"Sister Candace."

"Ever worked on a farm before?"

"No, sir."

He looked at her with a speculatively reproving expression. "How long have you been in the movement?"

"A bit less than four months."

"Then you should know that you don't address anyone as sir."

"Yes, Brother."

"We're almost finished with the harvest," Brother Philip explained. "Soon we'll be moving on to the next field to begin planting. But for the time being, make yourself useful with the remainder of the harvesting. Just take a sack from that pile there," he said, indicating a pile of gunny sacks near an old truck which was already half full of the same sacks stuffed with heads of cabbage, "and pick cabbages as fast as you can."

"Yes, Brother."

Candy moved toward the truck, but Brother Philip called her name before she had gone two steps. "You'll reside in dwelling number twenty-nine," he said, glancing once again at his clipboard. "By the grace of the Prophet, you are wife to Brother Benjamin."

CHAPTER 24

The first hint the Prophet received that she still existed was a letter, written on cheap notepaper in her unmistakable, lovely hand, and mailed to him in a post office envelope.

Dear Manny,
   I always knew you'd make it big, but I had no idea you'd actually become God. I guess that means I own half the universe under California law. I'll be at the coffee shop next to the bus stop at noon next Tuesday. For old times' sake.

Your loving wife,
Peggy Boling Hartford

It was enough to discourage a man, even a prophet, and for the second time in a week the Prophet thought about pulling up stakes and moving to Europe. But things were going too smoothly, the money was rolling in too swiftly, for him to panic now on account of a cryptically threatening letter from his ersatz wife.

Ho thought about ignoring her, but realized that that would probably bring her to the farm, which could prove troublesome. He thought of sending one of his minions to slip her a few hundred dollars, but that could prove habit-forming on her part. The only course of action that would allow him the flexibility he needed was to go and meet her himself.

It was almost a new experience to drive a car for himself after all this time. He took the Cadillac, piling into it without ceremony and driving off the farm, leaving his slaves working in the fields. It always gave him a feeling of gratification to see the fools toiling away for his benefit. He could picture himself in Switzerland or South America one day, drinking their health.

The coffee shop was rather like that in which he had once met Peggy in their hometown. Had that been only ten years ago? It seemed like another lifetime. He pulled the Cadillac into one of the marked spaces and walked into the coffee shop.

It took him a moment to recognize her. At twenty-eight she wasn't the prom queen any longer, even in a more mature form. She had thickened at the waist and picked up a few wrinkles at the neck, as though she managed to keep herself from growing really fat only through austerity. Her eyes were no longer softly lustrous but shiny with an agate gleam that looked artificially stimulated. He wondered whether she had got herself on drugs, or perhaps some sort of medication. She smiled up at him sadly from a half-finished Coke. Another, untouched, rested on a paper doily across from her.

"Hi, Manny," she said when he stopped next to the booth. "I ordered Cokes for both of us. A kind of commemoration. I'll pay for them, too, just to make the occasion complete."

"When did you get into town, Peggy?" The Prophet carefully bloused his expensive suit pants and slid into the booth opposite her. "And how long are you planning to stay?"

She laughed, the sound full and throaty and just a bit rough. "That's my Manny," she said. Then she looked at him hard, studying his features. "You haven't changed in any way, really."

"You've changed a great deal."

"I guess I asked for that. You were always ruthless in going after what you wanted, Manny, but you didn't used to be deliberately vicious."

"Then I have changed. What do you want, Peggy?" She didn't answer at once, but stirred her Coke with the straw. It showed a particle of lipstick at the tip. The sight disgusted Manny, as she disgusted him. Finally she raised her gaze, tossing her head as he had seen her do many times, to throw her hair behind her. Those burning eyes looked into his with a touch of pleading.

"I need help, Manny."

"Why should I help you?"

"Well, after all, you made me what I am today."

"You were always what you are today. I only made you aware of it."

"All right." She trained her eyes on his. "Then help me because I'm your wife."

"An unresolved detail," he said.

She tried to hold his gaze but hadn't the will for it. Her eyes slid down to her Coke. "It's still a legality, Manny," she reminded him.

He chuckled softly, so startling her that she looked at him. She seemed to see something in his eyes that she couldn't confront. It gave Manny a sense of power such as he felt when he was on the farm, surrounded by his boobs. "What do you think your legality is worth, Peggy?" he asked, smiling with genuine pleasure.

She sat there, her gaze lowered, the long golden hair that had gone a bit stringy now, but still not entirely unattractive, framing her face. "Manny, please help me," she murmured. "It would mean so little to you. All I need is a little money, but I have to have it."

"What happens if you don't get it?" It was an ambiguous question, and he was curious to see which way she would take it. As he could have predicted, she took the coward's way.

"What do you mean?"

"You're asking me for money," he said. "I have a right to know why you need it." Manny couldn't imagine why he had dreaded this confrontation. He was enjoying himself.

"Do you want all the gruesome details, or just the bare outline?"

"Depends on how much money you want," Manny said with a shrug.

She gripped the sloped side of her Coke glass so hard she almost spilled it. "I owe the money to some people," she explained. "If I don't pay it back—soon—I'll be in real trouble."

"Getting-beaten-up trouble, or just working-it-off trouble?" She glanced up at him again, and he saw things in her eyes: a mixture of hatred, contempt, and pleading. He ignored the expression.

"Getting-killed trouble, maybe," she said. "Or at least hurt so badly that I'll wish they had killed me."

"How much do you need?" Manny asked, to keep the conversation going and to satisfy his curiosity.

"Six thousand dollars."

For a moment Manny thought of giving it to her, taking it out of petty cash and sending her on her way. But it was a foolish idea. It would only convince her that he was her bank. Besides, he couldn't see any reason why he should give her his money. "Peggy, Peggy," he sighed, smiling. "What was it? Gambling? Drugs? Loan shark?"

"Let's just say I got in over my head. If you'll give me this money, I promise I'll never disturb you again. I'll go to Reno and get a divorce. Sign away all my marital rights. Anything you say."

With this last she looked up into his eyes once again, and even laid a warm, slightly damp hand on his wrist. It was funny, really, Peggy trying to seduce him. He felt like a man who owned a gourmet restaurant being offered a bowl of potato chips. It might be a novelty to screw her at that; but the impulse fled. He had had all of Peggy Boling Hartford he wanted.

"Your marital rights don't concern me, love," he informed her, and threw a dollar bill on the table. "I'll take care of the Cokes this time, but if you want to earn that six thousand on your back, you'll need more than one man. I'd say at least six hundred of them." He had turned to leave when she spoke again.

"Manny, as your wife, I'm entitled to half of everything you own." Manny stopped and fixed her with his gaze. She looked away. "I don't want to press that. I don't want to make trouble for you. But I'm very scared. I might be able to hold these men off if I tell them I'm suing you."

Manny laughed. "Honey, you're welcome to half of everything I own. What do you want, my coat or my pants?" She looked at him blankly. "You married the wrong pigeon, sweety," he explained. "I'm a pauper."

She stared at him for a moment, her eyes betraying the first tinge of despair. "You're a millionaire," she whispered desperately.

Manny laughed again, thoroughly enjoying himself. "I live like a millionaire," he conceded. "There's a difference. And that, too, is a legality." Because this was too good to pass up, he slid back into the booth. "That farm I inhabit," he explained, "and all of its products and proceeds, are the property of the Church of the All-Moving Spirit. So if you want any of it, you should have married God. I'm only His prophet." When she didn't reply, he smiled into her dulled eyes and resisted an impulse to pinch one of her pallid cheeks. With a chuckle he rose again, adjusted his coat, winked down at her, and walked away.

He was at the door of his car when she tugged his sleeve. "Manny, you're the only chance I have left," she said, not looking at his eyes. Her gaze hung at his collar. She looked like a whipped pet, and her voice was whining and placatory. "I have to put these people off for as long as I can. If you won't give me any money, and if I can't legally get it from you, I'm still going to have to try." Then, without a backward glance, she spun and walked away.

Manny stood looking after her for a moment, unsure of what to do, what action to take. That she would carry out her threat he didn't doubt. Peggy had developed into an inconsequential woman, the kind of person with whom he was most accustomed to dealing; but she was terrified, and a terrified person could be dangerous.

He walked out to the sidewalk and glanced down the street in the direction she had taken. He saw her at the end of the block, awaiting a signal change. She crossed to the opposite side of the street and turned left, doubling back. Manny stood within the parking lot of the diner, where she would be unlikely to notice him even if she looked in his direction. The precaution was unnecessary. She walked with her gaze lowered, her head hung like a whipped hound's. Twice she almost bumped into people, then diverted her course without looking up. When she was almost directly across the street from the coffee shop, she turned into a collection of ramshackle frame cabins reminiscent of the dwellings in which Manny penned his human livestock on the farm. A faded sign in front announced that the place was a motel. Manny shifted his position slightly to keep sight of her, observed her stop, fish a key out of her coat pocket, and enter the third cabin on the left. For some reason he didn't think to question or articulate, he was pleased that her cabin was one of the rear ones, far back from the street.

CHAPTER 25

Dwelling number twenty-nine, like all the dwellings for the followers of the Prophet, was a shack, eight feet square, windowless and featureless except for the number chalked above the opening, with a ceiling too low to permit a tall man to stand straight. It was made of thin wood, the remnants of old packing crates and produce boxes, basted together by three-penny nails and wood staples. To have leaned against any part of it would have amounted to vandalism: It offered concealment more than shelter. In the summer, which was when Candy moved into it, the dwelling was abrasively hot, making the blistering hours in the field seem soothing by comparison. It had a dirt floor and four wooden frames which served as beds, one against each wall. To relieve his followers of the temptations of sex, or the propagation of disloyal talk, the Prophet had decreed that each dwelling was to house two couples. Besides, it was a more efficient utilization of resources.

When Brother Philip informed Candy that she was wife to Brother Benjamin, she hadn't connected the name to any person. Her mind was still too numbed and preoccupied by her sudden ouster from the Prophet's dwelling to allow for clarity of thought, or any attempt at deduction. She worked through the afternoon stolidly, looking up as seldom as possible, relishing the aches in her back and joints because they were a manifestation of her devotion to the Prophet, and vaguely guilty because it was sinful to take pride in the offering of that which she owed, and could never fully repay. The work was monotonous and exhausting, and it allowed one to switch off one's mind, which was one reason that so many of the

Prophet's followers accepted the assignment so gratefully. Candy was able to get through those few hours without focusing on her plight, or wondering what was happening in the big house, or which of the new girls was at that particular moment having her blood purified.

She was slow and clumsy at the work, being unaccustomed to it, but no worse than many others. And she certainly tried, never raising her head until that moment, after the sun had ducked behind the mountains, when Brother Philip and the other overseers decided it was useless to continue.

Then she found dwelling number twenty-nine, trudging among other zombie-like figures, all numbed with exhaustion. When she saw the interior of it she wanted to cry, but didn't. It was evil, the work of the devil within her, that she could feel such disappointment over something as trivial as her surroundings.

It was dark inside, and still hot with the undissipated heat of the day. The only light entered through the door, and through some cracks in the walls. The place was filled with dust and heat and the smell of unwashed bodies. Candy stood in the middle of the single room looking about, because she felt disoriented in the dimness after being out in the bright sunlight all day. Even the twilight had been bright compared to this unlighted hovel. She had never felt more miserable in her life, and the wretchedness fed upon itself because it was the occasion of greater guilt. This was where the Prophet wanted her, so she should be ecstatic to be in this place. The physical discomfort and sheer tawdriness of her surroundings had nothing to do with it; she belonged here, and it was unspeakable of her to place such import in trivialities like dirt and claustrophobic closeness.

She refused to cry.

There was a sound behind her, and she realized that someone had been there in the dwelling with her for several seconds. The previous sounds had registered only dimly: She had failed to respond to them even in her mind. Now she turned, prepared to smile, to show outwardly at least that she was a good follower of the Prophet. But the smile faded, soured on her lips like something left there and forgotten.

"Hi," the huge black man said, grinning down at her. He had

to hunch his shoulders and duck his head to avoid the flimsy ceiling. Had he stood upright with suddenness and determination he would probably have poked his head through the roof.

Candy regarded him grimly. "What are you doing here?" There was only the one entrance, and he blocked that.

As though he had read her mind he moved aside, sitting on one of the makeshift beds. "I'm afraid I live here," he said apologetically. "I'm Brother Benjamin."

The revelation made her head swim even before she had fully absorbed it.

By the grace of the Prophet you are wife to Brother Benjamin.

She couldn't help thinking, on a dim, involuntary level, that this was too much to ask of her, too much all at once. She supposed it was a test, and that she had already failed it in her heart. It never occurred to her that the union between her and the man who had mugged her was simply an example of the Prophet's jaded sense of humor.

Before she could think further the stocky man who had pointed her way to Brother Philip entered, just in front of a faded, old-looking woman. He glanced at Candy and then at Brother Benjamin. "The Prophet has provided you with wife," he said, smiling in a tremulous, diffident manner. The woman, apparently his wife, smiled fleetingly at Candy and without a word walked to one of the vacant beds and lay upon it, staring up at the low ceiling. "How do you do, Sister?" the man inquired with bumpkin politeness. "I am Brother Joseph. This lady is my wife, Sister Polly."

CHAPTER 26

Though she would never really think of herself as Brother Benjamin's wife, Candy Sterling had once thought of herself as wife to another man. Her affair with Vernon had started, in her mind, as a marital relationship, and continued that way until its termination.

Because he believed in Christianity and she believed in him, Candy had moved into the Jesus community bag and baggage. She had never been one to do things by half, and so within a few weeks she knew almost as much about the Bible as he did, and believed in it more strongly than anyone she had met. She could relate to the others not only the Scriptures but the books Vernon had given her explaining them.

There were other professed Christians who enjoyed sexual relationships outside marriage, even some who lived together. Candy steered Vernon and herself toward these people in order to help rationalize their own relationship. He went along with it nervously, never quite convinced of the probity of what they were doing but too captivated by the pleasures she brought him with such expertise to eschew any of it.

Candy was determined to be more than a bed partner and housekeeper to the man she loved, and so she bustled into other areas of his life in an attempt to make herself unobtrusively indispensable.

There was a man named Bauer who had made a fortune in electronics and was looking for ways to spend it without harm to his tax structure. A Christian radio station would fit in with his plans, and after their initial meeting Vernon came home with a spring in his steps.

"The Lord has brought us the means," he said to Candy as

she poured him a cup of coffee. "I know this is His intention!" Candy helped herself to a cup and stood across the kitchen bar from him, listening devotedly as he told her about Bauer. In months of endeavor Vernon and his friends had been able to raise only a tiny fraction of the money they needed for their station. Bauer could close the gap with the signing of a single check. "He's invited us to dinner," Vernon said finally. "Day after tomorrow."

Candy had saved her tips, and now she went to a nice dress shop in Anaheim and purchased a new dress for the occasion. It cost sixty-five dollars, more than she had ever paid for a garment in her life. Afterward she had her hair styled, then bought a new pair of shoes to go with the dress. When they went out to meet their host she felt ready, determined to be her most charming, to show Vernon that she could be an asset to him outside the bedroom.

Bauer lived in a huge house on a hillside. The living room was larger than Vernon's apartment. A servant admitted them, and Bauer came out a moment later, dressed in a silk suit and Elevator shoes buffed to a soft shine. He shook hands with Vernon and apologized for his tardiness. He gave Candy's hand a protracted squeeze and looked at her in a way she had learned to recognize when she was on the street. It thrilled her because she felt that if she played things right she could influence this man to part with his money for the Lord's work.

"I asked my daughter to join us," Bauer said to Vernon, and then glanced at Candy, including her in the explanation. "I hope you don't mind."

"Not at all, sir," Vernon said.

At that moment a tall, slender, almost exotic-looking young woman in a blue dinner dress emerged from the rear of the house. Her hair was upswept, and her eyes, slightly slanted, had been carefully made up. Candy disliked her at once, and rebuked herself for this all-too-human feminine reaction.

Bauer introduced her. "Connie, this is the young man I've told you so much about, Vernon," Bauer said. "And Miss Sterling."

"Candy," Candy corrected in a friendly tone.

"How do you do," Connie said to Candy in a voice that was predictably sexy. She extended a slender hand to Vernon, held his a moment longer than seemed necessary. There was such an obvious, instant rapport between them that Candy would think, in the months to come, that she had known instantly that Vernon was lost to her in that moment.

Bauer's car was all the Cadillac you could buy, and in the sophisticated custom of the affluent, they swapped couples on the way to the restaurant. Candy fought an impulse to turn in her seat and chaperone Vernon and Connie. She could hear the girl's husky voice, occasionally catch a glimpse of her sparkling eyes in the mirror. Her heart kept sinking all during the ride.

The night, from Candy's viewpoint, was a disaster. All the charm she had summoned for the event fled from her. She knew she was acting sullen and bitchy throughout dinner but couldn't help herself. When Vernon danced with Connie Bauer she wanted to run out on the dance floor and attack the woman.

Still, from Vernon's point of view, the night was a success. By the time they parted at Bauer's home the deal was almost completed, and Candy knew that Vernon had found a powerful ally. Connie, doubtless, would see to it that her father invested in the radio station.

She sat in silence throughout the ride home. Vernon was as quiet as she was. At the apartment she seduced him, approaching him with deliberate, calculated, and compulsive sexuality, knowing even as she drew him to her in bed that she was thrusting him away, irrecoverably.

A week later he asked her to move out.

"This just isn't right," he said. "What will people think? As Christians we have an obligation to make a good impression," he said prissily.

Candy felt her eyes widen, gave vent to the sudden, terrified anger that welled up in her. "You mean what would the Bauers think!" she accused. "Especially one of the Bauers!"

"Candy, don't be childish," he reproved her. "We can still see one another. We just have to behave with greater circumspection."

"Oh, bullshit! Do you think I can't see what's happening, you son of a bitch?" It got worse, with Candy shrieking through half the night, barely restraining herself from the violence that would have ended their relationship on the spot.

Finally, when both of them were exhausted, they fell into bed and slept like drugged strangers.

Vernon never mentioned breaking up to her again. A week later he didn't come home, and after two days it became obvious that he wasn't going to. His roommate was away on one of his protracted out-of-town stays. Finally, Candy took a knife from one of the kitchen drawers and wrapped it in a brown paper bag. She wandered for hours before figuring out where the Bauer house was. Her feet were globs of pain by the time she had found it and climbed the winding hill that led to the big parking area in front of the garage. She hadn't really formed a plan beyond that point, except for some vague intention to use the knife to make Connie Bauer less attractive to Vernon. There was a fierce coldness in her, and a clarity of the senses that she hadn't known since her days on the street, when she had dropped some acid from time to time.

It was miraculous that no one spotted her during the hour she stood there, waiting her chance. Some sense told her that Miss Bauer wasn't at home, that she would be driving in, and after an hour of waiting she spotted a powder blue Mercedes coupe through the foliage that lined the drive. Candy placed the paper bag under her left arm, arranging it like a shoulder holster, so that she could draw the knife with her right hand. A moment later the Mercedes pulled up and stopped. The garage door rumbled open, but before the car could move Candy stepped in front of it. She could see Connie Bauer behind the wheel, her hair down about her shoulders now, her perfectly applied makeup apparent through the tinted windshield. She looked back at Candy for a moment as though trying to figure out who she was. Then her hands shifted and tightened on the wheel. Candy didn't move from in front of the car, and after a moment the driver's door opened.

Connie was dressed in a tight dress, which was gratifying to Candy, since it meant she wouldn't be able to run. She faced her nemesis with an outward show of courage, but Candy, for the first time in her life, felt in complete control of the situation. Already she was planning her attack, deciding on the motion that would bring the knife's blade across one of those alabaster cheeks and up over one lustrous eye. If there was time for additional cutting, so much the better, but she intended to do the maximum amount of damage in the first swipe.

"Hello," Connie said, just a hint of a tremble in her voice. "Candy, isn't it?"

Something in the girl's manner tipped Candy off to the fact that she had just been with Vernon. Learning all the tricks she, Candy, had taught him, probably. "Hi," Candy said. "I came up to tell you that Vernon has left me."

"Oh? Well, I'm sorry."

Candy edged closer, and Connie started to step back, then apparently thought better of it, perhaps deciding that it could give Candy ideas she didn't already entertain. Candy came closer again, moving to within reach. Still, she would have liked to have closed the distance some more.

"Yes. He decided our relationship was immoral," Candy explained. Her voice was dead of emotion. She was like a sentient computer programmed to a single purpose, and she kept the emotions bottled down in her loins, where they belonged, where they couldn't do any harm, couldn't reduce her efficiency or swerve her aim. She moved a step closer.

"Look, Candy, I—"

Before Connie could finish, Candy swept the butcher knife out of the bag and brought it up, ready for a swift downward cutting motion. The only thing that thwarted her intent was that Connie, for some reason, perhaps just to emphasize her point, had raised her left hand to shoulder height and now, reflexively, she brought it up to protect her face. The knife's edge raked across the hand, cutting a superficial gash in it. Connie screamed and jumped back, looking in horrified disbelief at the wounded hand. Candy glared at her, triumph and frustration mingling in her breast. Then she closed the distance in a swift, surprisingly expert lunge. Connie was frozen, staring at the blood that oozed from the thin cut on her hand, and didn't turn to run until too late. Candy grasped her hair, that long, luxurious hair that had doubtless been spread across some pillow just recently, and hauled the distraught girl back, yanking her off her feet. One of Connie's high-heeled shoes came off, throwing her off balance, and then she went down on nylon-clad knees. Candy stepped in and laid the knife edge across the woman's cheek and eye.

"I'm going to cut your face," she warned. "I'm going to cut it to the bone, dear. But don't worry, you'll still have Daddy's money. Vernon will still want you. Only any time he fucks you, he'll look at that face, and he'll think about Candy, won't he?"

"Candy, please don't." The voice was so pathetic, so wheedling, that Candy felt a swift surge of pleasurable power. She had it in her hands to destroy this girl, and the feeling was an intoxicant. She savored it just a moment too long.

A powerful hand grasped her wrist, plucking it directly away from Connie Bauer's face. Candy gave a strangled, outraged scream and turned to face her attacker. The hand tightened and twisted, and in a moment she couldn't hold the knife any longer.

One of the servants had heard Connie's scream and come to investigate. It was too late now. She had come so close, had been right within reach of really doing something for once, something she had set out to do. She had come close to a genuine triumph.

No police report was filled out. The police weren't even called. Bauer came home when the servants called him. Candy was held in the house, under watchful eyes, until he arrived. A bit later Vernon showed up, too, and they held a conference, during which they talked about Candy as though she weren't present, or as though she were some sort of non-human phenomenon, incapable of comprehending their speech. Vernon's chief worry seemed to be that he would lose Connie, that this would reflect on him. Or perhaps it was his precious radio station that he feared losing. Finally, it was decided that Candy would be turned loose. She was admonished sternly, warned that a repetition of her behavior would lead to her arrest and prosecution. She didn't even nod to acknowledge their threats, but left the house silently, in a fit of sodden despondency.

She had some money on her, and so she took a taxi to the beach. Why she had chosen to go there she didn't know, but the sea seemed to draw her. Perhaps, in the back of her head, she entertained a notion of taking off her clothes and swimming out as far as she could. It was nightfall when she finally arrived.

CHAPTER 27

A dead gull lay in the surf the night of Candy Sterling's resurrection. She had come to the beach because she wanted to be alone to suck on her melancholy like a sick tooth, and the resolutely monotonous lapping of the waves against the sand seemed appropriate to her mood and to the point life had led her to. And there was the possibility that she would go for a swim, as far as her stamina would take her.

When she had first noticed the gull she thought it was part of an old newspaper that someone had scattered near the surf, but after sitting for a moment she had seen it for what it was. By then some creatures had lurched out of the darkness and begun to feed on the gull, tearing out feathers and nipping off bits of flesh. Candy couldn't see well enough to know whether they were crabs, but she supposed they must be. She thought they were fighting at first, but two of them had merely collided in their enthusiasm over the meal that God had provided. Candy tucked her skirt under her legs, making it a tight tube, to insulate her skin from the snappish breeze that had begun to whip up from the Pacific Ocean. She stared at the savage, quiet spectacle before her, watching the living creatures efficiently strip the dead one. There was little left of the gull by the time she became aware of someone standing beside her, towering above her seated figure. She looked up quickly, apprehensive because she was alone and in an awkward position with her skirt wound so tightly about her thighs.

He was a young man, probably not much older than she, tall and slender with slim, muscular-looking legs that were sprinkled with sparse blond hair. He wore fancy glasses, something like motorcycle patrolman glasses but not dark, and he was to her left. With a surreptitious gesture Candy scooped up a portion of sand in her right hand and looked up at him with a blank, uninviting expression.

"Hi," he said in a light, rather thin voice, and hitched up his plaid Bermuda shorts, smiling in a manner obviously meant to be seductive.

"Fuck off, turkey."

She couldn't remember when she had used such language last, and she fancied that she could taste it rolling across her tongue like wine. The young man stood looking down at her for an instant, apparently stunned by the violence of her outburst. Then he turned and moved down the beach, walking as fast as he could in the deep sand.

Candy allowed the grains to seep from her hand as the savage elation seeped out of her body. Dimly, she heard a feather snap as one of the crabs continued a desultory search for more that was edible. The other less enterprising or less optimistic beasts had moved off in search of new booty. Candy felt something flapping against her clothed thigh and glanced down to see that a page of the newspaper had been blown against her by the persistent sea breeze. She reached down, plucked the paper free, and tossed it away, but the breeze returned it without hesitation. Grasping it, she balled it between her hands and tossed it the other way, but with seemingly deliberate perversity the wind shifted, tossing it back at her. It was then, as she compressed it again between her hands, that Candy noticed the small heading: RESURRECTION NOW!

The page was from the classified section, the heading a part of the column devoted to "Announcements." Without quite knowing why, Candy smoothed the page and looked more closely at the ad.

RESURRECTION NOW!

For those willing to dedicate themselves totally to the All-Moving Spirit through His eternal and recurring Prophet, the rewards are instantaneous and eternal. Don't wait for spiritual fulfillment after death. It is within your reach at this moment.

There was a telephone number as well as a post office box, both within the Los Angeles area. Candy sat staring at the short advertisement, unsure of what she would do, unsure of the cause for her suddenly heightened emotions, the pounding of her heart and pulse, the tingling of her skin. She had felt like this before, but not for what seemed like ages. With infinite care she tore out the ad and thrust it into the single pocket of her dress. Then, with some difficulty, she pushed herself to her feet, unfurling her long skirt like a banner, feeling it whip and snap against her legs. She walked off, limping slightly at first, toward the row of pay telephones by the sidewalk. The tide had turned, carrying off the feathers and scaled feet of the destroyed gull.

Whether she had intended to call the number in the ad she was never certain, but by the time she reached the telephone she had forgotten about it. Slipping a dime into the slot, she dialed an old number from memory. The young, slightly hoarse voice answered after the fourth ring. Candy could hear other voices, all young, in the background, and felt a sick nostalgia. "Cliff?" she asked.

He didn't reply at first. She was ready to repeat the question when he finally answered, "Candy? That you?" His voice was slightly slurred.

"Yes, Cliff. I wondered if I could come over and crash. I don't have any place to stay."

"I heard you got religion," he said, a slight lilt of amusement in his tone.

"I'll tell you all about that trip," Candy promised.

"Shit, I'd love to hear it," he said, and she knew she was in. "You got a way to get here, love? 'Cause there's nobody around this place who's fit to drive."

"I can get there," Candy assured him. "And thanks, Cliff."

"Sure thing, cutey."

Candy pressed down on the cradle for a second, then dialed Yellow Cab. A half hour later she was at Cliff's place.

It was an old frame house that had been divided into two dwellings with separate entrances. It looked a bit disoriented as a result, which was very appropriate. Its chief attraction, aside from low rent, was that it stood in a neighborhood which didn't much care what people did. From long habit Candy tried the door. It was locked, so she knocked.

After the third knock Cliff opened the door. He was stripped to the waist, wearing ragged shorts and zories. His tiny string of a beard was sopping with perspiration. He smiled at her glassily, apparently not recognizing her at first. "Come on in," he said finally. "You got here quick enough."

Candy knew he had no idea of how much time had elapsed since her call. She closed the door behind her and followed him into the living room. There were wall-to-wall people, dressed, half-dressed, and a few naked. The walls shook with rock music from a cheap stereo in one corner, and the old, dented coffee table held a platter of tabs. It had been a long time since Candy had dropped any acid, and it was inviting. Cliff left her immediately, not bothering even to introduce her. A few of the people she knew anyway.

The heat of the room felt good after the chill night air. She walked to the coffee table, found an open place on the floor, and sat, winding her skirt about her.

"Hi, lovely lady," a kid next to her said. He couldn't have been more than sixteen. Candy smiled and looked around, then helped herself to a half tab lying on the edge of the platter. The kid grasped her wrist, and she fixed him with a withering glance.

"Hey, that's pure stuff, lovely lady," he cautioned. "You're only supposed to take a quarter tab."

"Don't be chickenshit," Candy said, and popped the half tab. The kid stared at her for a moment, then shrugged.

It was delicious at first, feeling things come apart and go together again, all compartmented. Candy stared at a lamp across the room, watching it change shape and turn into things. She laughed softly, not even minding when the kid beside her started copping feels.

She had never had a bad trip, and it took her by surprise. The first indication of it was when, in mild curiosity, she glanced down at the hand that was clutching at her thigh and pushing back her long skirt. It wasn't a hand at all, but a big green snake with wild markings all over its back. The markings were animated, changing shape constantly, independent of the snake's muscular flexing. Candy stared at the snake for a long time, cold terror running through her. Then its head opened like a vagina, and tiny spiders came out in a writhing cascade, covering her skirt. She shrieked and slapped at them, trying to brush them away, but there were too many of them, and they kept coming back anyway, as though they had marked her somehow.

"What's the matter, lovely lady?"

She looked up at the kid next to her, but now he was a skeleton, his skull of a head staring at her, the jaw flapping as it talked. Candy screamed again and struck out at the skull. When her hand struck it, it broke, cracking into a thousand pieces each of which turned into a scorpion. The scorpions attacked her in an angry mass. She was dimly aware of some sort of commotion around her, and felt grateful that the others saw her plight, and would come to her rescue.

Hands grabbed her shoulders and pulled her back and up, and the room seemed to rock and sway, and the walls were bleeding some sort of rank pus. She felt herself carried away, out of the room. The sounds died around her. For just a moment she saw herself placed on a swaybacked bed in a darkened room. She saw Cliff standing above her, with some other men.

"Help me!" she wailed. "Cliff, don't leave me alone! I'm on a bummer, Cliff!"

But Cliff seemed unmoved. "You'll be all right, girlie," he said in perfunctorily soothing tones. "I'll leave the light on for you."

"Cliff, for Christ's sake!"

In a mild effort at comforting her he reached down and squeezed her shoulder. The hand was a big lizard, the fingers its jaws. Candy drew away, certain she had felt the lizard's teeth sink into her skin.

Cliff apparently misunderstood her withdrawal. "I'm not gonna do anything, Candy," he said, and chuckled mildly, as though at some private joke. "You just stay here an' sleep it off, right?" Before she could protest or point out that there was no way she was going to sleep anything off when she was in the middle of a bad trip, he was gone. The door, a huge steel gate, slammed behind him. It was at least three hundred feet high, and carved with gargoyles that suddenly came to life, laughing and gnashing their teeth. Some of them began to spew blood from their mouths. It ran down the length of the door and spread across the floor, oozing toward the bed on which Candy lay. She wanted to scream, but she remembered the way Cliff had acted, and she feared that too much commotion might prompt him to have his friends tie and gag her or, worse, throw her out. On the street she would be helpless now.

The steel gargoyles began to emit tiny sparks. They flew off the gargoyles' noses and foreheads and chins. Most of them died an instant later, but a few of the sparks survived, waxing into spots of light that flew about the room in lazy holding patterns, occasionally dropping close to Candy's face. The motion seemed rationally directed, as though the spots of light possessed independent intelligence. Gradually she came to realize that they were assembling, forming into an oval above her, dancing around and around but holding that same oval formation. Once in a while one of them would drop down to look her over, sometimes contenting itself with a glance at her face, other times traveling over the length of her body. It was as though they were assessing her, checking her out to see whether there was enough left to be worthy of salvage.

"It's obvious," one of them said finally. She wasn't the least bit surprised to hear one of them speak. She even knew which one it was, and that he was the chief among them in some way. There was no movement, as of lips, nor any variation in shape or brightness of the blob of illumination, but she could tell the source of the words. "It's obvious," he said. "She is useless."

"I'm not certain," objected one of the others diffidently. "She seems salvageable to me."

"No doubt she is," said the leader in a yawning tone. "But who would want to salvage her? The effort would be disproportionate. She's got herself to the point where we would have to expend more energy and time on saving her than it would cost us to start from scratch."

"She's taking up valuable living space," said a third in quietly thunderous tones. "The sooner she kills herself the sooner we can get on with some new project."

"And I hope the next one is more successful," said another blob of light in a businesslike voice Candy hadn't heard previously.

"I just don't think we should be hasty," said the first one in a tone that showed he would be outvoted and wished to go down gracefully. "Perhaps there is some good in her, and we should take some additional time before deciding."

"Oh, come now," said the leader with a touch of impatience. "Just look at her! Any amount of good to come out of that would certainly be inconsequential. I think we've wasted too much time discussing the matter already."

Candy wanted to speak out in her own defense, to tell them that she was a living being, after all, and had some right to continue living, but she knew that speech on her part would be impertinent, and anyway she seemed to have been rendered incapable, as though these beings had decided beforehand that she might try to disrupt their objective discussion with some sort of impassioned plea.

"I take exception to that last remark," said another of the lights. This one had not spoken previously, and its voice was as authoritative as that of the chief. "This body has a responsibility, after all, and must deliberate at its own pace."

"Well, I'm not denying that," said the leader in a somewhat chastened tone.

"Perhaps not, but that statement about wasting time sounded to me like an effort at gagging us and forcing a hasty decision."

"Here, here!" shouted another light. "Personally, I believe the girl is a total loss, but let's not try to silence discussion prematurely."

"I wasn't trying to do that at all," said the leader, who had taken on a defensive tone. "I merely referred to the fact that we have a very full agenda, and can't spend as much time as we should like on every trivial matter that comes along. This one seems to me to be cut and dried, and I can see no reason to go on with it. Since most of you agree with me on that matter at least, perhaps we can just throw the matter open to discussion for those who feel that this Candy person is better than a write-off." There was a protracted moment of silence. Even Candy's former defender said nothing. "Very well, then," said the leader with something of his old vigor. "I call for a vote. All in favor of suicide, so signify."

There was a chorus of ayes.

"I think that constitutes acclamation," said the leader in a tone that was almost smug. "The girl is to kill herself."

The lights fell silent. There was an expectant air to their stillness. They didn't move or flicker, and nothing more was said.

With supreme reluctance Candy pushed herself up from the bed. The lights blinked, not quite synchronously. It seemed approving, as though there had been some doubt as to her obedience. She couldn't imagine what they had expected her to do. They wouldn't let her argue her own case, and anyway, the vote had been taken. It was very, very sad, but nothing could be done about it.

The door was a door again, worn and scratched and with a little nail in the center that had once held a little humorous sign Cliff had bought in a dime store. Candy opened it and moved across the hallway very quietly, not wanting to disturb the party any more than she already had. This was a matter that could be disposed of quietly and with dispatch, after all. She opened the door to the bathroom and stepped inside. Fortunately it was unoccupied at the moment. She closed the door behind her but didn't lock it. It would be a shame if someone had to break it down just to retrieve her body.

And it was such a shame that she had to kill herself. She really didn't want to at all. But there was no good in dwelling on that part of it.

Cliff had taken to using disposable razors, and so she had to pull one apart to get a blade. It took quite a while, and she lacerated the tip of her thumb. Though she couldn't see the lights any longer, she could feel their impatience, and it made her nervous. Finally, the blade came free. She held it in her right hand, between thumb and second finger, with her forefinger behind it for pressure. She laid the keen edge against her left wrist and pressed inward until she felt the blade cut her skin. She had placed it at one side of the wrist so that she would be able to get a clean cut across its width. She didn't want to botch the job, because she was certain that they would be very angry, and she wasn't certain she would have the physical strength to cut again if she didn't do it cleanly enough on the first try.

It didn't even hurt much. Just a little burning sensation as the steel cut through her flesh. The worst part was all that blood. It came spurting out like vomit, all over her and the bathroom. Candy looked at it with mild shock, and then realized that she had better get off her feet before she fell. So she sat down on the floor, there in the middle of Cliff's bathroom, and watched as her blood spurted all over the place. She hadn't realized there would be so much of it.

Then, all of a sudden, she realized what she had done, and the horror of it struck her. She began to weep, and wished she had argued with the lights. But they wouldn't have let her.

"God," she whispered. And then, from somewhere deep in her mind: "All-Moving Spirit, I'm sorry. I don't want to die. I didn't mean to do this, I swear."

The floor parted with the suddenness of a drawer yanked by an impatient hand. There was no sound to it. Suddenly the entire universe was poignantly silent, like a movie with a sound track that has recorded nothingness. Candy's feet and half her thighs hung over the abyss that had opened down the middle of Cliff's bathroom, and she could feel herself slipping gradually into the opening. There was no bottom to it that she could see. It just went down and down until she couldn't see any more. She grasped at the tile, trying to hold onto it, but it was slippery with blood, and she was weak and drowsy. Only fear made her try. She didn't know what was at the bottom of this abyss, but she knew she wouldn't like it.

"Help me!" she wailed. "Please, All-Moving Spirit, help me!" But her words were silent, caught up and smothered in the vacuum of that mighty stillness. She had only a second to go, maybe two seconds, and then she would be falling, and there would be no stopping short of the bottom.

"I'd never have killed myself," she said silently, imploringly. "I wouldn't! They made me do it. They . . ."

Something grasped her wrist just as her buttocks slid over the edge of the crevasse. She had felt herself falling for a moment, and then a giant hand took hold of her, and she knew that it was powerful enough to hold her forever if it chose. And she knew it could let her go.

"Please don't let me die, All-Moving Spirit! I'll do good from now on. I promise, if you'll just give me another chance,

I'll salvage myself. . . ." Her words were silent, but she began to hear other voices above her.

". . . all right," said a young woman. "She cut in the wrong place. And not very deep. There won't even be a scar."

"Shit, what a bummer!" That was Cliff's voice. "Man, she coulda fucked me up royal!"

"What do we do about the cut?" someone else asked.

"Put a Band-Aid on it," said the first young woman, who spoke with some authority. Candy wondered if she was a nurse. "She won't die from this."

"Then we can get rid of her?" Cliff asked.

"Let her sleep it off," said the first girl. "Will someone get me a goddamn *Band*-Aid? Let her sleep it off and then send her on her way when the sun comes up."

Obediently, Candy let herself drift off to sleep again, wonder-filled at the miracle that the All-Moving Spirit had worked for her.

CHAPTER 28

It would have been difficult to isolate the precise time when Polly Chambers began to die. A frail woman who had been a frail child, she had suffered from the trek westward. Her response to the Prophet's personality, the burst of faith and determination it engendered in her, brought an artificial blossoming of health for a while. But the work in the fields would have sapped a much stronger woman; she was no longer young; and she drove herself even harder than the majority of the Prophet's fanatical converts. Had she left the farm and sought rest, or placed herself under the care of a physician, she might have survived the wasting process that had taken root in her; but there was never a chance of that. Within days after her family's arrival at the farm she began to lose color and to experience dizzy spells which she strove to ignore. She seldom spoke, and ate even less than was allowed by the Prophet's rations. A week after the addition of Sister Candace to the dwelling she shared with her husband and Brother Benjamin, Sister Polly began coughing in the night. In the morning flecks were seen on the front of her dress, flecks which she insisted were stains left over from before the dress had been entrusted to her. The flecks were brownish in hue, and a cause of concern to her husband, who wanted to speak to the Prophet about the matter.

But Sister Polly would hear none of it. "The Prophet has more to do than listen to your silly worries," she admonished Brother Joseph. "I'm certain he knows about it, if there is anything to know. I won't have you bothering him on my account."

To Brother Joseph, who was still accustoming himself not only to life in the movement but to this stolidly determined and intractable woman who was not at all like the submissive Polly he had married twenty years earlier, the matter was bewildering. He told himself that the matter could wait awhile. If there were more symptoms, then he would go to the Prophet about it, regardless of his wife's feelings. It was believed that faith in the Prophet would heal any ill, and if that were true, then, he assured himself, his wife was impervious to harm; for she had certainly displayed an impressive degree of faith.

While Sister Polly was fighting for her glorious death, her daughter was fighting for something else. Sister Virginia, still trapped within the confines of the Prophet's dwelling, found herself the subject of that man's constant scrutiny. She would work herself into exhaustion, keeping her mind from the dilemma in which she had been placed, and avoiding conscious consideration of the outcome she must have known, on some deep level, to be inevitable. Suddenly, having crawled on hands and knees under a table to scrub the floor beneath it, she would turn her head to see him sitting in a chair, watching her with the admiration of a proprietor. She didn't know how much of her he had seen. The skirts of the handmaidens' dresses were brief, and they were not provided with undergarments. It didn't matter, really, because he had seen her naked body at least once. But Virginia couldn't help shuddering at the icy caress of those eyes. She said nothing on that occasion, but went about her work as though she were alone. To have confronted him would have been worse than fruitless, because he was surrounded by people who were fanatically devoted to him, including Virginia's sister.

Mary seemed to have fallen prey to the Prophet's rancid charisma as readily as the rest of the Chambers family, or as any of these other pitiful girls who accepted sexual slavery with the same depressing acquiescence they displayed in their daily work. Mary moved about the house, apparently placid and content. Though Virginia hated to think of it, she supposed that Mary had consented to his advances as easily as the rest of the handmaidens. It was simply incredible to Virginia that so many girls had accepted that as part of their spiritual duty, a necessary step on the road to salvation.

A week after her confrontation with him, Virginia finished her workday and entered the dormitory. The space that had been occupied by her cot was empty, leaving a mocking gap between the cots that had flanked it. She turned to Sister

Penelope, who had just emerged from the shower and was walking, naked, toward her own cot nearest the entrance.

"Sister, my bed—"

"The bed you occupied has been removed by order of the Prophet," Sister Penelope informed her. "By order of the Prophet," she repeated with arch satisfaction.

"I don't under—"

"The Prophet has decreed that your wickedness is too deep and too vast not to be contagious," Sister Penelope replied, apparently quoting him directly. "To allow you to share quarters with the rest of the handmaidens would be to endanger the souls of all of us."

"Does this mean I go to the fields?" Virginia asked with a touch of hope.

Sister Penelope yanked down the cover of her cot with an impatient snap of her arm. "Of course not," she snorted derisively. "If you're a threat to us, in the direct presence of our Lord, how could you be allowed to mingle with those outside this dwelling?"

"Well then—?"

"You are to be placed in isolation," Sister Penelope said with obvious, if preconscious, relish. "You will work alone from this time on, and you will eat alone. And you will sleep alone. A room has been set aside for you, by the grace and mercy of the Prophet. The room at the head of the stairs, on the second floor." She lay down on her cot and rolled over, terminating the discussion and dismissing Virginia.

Virginia stood for a moment. She was aware of the other girls as they got into bed. They avoided looking at her, as though they dreaded the fate of Lot's wife. Virginia had felt alone here from the outset, isolated from the others by her refusal to accept their version of reality. But she hadn't realized how much more total the isolation could be. Something settled deep in the pit of her stomach, something hard and painful. She knew it would be worthless to appeal to any of these young women, so she turned and left their physical presence, trudging up the stairs to the room that had been set aside for her.

It was a lovely room, but she could take no joy in its furnishings or appointments because to her it was a cell, where she had been placed in solitary confinement. She undressed and went into the private bathroom, where she showered. It was growing late, she was exhausted, and she would have to rise in a few hours to begin another eighteen-hour day. Stumbling almost blindly to the large bed, she pulled down the covers and crawled in. Then she thought of the door, and the fact that it had a lock on it, and rose and set it. In the dorm she had felt safe because of the presence of the other handmaidens. She had supposed that the Prophet would refrain from any act in their presence that might impair the serenity of his image. But now she was glad for the sturdy door and the lock on it. In her exhaustion, and in her fifteen-year-old innocence, she never considered the fact that this house had no doors to which the Prophet lacked a key.

CHAPTER 29

Candy had vaguely noticed when her husband was called out of the field during the workday, but aside from an almost subliminal relief, she felt nothing about it at the time.

It was almost quitting time, and the sun threw long shadows across the ground, when Brother Benjamin emerged from the Prophet's dwelling and, crossing to the field, approached his wife. "The Prophet wants to see you," he informed her. There was always that little lilt to his voice when he spoke of the Prophet.

Candy sensed that the man didn't really take the Prophet or his movement too seriously, and she felt vaguely guilty for consorting with him, though it had been the Prophet himself who had decreed their marriage. At the moment she was too stunned to think much about any of this.

"Me?" She was so excited she thought her heart would pound its way through her chest. "But why—?" Of course it was foolish and wicked to ask why. Brother Benjamin wouldn't know the reason, and she had no right to ask anyway. She laid down the half-full sack she had been loading with cabbages and set out for the house. She was so lost in her ecstasy that it took her several strides to realize that her husband was keeping pace with her. She glanced up at him.

He shrugged. "I'm supposed to come with you," he explained.

It disappointed Candy to hear that, but at least she would get to see the Prophet again.

She was in the foyer of the dwelling when the glances of the handmaidens reminded her of how she must look. Her hands, once so soft and smooth, had grown red and raw from the work in the fields, and her skin was red from exposure to the sun and wind for these past weeks, and filthy from lack of bathing. The field hands were allowed to bathe only once a week, and it had been five days since Candy's group had had their turn.

In a moment Sister Penelope approached them, that arch look in her eyes as she glanced at Candy's clothing and scratched and roughened skin. It seemed the look of one who sees a once feared rival brought low. "The Prophet will see you now," Sister Penelope said. "This way."

Candy knew the house as well as Sister Penelope, but she allowed herself to be led to the Prophet's den like a stranger.

The Prophet wore a silk dressing gown and soft leather slippers, and smoked a huge Jamaican cigar. As he removed it from his mouth Candy saw his saliva glisten on the tip, and felt a lump of excitement in the pit of her abdomen. He was stretched out on the couch, and glanced toward them with haughty nonchalance. "Approach," he commanded.

Candy moved forward, scarcely aware of the man beside her. She felt like crying, though she didn't know why, and her body was covered with perspiration. It ran down her back under the thick nondescript dress she wore, and down her legs.

"Sister Candace, I am pleased with the progress toward grace which you have shown while in my service," the Prophet said in sonorous tones, not looking at her but staring at the ceiling. He took another puff on the cigar.

Candy was uncertain of whether she was supposed to reply or hold her peace. She compromised by shifting her body slightly in mute acknowledgment of the compliment.

"There is great wickedness in the world, and great wickedness in you," he went on, "but you have diminished it to a considerable extent in the past few weeks."

"Th—thank you, Lord," Candy said, stammering a bit from nervousness and because she was still uncertain of the proper etiquette demanded by this situation. It had made her nervous to be praised by her Lord, and she was reassured by his assertion that she still contained great wickedness.

Suddenly the Prophet sat up, placing his feet on the thick carpet. He was looking directly at Candy. "Now I have decided to grant you an opportunity to diminish the evil in the world still further." He fixed her with that gaze that always made her want to run, and made her too weak to do anything but barely hold her upright position. "Are you willing?"

"Let it be done according to my Lord's will," Candy said, casting her gaze on the floor.

The Prophet rose and paced to his desk, waving the cigar like a baton as he spoke. "There is a misguided and very evil woman in town," he said. "She has come here to damage the movement, and to do ill to me, your Lord." The cigar had died. He revived it with a lighter snatched from his desk. "She must be convinced of the unwisdom of her course of action," he said, looking directly at Candy again. For some reason she was vaguely aware that Brother Benjamin was also looking at her intently. "You may earn additional grace by undertaking this task for me," the Prophet informed her. "If you wish to do it, that is."

Candy's heart was palpitating, but she was surprised at the strength and steadiness of her own voice as she replied, "Of course, Lord."

"It will be unnecessary to harm the woman," the Prophet informed her. "But she must be made to realize the foolishness of threatening harm to the Prophet of the All-Moving Spirit."

"I understand, Lord."

"Very good." The Prophet walked around behind his desk and picked something up from the middle of the green blotter. It was a lumpy article wrapped in a towel. He placed it on the front edge of the desk, leaning over and grunting slightly to do so. Then he pulled back the towel to reveal a spidery-looking pistol. It was old and worn but seemed in good repair.

Candy had never held a pistol in her life, and had always been afraid of them, but without hesitation she walked to the desk and picked it up. It felt cold under her fingers, and surprisingly heavy. The Prophet had turned his back, staring at the wall behind his desk. Candy hugged the gun to her body, hiding it behind the heavy, voluminous sleeves of her dress.

"There is a pad on my desk," the Prophet continued. "On it you will find the address at which this unregenerate woman is staying. Outside is a car with the keys in the ignition. Brother Benjamin will gain grace by accompanying you." He turned once again, relit his cigar, and repaired to the couch, stretching out with a sigh of deferred comfort.

* * *

Why he had chosen to enlist the black man's aid in this, the Prophet was unsure, except that he had the feeling that this particular street-wise young man was smarter and cannier than the boobs who usually showed up there. He wasn't even certain of why Benjamin was on the farm, but he might be put to some use. It had been Benjamin's advice that had prompted the decision to use Candy Sterling for this job.

"In your religion, she's a saint," Benjamin had said.

Tonight would tell. Meanwhile there was a new girl in the house, a Hispanic fourteen-year-old named Carlotta, whom he had yet to sample. This might be a good time to purify the girl's blood.

No words passed between Candy and her husband on the way to town. She sat on the right side of the car seat, staring straight ahead and occasionally laying her hand on the gun in her lap. It was odd how the feel of it, the weight and shape, conferred comfort on her. She had found an envelope on the car seat, containing two one-dollar bills. She knew exactly what the Prophet intended her to do with that money.

They stopped at a sporting goods store in town. She took the gun inside and showed it to the young man behind the counter. He sold her a box of .22 Long Rifle ammunition, high-velocity hollow point, and showed her how to load the little gun, which he called a Ruger. Somewhere, on TV or in the movies, Candy had heard of a gun called a Luger, and wondered if he meant that.

They pulled to the curb a half block from the motel. Candy thrust the gun, fully loaded and with the safety engaged, under her left arm, holding the grip with her right hand.

"You sure you want to do this?" Brother Benjamin asked when they were at the sinner's door.

Candy looked up at him blankly. She was in the grip of such excitement that she wasn't certain she had heard him correctly. Besides, the question was too farfetched to credit. "What?" she asked, looking at him through glassy eyes.

He shrugged, raised a huge, hard fist, and knocked on the door. At first there was no response. A light shone through the single window, but that was no proof that the woman was there. Candy was about to move to the window to peer in when the door opened. It opened almost halfway. The woman was apparently without suspicion. She stood there in the doorway, the dim lamplight behind her. She had donned a cheap cotton robe, which she held about her with one hand. She looked to be in her late thirties, blond—probably, Candy admitted to herself, natural. Her hair was damp, and Candy saw little beads of water on her hands and face.

"Yes?" she asked.

Brother Benjamin, who was operating in his own field after all, threw out his right hand, hitting the woman directly over her mouth. The blow was hard enough to propel the woman back several steps, nearly upsetting her. Because Brother Benjamin had been wise enough to direct his blow at her mouth, she hadn't cried out. A muffled, vocalized gasp was all that emerged from her. Through widened eyes she stared at the two of them. Brother Benjamin, following his advantage, moved inside, blocking off any potential attempt to close the door. Candy followed him inside. The woman opened her mouth to scream as Candy was closing the door. Candy heard another blow, a slap this time.

"No noise, baby," Benjamin said in the same soft, ugly voice he had used on that night when he had threatened Candy. "You dig?"

Candy turned toward them again and saw the woman nod. She opened her mouth to say something, closed it again, and swallowed twice, hard.

"W—what do you want?" she asked. She was hugging the robe about her with both hands now.

Candy moved toward her, keeping the pistol hidden until she was within reach. Then she jammed the pug-nosed barrel into the woman's midriff, eliciting a short cry. The woman stared down at the gun, apparently incapable of accepting its existence. Candy's finger tightened on the trigger until she could feel the grooves impressing themselves on her flesh. Then she remembered that she had left the safety engaged. The excitement she had felt outside was erupting now, like something volcanic. Stepping close to the woman again, she snapped off the safety, deliberately doing it with a smart, quick movement that made a loud click in the tomblike quiet of the room. The sound was followed instantly by a gasp. Candy smiled and jabbed her once again, harder this time, making her bend a little and step back. The woman looked at Benjamin once, as though hoping insanely that he might be of some help. Then she returned her gaze to Candy and opened her mouth to gargle something incomprehensible.

On the second try she managed to articulate a few words. "I —I don't ha—have a—ny—"

Candy slapped the woman across the mouth with the back of her left hand, keeping the pistol trained with surprising steadiness.

"Oh, please," the woman whimpered, belatedly protecting her mouth with her right hand. The left hand held the robe closed. The pathetic modesty of that annoyed Candy for some reason she herself couldn't fathom.

"Get over there," she commanded, gesturing toward the bed. The woman looked in that direction, then at Candy again. She moved reluctantly in the direction indicated. Candy raised the pistol, aiming it directly at the middle of her face. "Move!" she hissed. The woman sidled to the bed with crablike haste and stood beside it, staring at Candy woozily. Candy gestured with her free hand and her victim sat on the edge of the bed. Candy moved close to her, pointed the gun at the center of her face again. It was an attractive face, and had probably once been beautiful. The woman's terror seemed amplified at the thought of being shot in that particular part of her anatomy. "On your belly," Candy ordered, more excited than she could remember having been previously except for a few times in the presence of the Prophet.

"Please, I—"

Candy jammed the pistol's barrel against the woman's face, just below her nose. It had to hurt, because she thrust it hard enough to bob her victim's head back. Tears streamed down the distraught woman's face and sobs shook her. She seemed to be maintaining some control over herself by sheer force of will. Candy knew that much more of this would send her into an irrational panic, probably start her screaming, perhaps precipitate a frantic resistance that could force Candy to shoot her. She recalled, dimly, the Prophet's injunction against actually hurting her.

"Lie down," she reiterated in a voice very slightly more gentle. The woman, weeping freely now, did as she was told. Benjamin stood on the opposite side of the bed, looking slightly tense, ready to lend a hand should it prove necessary. Candy was sorry he had come, sorry that his restraining presence might render things difficult. She had never dreamed that it could be this easy to terrify someone, or that doing so could generate such a feeling of exhilaration. She reached down with her free hand and tore the pillow from beneath the prostrate woman's face, bringing forth a freshet of tears, an explosion of sobs. Grabbing the pillowcase, she shook it free of the pillow, then tossed it on the bed near Benjamin. "Tie her up," she said peremptorily.

Benjamin stared at her for a moment, his face too much a jumble of expressions to be readable. Leaning across the bed he grasped the woman's wrists, crossed them behind her and knotted the pillowcase about them efficiently. "Now her ankles," Candy ordered.

"You don't have to," the woman sobbed, her words muffled by the mattress. "I won't—"

Candy rapped the back of her blond head with the butt of the pistol and she subsided, burrowing her face into the mattress as though she could escape through it. Benjamin stripped the pillowcase from the other pillow and tied the woman's ankles together. He did a thorough job of it.

"Now turn over," Candy ordered. It took the woman a moment to respond. Then, grunting a bit, she turned onto her back. The robe fell open, exposing her, and she stared up at Benjamin, looking embarrassed and oddly apologetic. Her figure wasn't bad, though she had some flab on her, and stretch marks impaired the smooth whiteness of her belly. Her nipples, brownish and swollen, seemed distended, as though her terror had brought her a tinge of involuntary sexual excitement.

Engaging the safety, Candy placed the pistol on the bedside table and sat on the edge of the bed, feeling that exhilarating, formless excitement swell in her once again. She had no idea of why the sight of this helpless victim excited her so. "Now," she said, leaning down until her face nearly touched that of the older woman, "we're going to have a little talk, dear. We're going to settle something."

"Are you from—?" the woman started. Candy grasped one of her nipples between thumb and knuckle and pinched it hard. The woman opened her mouth and let out a short, ragged screech.

"Shut up!" Candy rasped into her face. She looked around. "Find something to gag her with," she ordered Benjamin. The woman looked more panicky than ever at that prospect, and tried, reflexively, to sit up. Candy shoved her back with ease.

Benjamin walked to a suitcase that lay open on the dresser, rummaged for a moment, then returned to Candy with a pair of panties. They were thin nylon bikini panties.

"Perfect," Candy chortled. She pressed them against the woman's lips, but her victim wouldn't cooperate for once. Candy picked up the pistol once more, pressed it against the woman's temple, and snapped off the safety. With a strangled sound the woman on the bed opened her mouth and let Candy shove the panties beyond her teeth. Candy engaged the safety once more and replaced the pistol on the table, then yanked the sash from the woman's robe with three heavy tugs. She wrapped it around her head several times, crossing her mouth, and knotted it securely. "Now," she whispered, "I'll do the talking, and you'll do the listening." The woman stared up into Candy's eyes, apparently fascinated by something she saw in them.

"You've been a very wicked girl," Candy said, gently brushing back a lock of gold hair that had strayed down the woman's forehead. "You've threatened the greatest man in the history of the world. You've tried to harm him. We can't let you do that, now can we? You have to understand, to look at things through the proper sort of eyes. Your safety, even your life, doesn't matter at all compared to the Prophet's work, or his peace of mind. It only makes sense to eliminate someone like you rather than to take any chances with the Prophet's safety."

The woman suddenly shuddered violently. For an instant Candy thought it merely the result of her quietly expressed threats, but then she realized, with some surprise, that she had been gently fondling the woman's nipple as she had spoken.

To emphasize her point, she mashed it hard between thumb and forefinger, causing her victim to arch her back and cry a muffled scream into her gag. Candy felt the excitement well up in her again, and she pressed even harder on the nipple. The woman thrashed briefly, found that that only increased her anguish, and lay still and rigid, every muscle in her body taut. Then her head lolled, and Candy realized that she was about to lose consciousness. Drawing back her hand quickly, Candy grasped her victim's hair and shook her head back and forth violently, wrenching her into awareness.

The woman stared up at her with eyes that were frantic, doe-wide and limpid. She cried into the gag, sounds that could have been words except for the restraint of the garments stuffed into her mouth. She seemed to be pleading.

Candy shook her head, assuming a look of mock sadness. "What's the matter, dear?" she asked, brushing back that rebellious lock of hair again. "Don't want to die? Well, what a shame. But we should have thought about that earlier, shouldn't we?"

The woman's head had come clear of the bed, as though she were trying to sit up and talk, to communicate with this person who seemed bent on destroying her. Candy reached over and picked up the pistol again. Pressing it against the woman's sweat-drenched temple, she worked off the safety loudly. Her victim shook her head vigorously, as though trying pathetically to shake loose the muzzle. Gradually, Candy increased the pressure her finger exerted on the trigger. She felt it move slightly, felt a gritty creep as metal slipped against metal inside the weapon. Just one more little pull, she thought, just a tiny bit more pressure, and this evil woman's life would be terminated. Forever. Candy felt an excitement of sexual intensity deep inside her loins.

Why, she wondered, did people tell lies about this matter of killing? She had been led to believe that it would be a hideous experience, that it would make her ill. Instead she felt the most exhilarating, liberating emotion of her life. She supposed it must be because she was doing it for the Prophet, and that blessed the act.

A shadow fell across her. It annoyed her at first. Then, a second later, she realized that it must be Benjamin. She knew even before she looked up why he had approached her and felt a mixture of gratitude and annoyance. He looked down at her with an expression of concern. Candy released the trigger on the little pistol and withdrew it from the woman's head. The woman was still rigid, as though she had fallen into some sort of seizure. Her eyes, clamped shut while the pistol had been about to fire, now opened, rolling about, unfocused.

"I think I'll look around a bit, dear," Candy said softly, stroking the victim's forehead. "I'll be back." She rose and carried the gun to the bathroom door, smiling at Benjamin. His expression was only slightly less distressed than before.

Candy entered the cabin's bathroom, closing the door behind her. It was much as she had expected, much like the bathrooms in which she had showered after a hundred tricks. The stall shower was metal, and the basin was ancient, with bare and pitted pipes anchored in the wall. A pair of nylon panty hose had been hung over the shower-curtain rod. A woman's razor lay open on the basin, its blade removed and laid out to dry. Candy picked up the blade, holding it close and gazing at the still keen edge. She caught a glimpse of herself in the smeared, discolored mirror and smiled.

Turning to the shower stall, Candy placed the gun on the edge of the basin. She pulled the panty hose down and began slicing them with the razor, mutilating the crotch before she cut long, straight slits down the legs. She cut open the bottoms of the feet and ripped them wide, then replaced the hose on the rail, winding them about it and tying several knots in them, pulling the knots as tight as she could. She was breathing hard, and not from exertion.

Retrieving the pistol, she removed the magazine and worked the slide as the young man in the sporting goods store had showed her. She bent and picked up the ejected cartridge, then slipped the magazine back into the gun. The single cartridge she placed in the pocket of her dress with the box holding the others. Then she picked up the razor blade and returned to the bedroom.

Benjamin was standing near the bed, looking as though he didn't know quite what to do. The woman on the bed had recovered her faculties a bit, looking more normal, though still terrified. Candy walked straight to the bedside, holding the pistol out in front of her, while she concealed the razor blade in her left hand.

"Well, I guess it's time to finish up," she said in a voice almost merry. She said it to Benjamin, as though the woman were some inanimate object. Then, unceremoniously, she pressed the muzzle of the pistol against the prostrate woman's temple.

The victim began to make those pathetic mewing noises again, and tried to turn her head away. Candy shifted the pistol, maintaining the pressure against the woman's temple, and began once again to press the trigger. Benjamin moved toward her quickly, apparently frightened that she intended going through with the act of murder. The trigger released, making a clicking sound that must have been horrendously loud to the woman.

Candy threw back her head and laughed ringingly, peals of glee that blotted out the woman's sobs and muted screams. Benjamin looked stunned by her actions and mood, and that made it all seem funnier. She worked the slide of the pistol, injecting a cartridge into the chamber.

Leaning down, she spoke in the woman's ear. "You see, honey? I could have killed you so easily. It's not hard at all. It's ridiculously simple. And I may do it yet." She tossed an impish grin at Benjamin, then dropped the pistol to the bed and, with a movement that surprised even her with its swiftness, brought the little razor blade against the woman's cheek. "You know what that is?" she asked. When the woman made no effort to respond, Candy slapped her across the breasts with her free hand. "Do you?" she demanded. The woman nodded carefully, apparently afraid that too generous a movement might cause the blade to cut her. Candy pressed harder with the razor and then, slowly, drew it down the woman's cheek. The cut it made was superficial, though it would have been very easy to cut clear to the bone. A thin line of blood traced across the cheek from cheekbone to chin. Benjamin was standing stock still, as though afraid to move. The woman whimpered, lying rigidly with apparent effort. Finally Candy tossed the blade to the floor. She picked up the pistol once again, hefted it in her hand, and gazed down into the woman's expressionless eyes. Candy's own eyes glittered.

"That's just a little something to help you remember this evening," she said. Her voice came in ragged puffs, broken by the fierce, almost sexual excitement she felt. "Maybe we'll let you live after all. This time. But you must go away. You must never annoy the Prophet again. Next time it will end differently. Do you understand?" She grabbed the woman by the hair, pulling her head up from the bed, extracting a muffled whimper of surprise. "*Do* you *understand*?" she almost shrieked into the woman's face. The woman managed a frantic, restricted nod. "Well, you'd better hope you do," Candy said. "Personally, I'd just as soon you gave us reason to come back and finish you off."

Candy brushed past the dazed Benjamin and walked toward the front door. Benjamin finally moved to join her, apparently relieved to find that she intended to terminate the proceedings.

Candy opened the door, then turned back to her victim. "You can work yourself loose before checkout time if you try hard," she said. The woman wasn't looking at her but stared at the ceiling. "You wouldn't want them to find you like that, because then you'd have to think up a story. Whatever you do, don't tell anyone about this night." Candy slipped the catch on the lock. "We'll leave this unlocked," she said. "Just in case we decide to come back."

CHAPTER 30

Virginia Chambers had never known what exhaustion was until the past few weeks. She had been tired after working hard on her parents' farm. She had come to know that such tiredness was less than considerable since coming to the Prophet's quarters, where a young girl was expected to put in sixteen hours a day without sitting down once. But even then she had been able to get in five or six hours' sleep each night, lying in sodden weariness between the equally fatigued bodies of other girls. Then she had slept as though she had been anesthetized, her slumber not even disturbed by the knowledge that she would have to get up the next morning and do it all over again. Or even that she would have to face the Prophet, with his tricky ways of getting her alone and his quick, inquisitive fingers.

But even then she hadn't been exhausted. Exhaustion was something she had learned of later, when he had pulled his masterstroke, removing her from the handmaidens' dormitory and placing her in the private room. She had been fooled by that at first, lulled by the fact that the room wasn't even on the same floor as his, and was near the head of the stairs, while his bedroom, only a part of his private quarters, sat in solitary splendor at the back of the top floor. It had never occurred to Virginia that he had moved her for his own evil purposes. She had supposed it was a sign of his official disapproval, intended to weaken her resistance by making her a pariah among the handmaidens. She had even been slightly amused at such a futile, weak ploy.

The ostracism Virginia suffered during the day was of slight importance compared to the things that had begun to happen at night. The first night had been just fine. Virginia had showered in her new private shower and had slipped, naked, between the sheets of her huge bed. She had slept the night through, it seemed, without turning or stirring. In the morning, at the regular time, Sister Penelope had pounded on the door. When she woke, Virginia had the impression that the pounding had been going on for some time, and Sister Penelope's voice, driving through the thick door, sounded irate. Virginia had scrambled to her feet and run over to unlock the door and open it a crack.

"Get dressed and get to work," Sister Penelope ordered. "You're already too late for any breakfast."

Virginia put on one of the fresh dresses in the closet after taking a quick shower, ran a comb through her hair a few times, put on some makeup, and reported to Sister Penelope to be duly told to begin her day by scrubbing all the toilets, as she had known she would be. She was on the third one, on the top floor in the Prophet's private quarters, when he walked in on her. She had been on her knees, bent double over the rim of the toilet, rubber gloves drawn halfway up her slender arms. She started as he entered. It seemed unnatural, the way he could move so quietly. Virginia turned her body away from the direction of the door because she knew that he could look up her short skirt, and like all the girls in the house, she wore nothing under it. He smiled patronizingly, as though her modesty were childish, her obstinacy fruitless against his patience.

"Well, Virginia, how do you like your new quarters?" the Prophet asked.

"I have no complaints," she answered flatly.

"Think of it as a quarantine. We can't let your disease spread throughout the house, can we?"

"I said I wasn't complaining."

"I should think not. For someone like you, a recalcitrant sinner who refuses even to admit her guilt, I should think the move would be most welcome. Privacy and luxury. What more could you ask, since you reject the grace of the All-Moving Spirit?"

"Yes, you're right. I like it much better. I suppose I should thank you."

"If you did it would be insincere. But the time will come when you will thank me, Virginia, and with solemn gratitude."

His pompousness irritated Virginia even more than his horniness and lack of decency. She turned on him. "Don't hold your breath," she said, twisting at the waist so that she knelt facing him. And then, with uncharacteristic profanity, "You bastard!" She hissed these words at him, afraid that if she voiced them they would come out as a shriek that might be heard all over the house, thus convincing the other hand-maidens all the more that she was the ultimate in culpability.

The Prophet had grown unaccustomed to such straight talk and now he moved toward her reflexively, his hands curling into talonlike fists, his entire body stiffening. Virginia whitened, drawing back in spite of herself so that her elbow barked painfully on the wall.

But he had already regained control. He smiled down at her, obviously amused at her fright. "You'll see, dear," he said with that same silky pomposity. "The time will come when you'll implore me to purify your blood." Then his eye took on a cryptic twinkle, emphasizing his double entendre. "You obviously need it so desperately."

It began that night, her second night in her private room. After eating her meal alone, she locked the door of the room, took off her clothes and showered, then fell into the huge bed. She was asleep before the sheets had settled over her body. It could have been minutes or hours later that she felt herself in the grip of a horrid dream. Something was grasping at her, trying to smother her. She was sweaty and weak, and the thing was all bristly, and much stronger than she. She twisted and tried to resist, and then, nearly too late, realized that she had awakened, that the dream had become reality. The thing was a man, and he was in bed with her! His body pressed down on hers, holding her pinned to the mattress, while his hands groped between her thighs, trying to insert himself into her. Virginia tried to scream, but the man lay upon her with such force that she couldn't gather enough wind. All that came out were little whimpering yips. His breathing was loud and ragged in her eyes, disgusting her. She had never felt such fright in her life, and it lent her strength. She jammed her legs together hard, crossing her ankles and immobilizing his hands.

Finally, he pulled the hands free and clamped one over her mouth. The hand was soft and smooth, not the hand of a man who had worked, like her father. She caught a tinge of sweat mixed with expensive cologne, and finally recognized him.

Rising above her, he jammed his knee between her thighs, trying to open them. It was bruisingly painful, but Virginia rolled to one side, keeping her legs locked together. She tried to bite his hand but couldn't reach it with her teeth. The cries she sought to emit died faintly in her throat.

"Damn you, put out!" he snarled in her ear. "I'll kill you!" The words, the threat, hardly registered. Virginia was so caught up in the horror of the thing he was trying to do to her, the one thing that, for some reason, she had failed to anticipate, that other fears couldn't penetrate her numbed consciousness.

Then, after a time she couldn't estimate, he stopped trying to penetrate her. He simply lay atop her, his hand still clamped over her mouth, while he breathed roughly, loudly, in her ear.

"All right," he wheezed. "All right, Virginia. I'll leave you now. Just don't scream or I'll throttle you." He was still then.

She could feel him atop her, hear his breathing and vaguely see his shape, but he made no more effort to rape her. It finally occurred to her that he was waiting for some acknowledgment on her part. She nodded briskly, so that he could feel it with his hand. The hand lifted tentatively from her mouth, hovering a scant inch from her lips. Virginia felt an immense relief at being able to breathe normally again. She didn't make a peep, utilizing all her will power to keep in the scream that bubbled in her lungs. Finally he rolled off her, lying there beside her on his back, catching his breath. She had the feeling that he was badly out of physical condition, and that that had saved her.

"I'll be back," he said. "If not tonight, then on other occasions. After tonight it won't even matter if you scream, because I'm going to see to it that the others expect you to. You know they'll believe anything I tell them."

It was true. Virginia felt the futility of her position. All she could do was fight for time, and hope that he would give up, decide that she wasn't worth the effort. And yet somehow she didn't believe that would ever happen. The one quality he possessed that seemed almost supernatural was his persistence.

He was like a man obsessed. Falteringly, she found some words to answer, aware that they masked her hopelessness, and that he would know it. "I'll barricade the door," she said. "The furniture—"

"Do that and I'll have the other girls remove the furniture."

"They'll wonder why," she said, starting to cry.

"No they won't." He said that simply, rising from the bed. Standing there for a moment, he managed to tame his breathing.

Virginia had the outlandish feeling that he really did possess some sort of powers, that he could see her nakedness clearly in the darkness. She was scarcely aware of his departure.

The Prophet proved true to his word. The next night he returned, not once but twice. She fought and screamed, and quickly learned the hopelessness of the latter. Most of the handmaidens were asleep in the basement and would be unable to hear her cries, but there were always some awake. The Prophet had decreed that there must be at least two girls awake and made up, puttering about the house and ready to serve him personally, at all times. Still, Virginia's screams accomplished nothing except to rob her of wind and strength. She learned to fight in silence after that.

The third night she slept in her dress. There were no other clothes, no underwear that might afford her some flimsy protection. The dress ended in tatters.

And so it went for more than a week, Virginia growing progressively exhausted, robbed of sleep even between bouts because she hovered always on the verge of wakefulness, occasionally coming upright in the bed with a start, thinking that she heard his approach or felt his weight in the bed. She could see the results in her mirror in the morning: her haggardness, the lines around her eyes growing deeper with each day, the sag of her mouth and the dullness of her eyes. And then dullness vanished, displaced by a burning glint. She went about the house in a veritable trance, barely aware of what she was doing, frequently scolded by Sister Penelope and made to repeat tasks during the mealtimes.

She supposed she had been pretty in the beginning, but now she couldn't imagine why he still wanted her so badly. She supposed it was simply that she was the one girl he hadn't been able to possess, and so he was determined to return his score to one hundred percent.

On the tenth day Virginia Chambers rose from her bed and entered the connecting bathroom, where she showered, nearly falling asleep under the nozzle. She was hungry. Her ravenousness was the only sensation that competed with her weariness. She hadn't eaten since breakfast the previous day. She turned off the shower and plodded to the bedroom, toweling herself. Then she sat at the little vanity and applied her makeup carefully, driven by some stubborn streak of feminine vanity. Her hands shook so that she had to steady her wrist with her other hand as she applied her lipstick and eye makeup. Pushing on the top of the vanity with both hands, she dragged herself to her feet and walked to the closet, opening it wearily.

It was empty.

She stood staring into the closet for half a minute, her dulled mind incapable of absorbing the fact of its barrenness. Her hand tightened on the doorknob and her heart accelerated as she finally computed the evidence of her eyes. Then, suddenly, she spun and looked at the little chair where she had thrown her dirty dress the night before. The dress was gone. Someone obviously had removed it. Her shoes too were missing.

Too exhausted even to react, she walked back to the vanity and sat on the stool, staring at her haggard reflection.

Was she to be a prisoner in the room now, forbidden to leave it? If that were the case at least she could try to sleep during the day, though she supposed the Prophet would simply extend his intrusions to the daylight hours. Or was there some other, even more ominous meaning to this latest turn of events? As though in answer, there was a rap on her door. Virginia started dully, looking at the door, saying nothing.

Someone tried the knob, opened the door, which she hadn't bothered to lock after the Prophet's latest visitation. "You're already too late for breakfast," Sister Penelope informed her crisply. She was expected to go down and get her breakfast on a tray, then eat it alone in her room, lest she infect the other girls with her wickedness. "Get to work. You'll start on the bathrooms as usual, and this time don't—"

"I can't," Virginia objected. "I don't have any clothes."

"They were removed last night," Sister Penelope informed

her with an arch little smile. "By the Prophet's holy decree. Because of your perverse wickedness you are to go without clothing, so that all may know and avoid you."

That made no sense, since they all avoided her anyway, but Virginia was too befuddled to think of such niceties at the moment. She hugged herself in belated modesty. "I will *not* go around naked!"

"You will do as the Prophet decrees, Sister Virginia. If you won't do it willingly, then I'll just bring up a few of the handmaidens and we'll drag you out of this room." From the glint in her eye and the lilt in her voice, Virginia deduced that Sister Penelope would not hesitate to carry out her ultimatum.

What did it matter now, anyway? He could see her naked, as he had so many times, whenever he wished. They were all his accomplices, all the people he had somehow turned into robots. Even Virginia's parents. She had no one on whom she could rely except herself. But if he thought this meant she was going to give up . . .

It would be easy to give up. Then he would tire of her, as he had tired of most of the others, and send her out to the fields. There she could work her sixteen hours and sleep at night, unmolested. It would require such a little act on her part. No act at all, really; just a supine acceptance. Surely he would tire of her quickly. No more than a few times. Now the only attraction she had to offer him was her resistance. No one would care. They would all think she had risen above her corrupt nature. To everyone here it would be an act of virtue.

Everyone but her.

Lifting her chin, Virginia rose and walked toward the door, and Sister Penelope, with a firm, reinvigorated tread. "All right," she said. "Do you want me to start upstairs or downstairs?"

CHAPTER 31

Candy had kept the gun. Nothing was said about its return, creating a dilemma for her. To return to the Prophet's quarters without invitation would be unthinkable; yet she was very much aware that the pistol belonged to him and that it had been entrusted to her only pending the fulfillment of her appointed task. The Prophet's followers were forbidden to own or keep any articles other than their clothing and the little bit of matting on their beds.

She thought of giving the gun away, but the fewer people who knew of its existence the better. So she had placed it under the matting on her bed, together with the box of ammunition, in which she had replaced the cartridges taken from the magazine, all neatly alternating between points up and points down, the way they had been originally. At night, as she dozed off, she could feel the lump of steel through the rags under her head and shoulders. It was an odd feeling, both comforting and exciting. Somehow it seemed to bring her closer to the Prophet; and she could think back, as sleep closed in on her, to that night, that trip of a night when she and Brother Benjamin had brought that silly, misguided female to her senses.

Sister Polly grew worse. Her coughing had become so bad that sometimes she actually awakened Candy, and Candy could see that Brother Benjamin and Brother Joseph were also awakened by it. Brother Joseph would rise from his bed and approach his wife's. Sometimes he would forget himself nearly to the extent of touching her, but she would draw away, more terrified of breaking a holy decree than she was concerned about her health. She insisted, when her husband expressed his care, that she would recover in good time, provided that she kept the Prophet's faith. In the morning she was always the first one to sit up, though it took her longer to gain her feet than any of the others. She would trudge to the fields and work slowly but with determination all through the day.

Then, a week after Candy and Brother Benjamin had terrorized the recalcitrant woman, Sister Polly collapsed in the middle of the workday. It was ten o'clock in the morning, and very hot. Others had passed out before, and were usually allowed to lie in place until they came to, or their presence began to hinder the work of others. Normally they would regain consciousness and resume their duties. But this time Brother Joseph committed a serious breach. When he saw his wife collapse he dropped the bag he had been filling with lettuce and ran to her in a kind of loping gallop, showing surprising speed for a man of his years and girth. Although everyone else had lost weight working the farm on the subsistence diet the Prophet allotted, Brother Joseph had somehow maintained his beefy physiognomy.

The moment he reached his wife, he scooped her up in his arms and carried her to the dwelling. It hadn't escaped Candy's notice that he managed to work near his wife all the time. She had come to feel a kind of contempt for the man and his lack of faith and poor sense of values. Now she was shocked, as she could not remember having been shocked before in her young life. Of course she did nothing about it, but continued to work, stuffing lettuce heads into her bag as quickly and vigorously as she could. Her resentment of Brother Joseph's perversity showed through only in an increased stiffness to her stooped body, an extra force to the plucking of the lettuce heads and the thrusting of them into her gunny sack. She was vaguely aware of her own husband nearby, glancing at her from time to time, as though fascinated by her behavior, though she couldn't imagine why he should be.

That night Brother Joseph was called to the Prophet's quarters. Candy was certain that he and his family would be expelled from the group, which filled her with a feeling of satisfaction. She had never liked Brother Joseph, though his wife was all right. She had never believed that his faith was up to standard. She knew that he had two daughters, both of whom had been demonstrated to be especially sinful by the astonishingly long time they had been kept in the Prophet's direct presence. She had seen the Chambers's son from time to time, working along with the others. He seemed a nondescript boy who worked with no greater zeal than necessary, as though he was there simply because he was a minor, and required to remain with his parents. It was too bad about Sister Polly, or Mrs. Chambers as she would soon be once again, but the Prophet's will would be done. And Candy felt warmed by the thought that some corruption would soon be cleansed from the Prophet's holy movement.

When the Prophet heard about Brother Joseph's reaction to his wife's bit of malingering, he reacted angrily. The Chambers family had just about run things into the ground with him, and he was determined to see to it that they learned their lesson.

That was why he ordered Brother Joseph brought into his holy presence. He saw to it that Sister Virginia knew nothing about her father's presence, and that she was kept sequestered in another part of the house during his visit. It occurred to the Prophet almost too late that it might be wise to put the other Chambers girl away too.

Sister Penelope ushered a somewhat chastened but not entirely subdued Joseph Chambers into the Prophet's presence just after dinner. The Prophet was enjoying a Jamaican cigar, sitting behind his desk with his swivel chair tilted back, and he fixed his minion with a piercing gaze.

"Brother Joseph," he said in a voice quiet and controlled but devoid of cordiality, "I am aware that you have committed a serious breach of my holy decrees. Please don't deny it, because the Prophet knows all that occurs."

"No, sir—I mean, Lord. I don't deny it," Brother Joseph said. "But you see, my wife—"

"I know all about that. Do you think I would allow a faithful servant to come to any serious harm?" The Prophet fixed Joseph with a glinting eye and awaited a reply.

Brother Joseph shifted his feet. "Well, no, Lord, but she's my wife."

"And you have brought her and yourself very close to expulsion from this community. I simply cannot allow people to do as they choose. If I did, anarchy would reign, and my holy covenants would come to nothing. Were you not aware that contact between males and females is forbidden?" Once again the Prophet awaited a reply.

"Yes, sir, I know that. But she had passed out. People were just gonna let her lay there in the hot sun." Brother Joseph's tone took on some strength, even a touch of defiance.

The Prophet was startled by this show of independence but managed to maintain his composure. Apparently Virginia Chambers had taken after her father more than her mother. They were an insubordinate crew, and he ought to order them off his property. Had he done so, subsequent events would have been entirely different. But though he went so far as to open his mouth to issue the order, there was never any chance of it. He had not yet possessed Virginia Chambers, as he had determined to do. So slowly he had not noticed it, his personality had lost its flexibility, until now he was as much a prisoner to compulsion as the people who tilled his fields.

"You have little faith, Brother Joseph," the Prophet said in a weary tone. "After all I have brought you: the grace of the All-Moving Spirit. Still you believe that your wife could come to harm in my holy service. Don't you know that we have had people like your wife in this place before? People even sicklier. They obeyed the covenants and decrees, and they waxed strong and healthy because of it. Many of the people who work around you were weak, consumptive creatures when first they devoted themselves to my service," the Prophet said, warming to his topic, and his story. He had almost begun to believe it himself. As he spoke he could see the ranks of wan, pale people growing ruddy-complexioned and strong as a result of his grace.

"Your wife will grow worse now, for a while," he said, "because of what you have done. If I decide to drive you from the midst of this holy assemblage, she will die." He rose as he spoke this last sentence, punctuating the final word by pounding the desk with his fist. "And you, your sin, and that of your willful, rebellious daughter will be to blame for it."

"My daughter?"

"Sister Virginia," the Prophet railed, slamming his fist on

the desk once more. "A fractious, wicked child who courts damnation and lusts for disaster!"

He caught himself raising both arms high over his head, felt the pounding of rushing blood in his temples. Brother Joseph was looking at him strangely. The Prophet thrust his right hand forward, forefinger jutting, succeeding fairly well in making it look as though he had intended that gesture in the first place.

"If I expel you from this place and excommunicate you from the grace of the All-Moving Spirit, beware, Brother Joseph! Your wife will surely die, and you and your wretched offspring will wander the earth, unloved, alienated from God and man, helpless to alter your fate, mere spectators at your own damnation!"

The Prophet lowered his arms and stood, breathing in heavy, ragged puffs. His face was purple and his eyes distended and bloodshot. Brother Joseph had backed away a step and stood staring, awestruck, though the Prophet wasn't certain of whether the man was awed by his divine anger or by the suspicion that he had gone insane. The Prophet turned his back on Brother Joseph and walked around his desk to sit in his swivel chair. He took his time, settling, rekindling his cigar before speaking again. He gave himself plenty of time to regain control of his faculties.

"Now," he said in a soft, even voice, "is that what you wish?" For a moment he was uncertain of the reply he would receive. Brother Joseph stood there, looking down at him as though actually trying to make up his fool mind. The Prophet felt exasperation rise in him once again, but bottled it, staring at the man with cold outward indifference.

"No, Lord."

"Fine. I intend to give you one more chance. I do this because I know that your wife is a devoted follower, and I will not turn away one who needs my sustenance and who knows her place in the scheme. But break no more covenants or decrees, Brother Joseph. I may decide to oust you and let your good wife remain." He let that sink in, watched the meaning dawn in the other man's eyes, before continuing. "Do you need to speculate on her decision were she required to choose between us?" His voice purred the threat. The Prophet found himself enjoying the discomfiture he was inflicting on a member of the Chambers tribe. They all had it coming. He just wished he could show the old fool his precious little Virginia, stumbling about the house ass-naked, half crazy from fear and exhaustion. That would put both of them in their places. "Now get back to your dwelling," he commanded peremptorily. "And neither touch nor speak to your wife again."

"Yes. All right. Yes, Lord." There was a grudging note in Brother Joseph's voice, as though he were unsure of his or the Prophet's status but must, for practical reasons, bow to him. He backed to the door and let himself out.

Well, the Prophet decided, until he had fucked little Virginia Chambers it would be to his benefit to take at least minimal steps to keep the old lady breathing. He reached across his desk and pressed the button that would summon Sister Penelope. He would give the order that the old Chambers woman was to be excused from manual labor for a while, to meditate and recover from her and her husband's unconscionable iniquity. That should keep the old buzzard happy and ignorant until his daughter learned to get screwed like a good girl.

CHAPTER 32

Brother Joseph got precious little sleep that night. He sat by his wife's bedside until past midnight, and then awoke at three o'clock to take up the vigil once again. The one room of the dwelling was redolent of unwashed flesh. The air itself seemed fetid, stagnant. He couldn't believe that Polly would recover in such an atmosphere; yet he knew that to speak of moving her would be futile, and to move her contrary to her will, even if he could manage it, might prove more harmful than keeping her here.

What had he done? To his wife and to his family. And how could he rectify it?

At four-thirty the supervisors came by, peeking into the dwellings to ascertain that everyone was stirring. Joseph was ready to fight any of them who insisted on waking his Polly, but no such attempt was made. Instead he was informed that the Prophet had decreed that she was to be excused from labor for an unspecified period of time. This permissiveness did not, however, extend to her husband.

Joseph thought about that as Brother Benjamin and Sister Candace rose and stumbled out of the hut to begin the day's labor. He didn't want to leave his wife alone. Yet if he refused to work there was no telling what that crazy man in the mansion would do. He agonized for long minutes over the dilemma before his wife stirred.

"Joseph?" She looked up at him for a moment, initiated a tremulous smile, and then seemed to remember where she was. Panicky, she looked about the dwelling, uninhabited except for the two of them, then at the door, through which streamed a ray of dusty light. "We should be—"

183

"I stayed behind to tell you," he cautioned her. "The Prophet has excused you from labor until he can heal you."

She stared up at him, apparently more frightened at being any kind of exception than of working while she was ill. "Oh, no, I mustn't—"

"Now, Polly, it's a holy decree. You have no choice, do you?"

She stared searchingly up at him. "You aren't making this up, are you? Just to keep me here? I know you mean well, Joseph, but that would be wicked and evil."

"No, Polly. It's true. I swear it."

"Oh. Well, all right, then." She lay back, working at relaxing. "What about yourself?"

"I'm going out right now. I just wanted you to know of the Prophet's decree, so you wouldn't fret."

"I'll try not to."

She closed her eyes, and he was almost certain that she was asleep. He leaned down to kiss her forehead, then pulled back. If he should wake her she would be scandalized at his having broken a decree of her damned Prophet.

At the very moment when Joseph Chambers was reluctantly leaving his prostrate wife's bedside, two boys armed with .22 rifles and provisioned with lunches packed by their mothers happened on a clump of something in the ditch in which they were stalking bullfrogs. Curiosity brought them closer, until the boy in the lead suddenly raised his Remington Nylon 66 in the air and fired three shots, without knowing exactly why he was doing it. He turned to his friend and gaped at him through wide, blank eyes.

"Well, what is it?" his friend demanded irritably. The first boy simply stood staring at him, uttering not a sound, until the second boy pushed by him impatiently. Then it was his turn to yield to shock. He didn't fire his rifle, but just stood staring for a moment, too stunned by the apparition before him to turn away, though he wished mightily that he could stop seeing it. He had never seen a naked woman before, and this was not a pleasant initiation into the mysteries of femininity.

The woman's skin was caked with mud and shriveled by the water in which it had lain. Something had got at her eyes, which were wide open. Whatever the something had been, it had eaten part of the eyes away, leaving jellylike masses sunken into the sockets. Finally the boy turned to one side, bent deeply at the waist, and vomited up his breakfast.

Peggy Boling Hartford had finally come to the end of the trek she had begun years earlier, when she had decided, albeit unconsciously, to allow Immanuel Hartford to blackmail her into being his girl. Candy Sterling, had she known of the outcome, would have been thrilled that wickedness had been so thoroughly scotched; and humbly proud that it had been she who had managed to frighten Peggy into giving up on her attempt to extort money from her estranged husband; and surreptitiously disappointed that she had not been allowed to take part in the finish. That had been left to Peggy Boling Hartford's creditors, masters at their trade, who had seen to it that her last service to humanity was to serve as an example to dilatory debtors.

It was astonishing to Virginia Chambers how clear everything had become. From the murkiness in which she had lived for the past weeks she had finally emerged into a blinding clarity. It was like an overexposed movie film. She had even lost the feeling of exhaustion from lack of sleep that had haunted her so. Things seemed to burn before her eyes, bright and hard-edged, like a particularly vivid dream.

She knew that they were all against her. All these girls who paraded themselves around in those little skirts and pretended to believe in the Prophet and his phony stories. They were just here to spy on her, and to see to it that she surrendered to the man and his disgusting desires. It was amazing how long it had taken her to figure that out. Even her own sister, who pretended to avoid her just like all the others, was obviously in on the whole matter, and must have been from the beginning. And that in turn meant that her parents were involved too. Oh, God, how they must have laughed through that whole ridiculous trek from South Dakota. How it must have amused them that she believed all those stories about a new life, and devoting themselves to God, or the All-Moving Spirit, or whatever they had called Him. She wondered if, when she wasn't around, they had joked and laughed about it all, ridiculed her behind her back for being such a patsy, and going along with things so readily. And they were right. But how could she have known they would go to such lengths just to give her, or probably sell her, to this evil little man?

But she had thwarted them. As she went about her daily chores she chuckled to herself to think of how disappointed they must be, and how surprised, that she hadn't fallen for it in the end. Just because she had found herself in a house full of whores, including her own sister, they had assumed she would become a whore herself. She wished she could see all their faces now that she had shown that she had no intention of playing their game out to the finish. It was priceless just to see Mary's expression—so guarded but so disappointed under all that makeup she wore. And, of course, best of all was that fake Prophet himself—so frustrated and outraged that there was a girl who didn't fall for his line even when he had so carefully prepared the scene for her. Well, he was never going to get her. She had decided that she would cheat him, cheat all of them, no matter what. If the time did come when she could no longer resist his advances, then she would kill herself rather than yield. Of course there was another possibility, and she had decided that that was more attractive, if she could manage it when it came right down to the wire.

She could kill him.

CHAPTER 33

The Prophet paid an unprecedented visit to the fields the next day. Workers paused momentarily to stare in awe, for most of them hadn't seen him in weeks or months. Some of the women reached up unconsciously to straighten their hair, or touch sun-scorched faces, in gestures of forgotten but not quite extinct femininity. Then, embarrassed, they bent their backs to their labors once again. The Prophet passed among them, smiling, glancing here and there in benign, vague acknowledgment.

The women were simply hopeless. There were the older ones, whom he wouldn't have touched with a pair of tongs, and the younger ones who hadn't met his standards in the first place, spindly little girls and chubby adolescents who wouldn't have been asked to dance at the prom. Then there were his castoffs, the beauties whom he had perhaps improvidently squandered here in the hot sun: dirty now, disheveled and coarsened by weeks or months of hard labor and exposure to the elements. It had been naive of him to think that he could find treasures here. These women, like the men, were worthless except to labor for him. Sighing, he turned toward his mansion, thinking of the air-conditioned interior, the chilled drinks, and the cool, silk-sheathed lovelies whose sole function in life was to serve him.

While he had been about getting all this for himself he had thought that the best part would be having things set up and functioning, with nothing for him to do personally except reap the benefits of others' labors. Now, ironically, he looked back on the days when he had been putting it all together with a kind of nostalgic fondness.

Hell, he thought, *must be an eternity of boredom.*

With this thought ringing in his cranium, the Prophet crossed the doorway of the hut in which that Sterling girl was quartered, and it crossed his mind that the Chambers couple also lived in there. The wife, what was her name? Polly? Yes, he was certain that was it. Polly. She was in there, he thought. He nearly walked on, but then it occurred to him that the woman might serve one more use before she had to be buried. She might just furnish him with a brief surcease from this terrible ennui.

The old bat was dying, and wouldn't last another week without medical care. It would be futile to waste money on her. No doctor would be able to make her useful again, and to bring a physician out here might give the other workers false ideas about their worth, and their rights.

He pulled his linen handkerchief out of his hip pocket and wiped away the perspiration that had already covered his face. He was turning to leave the dismal place when the woman stirred and opened watery, yellowing eyes, looking straight at him. He smiled at her, moved by a reasonless fear that she might suddenly blame him for her condition and begin to rail at him.

She sat up with astonishing energy, raised a hand as though to touch him across the several feet that separated them. She blinked twice, rapidly. "Lord, is it you?" she asked in a weak, incredulous voice as full of cracks as her skin.

"I have come to let you benefit from my presence," he told her. She stared at him adoringly, and the Prophet realized how silly had been his doubts. The worse he did to someone like her, the stronger would be his power over her. He had been a fool to doubt that principle, which he had formed intuitively about his followers, long since.

She raised her hand to him again. "Touch me, Lord. Please heal me, so that I may serve you again."

The thought of touching her made his flesh crawl. For an instant he was flustered, unsure of how to handle the situation and furious with himself for having come here in the first place. He fixed her with a stern gaze. "Do you think I must touch you to heal you?" he demanded.

She flinched, shrinking a little under his reprimand. The

Prophet warmed to his subject. This was the sort of thing he did best. This was how he gained and held the loyalty of these self-destructive twerps.

"Do you wonder, Sister Polly, that your condition worsens, when you lack so in faith? I could heal you in an instant, though I were across the world, but my faith is only for those who truly believe in me!"

She wavered, her frail body swaying a bit as she seemed to lose the strength that had come to her in such a burst at the discovery of his presence.

"When you truly believe in me, when your faith is genuine, you will be healed. You will rise and walk, and take your place among those who serve the Prophet. But until then you will languish here in your bed of pain and sickness!" His hand had risen before him, clutched in a fist about the handkerchief. He advanced upon her, suddenly remembering that it was this woman's daughter who had spurned him, her husband who had doubted him. "You will die!" he promised. "You will sicken and die, and your soul will writhe in eternal perdition unless you overcome your own doubt and the sins of those who are of your family, wicked woman!"

She collapsed, falling back on the bed and rolling her eyes downward to stare at him in panicky misery.

He was enjoying himself now, taking out on her the frustration visited upon him by her miserable little snip of a daughter. "I can already see you," he shouted, "churning and twisting in endless torment, repaid for the vileness of your unregenerate soul!" He had come within reach of her, and with surprising speed and strength she grasped at his hand. Her aim was poor, but her hand caught the handkerchief dangling from his grip. Impulsively, he pulled at it, trying to tug it free, but something deep in her hand generated incredible vigor, and she had a death grip on the fabric. He almost pulled her upright as he tugged on the handkerchief. Then he dropped it, let her fall back to the thinly matted bed with a distinct thump.

He stepped back, shaking a short, thick finger at her. "Mend your ways, whore of Babylon, or you perish, doomed and forgotten!" A single tear oozed from her dehydrated flesh as her eyes closed. Her head rolled to the side. The Prophet stood, recapturing his breath, beginning to feel a tinge of apprehension. Had his attack been too spirited? Had he killed her? He took a hesitant step toward the still figure, saw with relief that her flaccid, deflated breasts heaved feebly against the restriction of her filthy, tattered dress.

Emerging from the fetid interior of the dwelling, the Prophet smiled to himself. He had handled that quite well, he thought.

CHAPTER 34

The sight of the old lady had convinced the Prophet that he must act quickly if he was going to purify Virginia Chambers's blood. Once her mother was dead, her father's intransigence would erupt, and the fool would probably insist on abducting his daughters from the grace of the Spirit, and taking them with him into damnation.

He chuckled to himself, startled at his own thoughts. It was almost as though he had begun to believe his own line. But the major thing was not to let that stupid little girl escape with her virginity. It would be a rotten shame, a crime, an enormity, to let her get away with her perversity.

And time was short, if that old lady's appearance was any clue. So the day following his confrontation with Sister Polly the Prophet walked into a bathroom in his personal quarters while Virginia was cleaning it. She was hunched over the toilet, scrubbing it, her jiggly little fanny stuck in the air. She hadn't noticed his presence, and so he stood for a bit, admiring the view and growing miffed at her for keeping that little ass stingily to herself.

He had noticed a strangeness in her demeanor in the past weeks. It was as though her exhaustion and the constant pressure of anxiety to which he had deliberately subjected her had driven her to the edge of madness. Her eyes burned as though she could see some brilliant, raging flame that was invisible to others, and she seemed to look right through people. She responded to speech in a desultory, slightly retarded manner, as though the sound had to pass through some long channel to reach her brain. It was a bit scary if one allowed it to be, but the Prophet mad‍ use of it, as he was wont to make use of anything.

He had spread the word among the other girls that Virginia's wickedness and her refusal to yield to his grace had done this to her, that she was on the verge of eternal damnation, and the impairment of her soul showed through in her actions and appearance. Naturally the boobs bought it all. He had known they would, because it was true in a way. Through her foul pride she had brought it all on herself. And quite possibly, once he had fucked her she would relax and come out of it.

She was just finishing with the toilet, so the Prophet reached down and thrust his hand between her thighs, sliding it up to the crotch and getting a good feel. This time her response wasn't in the least delayed. Coming to her feet in an amazingly complex and swift movement, she spun, raking her nails across the Prophet's cheek. Her face was contorted, like something wild, and the Prophet was too taken by surprise to react before she drew back to lash out at him again. Some sort of animal wail, not nearly human, burst from her throat as her hands grasped for him. It all happened so fast that he was almost overcome by this little slip of a girl, who was showing not only astounding ferocity but astonishing strength as well. He pulled aside just in time to keep her grasp from closing on his throat, then backpedaled, opening up some distance between them. As she tried to close with him again, her face as ugly as before, that wild scream issuing from her lips again, he doubled his fist and thrust it against her breasts. The blow was considerable but it only made her wince and falter in her attack. As she made another grab for him the Prophet heard a gasp from the doorway. He had backed into the bedroom adjoining the bathroom Virginia had been cleaning. He glanced to the side for an instant, saw one of the other handmaidens, who had apparently been passing in the hallway. She held a cloth in one hand and a bucket of soapy water hung pendulously from the other. She was staring wide-eyed at her prophet under attack, something which obviously had never entered her mind.

"Grab her, you idiot," he gasped, trying with limited success to hold Virginia's forearms. She had begun to kick at him, and her tiny feet inflicted surprising amounts of pain through his pant legs. She still emitted that animal howl. The other girl dropped her rag and pail, which somehow landed upright, and plunged in with commendable courage. She locked her arms around the distraught girl's waist and tried to pull her back, but Virginia's strength was incredible, as though her state of mind had turned her into something superhuman. If the Prophet had hoped that this attack might divert his opponent's attention, he was disappointed. Virginia continued to lash out at him, as though aware of nothing else but his presence and the need to wound or destroy him.

Another girl entered, took one look and rushed forward to grab one of Virginia's arms, fighting vainly to hold it still. But she did manage to pull it away from the Prophet, allowing him to use both hands on the other arm. Then a third girl appeared, apparently drawn by the commotion. He noticed that she was Mary, Virginia's sister. She stood for a moment, drawn and pale at the sight of her sister, naked, thrashing like a maddened animal. Then she too plunged in. The three girls managed to pull Virginia away from him, but she continued to lash and struggle, the sounds coming from her now in hisses rather than wails.

"She's possessed!" the Prophet shouted. "The evil one has finally taken her for his own!" He felt his cheek gingerly, found that the scratches were superficial, hardly more than abrasions. His discomfiture turned to outrage, and he instantly formed a plan for turning this enormity to ultimate good. "There is only one hope for her," he stated, more calmly. "Take her to the bed." They stared at him, still struggling with the insane girl. "Now!" he roared. "There is no time to waste!" They dragged Virginia toward the bed. She wasn't too far gone to realize what was happening, to understand his intentions, and he smiled. She couldn't have played into his hands more neatly if she had intended it that way. Even her sister didn't question the Prophet's assessment of her condition.

"What—?" A feminine voice from the door prompted him to look in that direction. It was Sister Penelope. She was the biggest of his handmaidens, doubtless the strongest.

"Help them," the Prophet commanded, for the other three girls, having managed to haul the fighting girl to the bed, were encountering considerable difficulty in getting her onto it.

Sister Penelope, with characteristic efficiency, circled to the side of the bed opposite the others, leaned across, and grabbed at the shrieking girl. Virginia had been thrust partly across the bed by then, bent at the waist, her long blond hair hanging down to obscure her face. Sister Penelope grabbed a generous handful of hair and yanked hard, pulling Virginia off her feet. The girl fell to the bed, still full of fight. Her sister held her left arm while the other two girls held her right arm and legs respectively. Together with Sister Penelope they managed to shove her crosswise on the bed. Then, as she continued to thrash and fight, they worked her onto her back and turned her until she lay along the length of the bed. Sister Penelope still held her hair, but managed to grasp her right arm as well, thrusting her knee under it and locking it, the elbow thrust back against its own joint as Sister Penelope's weight held it in place. The girl opposite took her cue, doing the same thing with Virginia's left arm. The other two, including Mary, grasped her calves and pulled them outward until the girl's hips made cracking sounds. A surreptitious glance told the Prophet that Mary had moved into some sort of self-induced trance, apparently forgetting that this fevered creature was her sister. She performed this task the same way she cleaned his home and made his bed: stolidly, single-mindedly, without any sign of thought.

"Good," the Prophet purred. "Now hold her there." Virginia finally stopped struggling and lay staring at him with fear and loathing. He removed his coat and hung it neatly on the back of a chair, then pulled open the knot of his tie. She made loud grunting sounds, deep and guttural. "There is a demon in her," the Prophet explained. "She is helpless before it. You can hear it now, speaking in its own voice. There is only one way to drive it out, provided there is a shred of decency left in the girl." He sat down, having removed his shirt, and untied his shoes, then lined them neatly under the chair, stuffing his socks in them.

When he was nude, he advanced on the bed, moving slowly and with relish. This was the moment for which he had labored for weeks, and he intended to make it worth the effort and the wait. Stopping beside Mary, he laid a hand on her shoulder, slid it down the length of her body and up under her short dress.

"You do your sister a great service, my dear," he purred. "It may yet be possible to save her." The girl looked at him, her eyes uncertain for just a moment. Then she lowered her gaze and held onto her sister's calf all the tighter, leaning her full weight on it to make certain that it wouldn't work loose from her grasp. Suddenly Virginia began to fight again. That was good, the Prophet thought. It would make for a better fuck, and it would convince the nitwits who were holding her that she was really possessed. He sat on the edge of the bed, then stretched out on his side facing his victim. He brought his face a bit too close to hers and she snapped at him like a rabid animal. Her face was more contorted and ugly than ever, her makeup smeared all over it. It only made her the more attractive to him at that moment. Careful to stay clear of her teeth, he fondled her breasts for a moment, stimulating a fresh burst of resistance. Then he rolled onto her, snuggling his abdomen between her straining thighs.

CHAPTER 35

If it was impossible to estimate the time when Sister Polly began to die, it was very simple to determine the precise moment when she completed the process. It was on a Friday evening that her husband returned from his labors in the field and stood over his wife, looking down at the still, frail form. She was holding a handkerchief, clutching the white square of cloth to her breast as though she gathered some sort of solace from it. He had no idea of where it had come from, but he didn't think much about it.

Squatting on his haunches, he watched his wife closely, earnestly, for several moments. It was then that he grew disturbed, because she hadn't gone so long without stirring before. He leaned close to her, strained to hear her breathing. He couldn't be certain of whether he heard it; if so, it was alarmingly faint. Impulsively, he laid his hand on her forehead, found that it was even hotter than it had been before. He looked around, his eyes wide with panic, at the other two inhabitants of the shelter. Sister Candace was readying herself for her weekly shower and didn't seem to notice him. Brother Benjamin returned his gaze for a moment, then tiredly stretched out on his bed. Brother Joseph grasped his wife's wrist, shoving back the heavy sleeve of her dress, and felt for a pulse. It was there. He was certain of that. But it was slow and irregular. He had no watch with which to time it, but life on a remote farm had taught him the rudiments of health care, and his instincts told him that his wife was growing worse even as he stood over her.

Without thinking he swept up the woman in his arms, holding her close and drawing some comfort from the vague warmth of her body. Sister Candace was just going out the doorway. He brushed her aside, pushing her abruptly through. She gasped, turned, and looked at this apparition, a man carrying a woman in his arms, as though she had never seen or even imagined such indecency. But Brother Joseph was too intent on his wife's condition and his own intention to notice. Carrying Sister Polly toward the Prophet's quarters, he saw a car standing before the stately entrance. A man was nearby, raking leaves. Joseph walked around the car, opened the door, and set his wife in the right-hand front seat. Slamming the door, he walked around the front of the vehicle, determined to get behind the wheel.

"Hey, there!" The man's voice barely impinged on Joseph's consciousness. He was vaguely aware of a tone of surprise and mystification and of some dim satisfaction in himself, but he was intent on getting into the car and driving his wife off this unwholesome place. Then he felt a tug at his shoulder. Without even thinking, Joseph turned, driving his hard farmer's fist into the man's midsection, burying it almost to his thick, hard forearm. The man fell back a pace, his eyes bulging, his face puffing out piglike, and then moved forward once more. He was only stumbling, trying to regain his balance and reaching for Joseph's shoulders to support himself. But Brother Joseph interpreted the movement as a counterattack, possibly because he wanted to think so. Grasping him by the shoulders, Joseph grunted slightly, picking up the lighter man, lifting him until even his toes were clear of the ground, and threw him to the side as hard as he was able. The body struck the fender of the car, making a resounding thump, and slid to the ground. Joseph became aware of someone else nearby, to his left, and turned. He wasn't even aware of the frightening, joyously angry expression in his eyes. But he saw the man fall back after taking one look at him. Joseph turned this way and that, ascertaining that no one else was daring to question his actions. The few people who had approached, drawn by this unusual burst of open hostility, now fell back, repelled by Joseph's all-too-apparent eagerness to join battle. Finally he opened the car door and entered it. The keys were in the ignition, as he had known they would be.

It was a new car and an expensive one, and its engine

whirred into life instantly. The people were approaching once again, apparently fascinated by this demonstration of brazenness. Once again they leaped back as the car screeched into motion, showering those to the rear with gravel and dirt. The man, lying close to it, jerked back so quickly he almost threw his sacroiliac out of joint.

The country roads were almost unfamiliar to Joseph. It took him the better part of a fretful hour to find the way to town, and another twenty minutes to find the little hospital that served it. EMERGENCY ENTRANCE it said over the gate, and he took the turn at forty miles per hour.

The air-conditioned interior felt almost chilly after the baking heat outside. A middle-aged nurse in a green uniform summoned orderlies and took the necessary information from Joseph. Then Joseph sat on a bench and waited, impatient, agitated but queerly unaware of the passage of time. A half hour later a doctor approached him. The doctor was middle-aged, small in stature, with a tough look about him, as though he had seen too much and had had to develop a harsh resiliency to survive. Joseph rose to face him diffidently.

"Mr. Chambers, how long has your wife been in this condition?" the doctor asked in an almost accusatory tone.

Joseph fidgeted. "Some weeks," he replied.

The doctor looked at him with a lethal expression. "Why have you waited this long to seek medical aid?"

"Doctor, it's complicated," Joseph said. "I'll tell you about it if you want, but first tell me if my wife—how she—"

"She's dying," the doctor said bluntly. "I can't even tell you for certain what's killing her, either. Looks as though it started off as a minor respiratory ailment, complicated by exposure, exhaustion, and malnutrition. Right now she's got the worst case of pneumonia I've ever seen."

Brother Joseph stood staring over the little doctor's head, barely aware of any of his words after "she's dying." "But —there must be some—"

"Don't worry, we're doing everything that can be done, just as though we thought she could be pulled through." As though he had suddenly grown aware of his words' effect on Joseph, the doctor softened his voice. "Of course, I've been wrong before." Then, as if the injection of false hope into his speech had been too much of an effort, his voice returned to its former brusque impatience. "But it'll surprise the hell out of me."

An hour later a nurse came down the same hall, approaching Joseph with a resolutely blank expression that told him all before she began to speak. They filled out the death certificate, asked him about burial preferences. Joseph told them that the family had no money and no property, and they said that the matter would be resolved. He had the feeling that they suspected he was one of those queer ducks from the farm outside town.

Later he drove about the small town, reflexively dodging other vehicles and responding to traffic signals. When another motorist blinked headlights at him, Joseph was dragged into awareness of the passage of time. Absently, he found the switch and turned on his own lights, noticing that he still had half a tank of gasoline.

Finally he turned the car back toward the farm. His good sense of direction helped him to thread his way back, and by full darkness he pulled back onto the outskirts of the farm, turning down the dirt road that led to the center, easing along because there was no real hurry, ignoring the mechanical rumbling of his stomach, relishing what was to come. The needles of his headlights finally fell upon the Prophet's quarters and the row of shacks in which his suckers slept.

Suckers. Suckers. Joseph ran the word over and over in his mouth, savoring its sour flavor. He had been a sucker. Polly had been one, too. It had killed her, and God only knew what it had cost their children. He supposed he had gotten off easiest, losing a farm he now realized he had always hated, and a wife he had worshiped. But it wasn't going to cost any of the Chamberses any more than it already had.

Pulling up in front of the Prophet's quarters, Joseph switched off the engine and sat for a moment. He had never seen the place looking dark and deserted before. During the night hours he had always been asleep, recovering from his day of grueling labor and preparing for the next. He sat there for a few moments, just relishing the right to do as he pleased. Then he emerged from the car and moved toward the shacks. It took him ten minutes to find the right one. The interior was almost exactly like the one in which he had sat and watched his wife being murdered. He stumbled among the four people, feeling his way along the uneven dirt floor until he found his son, lying asleep on the cot farthest from the door. The boy's "wife" slept on the one to Joseph's right, her head toward his, as was the rule. It kept husband and wife from seeing one another while they lay in their beds, and thus discouraged iniquitous temptations. Joseph stood over his son for the better part of a minute. The boy looked so exhausted that he hesitated to disturb him, and for a moment actually thought of leaving him unawakened for the time being. But that made no sense, so finally Joseph reached down, clamping a hand over the boy's mouth. Henry jumped, his whole body twisting in surprise. It was as though even in his sleep he were on edge. Joseph leaned down, maintaining his grip on his son's mouth until he knew he had been recognized. Then he motioned to the boy to follow him outside. As they were moving toward the door one of the other occupants, a man in his forties, sat up, staring at Joseph with blank, awkward terror.

"Prophet's business, Brother," Joseph said in a soothing tone. His words woke the others. Henry's wife, a woman in her middle thirties, skinny and rawboned, sat up and stared for a moment and then lay back down. By the time Joseph reached the door she was as still as a corpse.

Joseph led Henry fifty feet from the shack in the direction of the big house. Then he stopped and faced his son in the moonlight. "Son, I've never asked you," he said in a soft voice. He could see Henry straining to hear, and raised his voice level. "I've never asked you," he repeated. "Do you believe in this Prophet?" He had kept his tone neutral without thinking of it, and his son shrugged, apparently not certain of what was expected of him. "I've just returned from the hospital in town," he said, laying a hand on the boy's shoulder. "Your mother has died." He felt a tremor move down the slender body. Joseph tightened his grasp. This was hard for a thirteen-year-old, but it had to be done. "She was murdered by this man. Oh, not legally. The law will do nothing about it, and we may as well understand that. But morally he killed her with his arrogance." Joseph took a deep breath. "And I killed her with my weakness. Now I'm leaving this place, and I want you to come with me." There was no verbal reply. After a moment the boy's head bobbed. Joseph thought he heard a sob from deep in his son's bowels, but he didn't acknowledge it. The two of them turned toward the Prophet's quarters.

Joseph left his son in the car, leaving the keys in the ignition and instructing the boy to leave and save himself should there be any trouble. He didn't really expect any, but it was always possible when one was dealing with fanatics and a madman.

CHAPTER 36

There were still lights on in the house, a few scattered ones on the ground floor and one on the top story. Joseph strode up the massive stoop and tried the door. As he had hoped and expected, it was unlocked. There was no need to lock it, since people on this farm were too well disciplined to enter the Prophet's holy ground without an invitation. They probably thought that doing so would result in death by lightning.

Joseph was halfway down the hall when he and the girl saw one another. She was no more than a child, perhaps fourteen or fifteen, with breasts still developing, and the smooth, glowing complexion of a little girl. Her bright round eyes seemed to look right through him for a moment, as though it were simply incomprehensible that he could be there. She had been dusting furniture, which seemed an odd occupation at this time of night, and was dressed in one of those little red dresses, revealing legs surprisingly mature in comparison with the rest of her. She stood there for a moment, slightly bent at the waist, her dust cloth, which appeared to be the remains of an old pair of man's briefs, poised over an end table. Then she straightened and walked toward him, her high-heeled shoes silent on the thick carpet. "Sir," she whispered, and then amended her mode of address. "Brother, you can't—"

"I've come to fetch my daughters," he told her. "Where are they?"

She only stood looking at him, those brown Bambi eyes looking shocked and confused. "Brother, you can't—" she began again.

Joseph moved down the hall, opening doors as he went. He heard her come after him, felt a tiny hand grasp his sleeve for a moment, then let go, apparently as she remembered the injunction against men and women touching one another. Old-fashioned good manners prompted him to turn around.

"You have to leave!" she said, her tiny immature voice rising almost to a squeak.

With a sigh of reluctance Joseph reached out and took the girl's thick brown hair in one hamlike fist, pulling her closer. He was firm, not rough, but she almost screamed, stopped by paralyzing fear. Her eyes grew even larger, which he had not thought possible. Conflicting emotions raged in Joseph. She was so frightened that he wanted to let go, to assure her that he meant no harm. She was so cute that he felt a chuckle in his throat, despite all that had happened. She was so foolish to be here in this place, dressed in those inappropriate clothes, that he wanted to shake her and then take her in his arms. And there was something else, something he didn't want to acknowledge in himself: It had been a very long time since he had touched an attractive female.

"I mean you no harm," Joseph said in a soft, steady voice. "But I want my daughters. Where are they?"

She seemed to reach deep within herself for the courage to perform her duty. "I—don't know."

"Where are they?" he demanded, a touch more loudly, tightening his grip on her hair. "Just tell me. I don't want to hurt you." Her eyes darted toward something behind him. Joseph turned his head and saw a staircase that went down into the basement. He hadn't even been aware that the house possessed a basement. Releasing the girl's hair, he stroked it twice in a gentle apology, then turned and moved down the stairs. He saw her move to the head of them and stare down at him, distraught, tearful, confused.

It was black at the botton. He felt his way down the last few steps, then groped for a light switch. It took him what seemed an hour to find one. Then he hesitated a moment, not certain he wanted to see what the light would reveal to him.

He had been wise to doubt. The place was a huge dormitory, the floor uncarpeted concrete. At the far end was what looked like a communal shower, with a shoulder-high wall separating it from the main portion of the room. Between the place where he stood and the shower room were a dozen cots. Two of them were empty. The other ten were occupied by young women, most of them just girls in their teens. They slept nude, as he could tell by the few whose covers had slipped below their breasts.

A vestige of gentlemanliness almost caused him to kill the lights he had just turned on. One of the girls, sleeping in a cot near the door, was his older daughter, Mary. Her light-colored hair spilled across the white pillow case and hung down over the edge of the cot. Her long, white arm lay gracefully across her body, which, mercifully, was covered by a sheet and a blanket. Joseph looked about him, studying the faces of the other women, but Virginia wasn't among them. He didn't allow himself to think about what that could mean, but moved to his daughter's bedside and clamped his hand over her mouth as he had done with Henry. Her reaction was even more pronounced. Her slim, tiny body seemed almost to erupt from the cot, her hand grasping at his with frantic strength. The covers slipped down, revealing fragile pink-and-white breasts. Her eyes finally focused on him, and she relaxed a bit. The other girls were beginning to stir and sit up.

"Get dressed," Joseph said. "We're leaving." She stared at him. His hand left her mouth, but she said nothing, pulling up the covers to her chin. She looked confused and torn rather than defiant. "Get dressed!" he repeated more strongly. He heard a chorus of gasps from the other girls. They were pulling their blankets up exactly as Mary had done. Mary opened her mouth timidly but found no voice. "No one is going to hurt you," Joseph assured her. "I'm taking you out of here."

"Daddy, I—I can't go—"

Joseph grasped the covers and tore them from her, then pulled her out of the cot by her arm. "Put on some clothes!" he roared. "Do as I say!" His free hand cocked slightly, without his volition or awareness. His daughter covered her nakedness with her arms as best she could. He reached out and stroked her hair gently. "Get dressed now," he said in a softer tone. Her gaze dropped, but she nodded. Joseph released her and turned away, allowing her some modesty. He turned just in time to see one of the girls, the one from the cot nearest the door, run up the stairs.

In a moment he was aware of his daughter at his side. He

turned to see her dressed in one of those scanty dresses and a pair of black patent pumps with four-inch heels.

"Don't you have anything else to wear?" he demanded. She shook her head, looking away from him. "All right," he said, modifying his tone. She seemed so fragile, and he didn't want to frighten her. He also didn't want to know, just yet, what had brought her to this state. "Where is your sister?" She didn't reply, but fidgeted, playing with the hem of her red dress. Joseph slapped at her hand, knocking it away from the offensive garment. Then he heard footsteps on the stairs and turned quickly, as reflexive as a boxer at the sound of the bell.

The girl who had run out a few minutes earlier stood there, beside the Prophet. He was wearing a silk robe and pajamas, and expensive-looking slippers. His hair was disheveled, his face shadowed by a day's growth of beard, but he didn't look like a man who had been awakened from sleep. He froze when he saw Joseph, stared at him sternly, and yanked at the ends of his robe sash, tautening them as though preparing for battle.

The girl was naked, but she wasted no time in opening the locker at the head of her cot and pulling out a dress. Hers was blue, and Joseph remembered that she was the one who had led him and his family into the presence of the Prophet for the first time. Sister Penelope, if he recalled.

The Prophet advanced on Joseph, walking with resolute majesty. "Is there no end to your sinfulness?" he demanded. "Are you *determined* to lead yourself and your family into everlasting—"

He stalked to within eighteen inches of Joseph as he spoke, which was all the latter had been waiting for. He drove a heavy fist into the little man's face, drove it forward with all his power, instinctively putting his shoulder behind the blow, as he had learned in the little bit of boxing he had had during high school. The blow knocked the Prophet three full steps back, prompting comical little dance steps on his part. But the dance was futile: His feet tangled and he went sprawling across the concrete floor. The silk robe fell open and the middle button on his pajama top popped off to reveal a soft, rounded, and hairy belly. One of the girls giggled with intolerable nervousness. Joseph saw Mary move forward reflexively, as if to lend aid to the fallen man. Then, catching herself, she stood looking down at her hands, which she had raised in front of her in a reaching motion that had also seemed supplicatory.

Joseph crossed the distance between them in one giant stride, bent down, and hauled the Prophet to his feet, grunting slightly with the effort of lifting the limp, dazed little man. He grasped the silk robe, wrinkling it, and tearing a few threads, and then cocked his fist and threw another punch. It landed almost exactly where the first one had hit. He felt a satisfying crunch of cartilage, saw a brilliant claret spurt, felt the warmth of blood drops on his fist. He had planned to hit the man a third time, but lost his grip on the robe. The Prophet slipped from his grasp, fell to the floor again, and immediately began to scoot backward, pushing himself with his slippered feet and his hands, sliding along on his buttocks.

Joseph grew aware of the sounds around him. The girls were squealing, drawing back in their beds. The legs of some of the cots scraped along the floor as they were almost upset by the violent recoil of their occupants. Sister Penelope rushed at Joseph, her hands curled into vicious-looking claws, a hideous animal sound bursting from her throat. Joseph had anticipated such an eventuality, and although it went against all his upbringing, the chivalry he had been taught as a boy, and which he had observed throughout his manhood, he brought his hand around in a vicious swipe. It was a fist until, at the very last moment, he thought to open it and slap the young woman across the face.

It was an authoritative blow nonetheless, twisting her head around, knocking her off balance so that she barely kept from falling. The girls screamed again, including Mary. The Prophet wiped his face on his silken sleeve and looked astonished, as though he had doubted that he could bleed like a mortal man. He looked up at Joseph, his face a mixture of reproach and dawning terror. Then, as Joseph moved toward him, the Prophet twisted his body about, tangling his robe for a panicky moment, and scurried to his feet. The soles of his slippers were slick, and he had to scrabble with them, scraping them along the floor several times like the creatures in animated cartoons, before he gained sufficient traction to reach his upright stance.

Then he ran, just as fast as he could, without looking back

once. In a moment he had left the room, tottering on his slippery soles, and Joseph could hear him thundering up the stairs, stumbling several times.

Sister Penelope, seeing her Prophet retreat so ignominiously, apparently decided that prudence was in order. She drew back to the vicinity of her cot, staring at Joseph with the wariness and unmitigated hatred one might expect from a person who had seen the devil incarnate. Joseph walked to where his daughter was standing and took her arm. He held it gently but with a firm grip.

She looked at him blankly for a moment, and then broke into a wide but odd-looking smile. "Did you see him?" she asked softly. "Did you *see* the way he tried to get up?" Joseph opened his mouth to answer but his daughter suddenly broke into peals of laughter. He felt a brief encouragement, then heard the intense, off-key ring to the laughter. Mary shook with it, laughing until her teeth chattered. As though she couldn't hold it in, or content herself with laughing, she caught up her brief skirt like a little girl and tossed the hem in front of her, exposing herself for an instant. "Did you see?" she repeated, clenching her tear-drenched eyes and pulling her mouth into an ugly sliver. Drool escaped from the corners of it and ran down her chin to fall in drops on the front of her dress. "Oh, God, Papa, did you *see* him?"

Joseph reached out and grabbed the girl's shoulders. Still she persisted in her hysterics until he moved one hand to her throat, grasping it and pulling her forward slightly. He was prepared to shake her into awareness, but suddenly her eyes focused and the laughter stopped as suddenly as though a switch in her bosom had been snapped off. He drew her close and slipped his arm around her slender shoulders. She began to cry softly, but at least it was normal crying. Joseph led her out of the dormitory and up the stairs.

The Prophet was out of sight when they gained the ground floor. Probably cowering in some room on the top floor, Joseph decided. He stopped in the hallway. Even the little girl whom he had scared so badly on the way in had vanished. He hoped she had run clear off the farm, never to return.

"Your sister," he said softly to Mary. His daughter hesitated for just an instant, then indicated the stairs leading to the

second story. When they had climbed the stairs, Mary led him
to the third door from the landing. Joseph tried the knob and
found it locked. There was no one else within sight, and he had
no intention of wasting time hunting for someone with a key. It
was a sturdy door, solid oak from the look and feel of it, but
Joseph didn't hesitate. He stepped back, raising one heavily
shod foot and driving it forward at a spot directly next to the
lock. He felt something give with that first kick, lowered his
foot to regain balance, then cocked it again and slammed it into
the same spot. This time wood splintered and the door moved
visibly. He probably could have forced it open with his hands
after that, but he had heard something inside, a dull sound,
muffled by the thick door, but definitely the scream of a young
girl. Raising his foot again, he drove it harder than before,
which was unnecessary because the tortured wood capitulated
easily, splitting and flying away in fractured shards. He was
vaguely aware of Mary standing next to him, her hands
covering her face, her eyes peeping between her fingers.

Joseph walked into the room. As he had imagined, it was a
bedroom, darkened, the form of a huge bed indistinct at the
opposite end. He could barely see the shape of a girl on the
bed. She sat up, staring toward him, and even in the gloom he
could see the rigidity of terror in her body.

"Virginia, it's me," he said soothingly. "It's your father,
Virginia." He walked toward the bed. The girl didn't seem to
hear him, or to understand his words. For a moment he
wondered whether it was his daughter after all. She didn't
seem to understand English. "It's all right, honey," he said in
the same soothing tone he had once used to quiet a skittish farm
animal.

When he sat on the edge of the bed she drew back violently
against the headboard. Her body struck it so hard the entire bed
rocked under the impact. Joseph put his hands on her bare
shoulders and pulled her forward. He had expected another fit
of resistance, but instead the girl's body went rigid, her back
arching like that of an outraged child being picked up against
her will. When he moved her toward him a splash of light fell
across her face, revealing a countenance taut and smooth with
terror. Every muscle in it seemed flexed to the straining point.
Her eyes were wide and fearful but carefully blank, as though

she were afraid to acknowledge even through her expression the fears and expectations that plagued her.

Joseph looked around at his other daughter. She stood in the doorway, the light behind her, an insubstantial wraith casting a long shadow across the bedroom's thick pile carpet. "What's happened to her?" His voice was a low rumbling croak, fearsome even to him.

Mary only stood for a moment, playing with the hem of her short dress again. Then, as though remembering his previous reaction to that gesture, she dropped her hands to her sides. "I —I—" Suddenly she turned away from him, ran into the hall to lean over the railing.

For a moment Joseph thought she was retching, but then he realized that she was only moving as far as she could from the source of her anguish. He couldn't believe that Mary had concurred in her sister's torment, but he had seen enough of this strange man's power over people, and especially over women, to allow for anything. Picking up his younger daughter in his arms, sliding his hands under the blanket, he found that she was nude. At the touch of his hands on her body she seemed to stiffen even more strenuously than before.

"It's all right, daughter," Joseph purred in her ear. "It's all going to be fine."

Wrapping her in the sheet and blanket, he lifted her from the bed. It was a giant bed, and the bedclothes wound around her several times. She lay rigid in his arms, still apparently not trusting him completely. But her own arms finally circled his neck, and her head lay against his shoulder. The feel of it there, so light, filled him with a surge of tenderness. It was as though she had become a baby once again: his baby. All the while he carried her down the stairs and out to the car, his other daughter following close behind, Joseph Chambers muttered an oath of vengeance against the man, the miserable excuse for a man, who had destroyed his family.

CHAPTER 37

The Prophet cowered in his private quarters for twelve hours, and then sulked there for an additional two days, refusing the solace of his handmaidens and even the food that Sister Penelope tried to thrust upon him. Since he refused to open his door to anyone, the food was left on trays outside his door and ultimately retrieved, cold, to be reheated and shared among the girls.

It was beyond his powers to absorb the fact that one of his minions, one of his suckers, would defy him, even raise a hand against him. The shock of it had numbed his powers to react for several seconds, and then all he had been able to think of was getting away from the lunatic who had dared to do such a thing. Later he had become aware of the humiliation attendant on such an occurrence. Although Sister Penelope showed up every four hours to knock at his door and implore him to take some sustenance, he was certain that the event of that night had precipitated some sort of mass exodus, with the girls who had seen it rushing out to tell others of the manner in which the Prophet had been demeaned, and the manner in which he had cowered under a physical attack. He wouldn't be surprised if by this time he had lost at least half his followers.

A glance out the window told him that they were still there, slaving away for his betterment, but that did nothing to ease his misgivings. He couldn't believe that his position could remain firm after what had happened. When his people discovered that it was possible for someone to mistreat the Prophet of the All-Moving Spirit with impunity, they would certainly begin to drift away. His work would be ruined as the people deserted him to return to their wicked and sinful ways.

He was well into his second day before it occurred to him what would have to be done. He supposed that Chambers had taken his son and daughters with him and left the farm. But he imagined that they were still in the area, and would be easy enough to find. If he could bring home to his people the cost that accrued to such behavior, then perhaps this unfortunate incident could be nullified, even turned to the service of ultimate good.

He remembered that girl, Candy Sterling. From all that he had gathered, she had performed admirably when he had sent her and her husband out to take care of that wicked little slut who had presumed to threaten him. Perhaps Candy Sterling could be trusted to perform an even sterner task. And her husband, who was obviously not a real believer but only here for his own obscure purposes, might be convinced to take part in the matter too.

It was almost noon, two and a half days after Joseph Chambers's act of insolence, when the Prophet emerged from his quarters, masking his timidity with an outward show of lordly nonchalance. He wore one of his most stylish suits, fashioned for him by a tailor brought in from San Francisco explicitly for the purpose. As he passed the girls scurrying about the rooms and halls of the huge house he sensed their relief at the sight of him, and by the time he had reached the door of his study something akin to his accustomed confidence had been restored. Minutes later a knock sounded at the door and Sister Penelope entered, bearing a huge tray on which she had brought him a breakfast of hotcakes, steak, eggs, and strong coffee. Although the Prophet hadn't thought about food before that, the sight of it made him aware that his appetite was immense. He had another appetite, too, which he slaked with Sister Penelope before sending her off to summon Brother Benjamin into his holy presence.

The Prophet had never doubted that there were those, probably amounting to the vast majority of the populace, who were simply not susceptible to his technique or charisma. It didn't really matter, because there were enough people subject to it that he had been able to swell the ranks of his followers to a workable extent. Others had drifted into the place from time to time, attracted by curiosity or propelled by the normal anxieties of life. They hadn't lasted long, but he had managed to get some work out of them before they had returned to their old sinful ways.

Brother Benjamin was an anomaly. The Prophet had never deluded himself that this man was a believer. There was a laconic humor about him, as though he could see something funny in all of this, but was withholding his laughter in order to be allowed to remain and see the show. Just what continued to attract him the Prophet couldn't imagine at first, though of late he had begun to entertain a theory on the matter.

This afternoon Brother Benjamin put in a prompt appearance in the Prophet's study, standing humbly before his desk, his twinkling eyes belying his stance, as though he were emulating the rubes who believed in this stuff because it amused him to do so.

The Prophet decided that it was time to be honest with this creature, at least to a point. Soon he would have no further need of him. "Brother Benjamin," he intoned after clearing his throat portentously, "I know why you have stayed here as long as you have." Brother Benjamin looked at him with idle curiosity. "It is quite clear that you do not believe in my movement. Please don't deny it."

"I ain't gonna deny it," Brother Benjamin assured him, relaxing noticeably.

"Good. That will save a good deal of time. I believe I know why you have remained here all this time."

"Well, I never figured you were dumb," Brother Benjamin said with a broad and ragged smile. "Say, you think you could spare one of those for me?" he asked as the Prophet reached into his humidor.

The Prophet retrieved a cigar for himself, left the humidor open. "Help yourself," he said with a shrug, clipping off the end of his cigar and handing the cutter to his guest. It was almost refreshing to talk to someone as an equal for the first time in so many months. It was relaxing not to have to be God for once.

Brother Benjamin selected a cigar, removed the wrapper, and cut it deftly, then accepted a light from the Prophet's desk lighter. "Now," he said, grinning again and lowering himself into a chair across the desk from his host. "Now, why have I stayed here all this time?"

"Because of Sister Candace, if I am not mistaken," the Prophet ventured.

"Now how could you be mistaken?"

The Prophet returned the man's grin and sat back in his swivel chair, looking at the juncture of wall and ceiling across the length of the room.

"You think I got the hots for my wife?" Brother Benjamin asked, and now there was something underlying his grin, something frustrated and resentful, which he managed to keep almost concealed.

"I could see to it that your marriage to Sister Candace was of more than symbolic significance," the Prophet reminded him gently, and thought he saw, on the lower edge of his vision, a quickening of interest in the man. The Prophet leaned forward, fixing Benjamin with a direct gaze that seemed to have no effect at all, but which at least gave the Prophet the benefit of a clearer look at the man with whom he was negotiating.

But Benjamin resumed his ribald, defensive grin. "You're not suggestin' that we do somethin' sinful, are you?"

"You forget that if I suggest it, it cannot possibly *be* sinful," the Prophet said softly. "To my people the only sin is disobedience to me."

"Yeah, that's a good racket, all right," Benjamin said, puffing on his cigar without looking at the Prophet. The Prophet was fairly certain he had the man then, because he was just too intently casual. He was awfully good at the act, but the Prophet hadn't got to his present position without refining his already excellent capacity for judging people, and reading their responses. "If I told her to, she would be your slave," the Prophet said.

Benjamin looked at him angrily. "No, she'd still be *your* slave, pretendin' to be mine."

"I fail to see the practical difference."

That stopped him. His type would never admit to such a mawkish sentiment as love, or to an emotional or symbolic need. If the Prophet was offering him access to the contents of Candy Sterling's panties, how could he acknowledge dissatisfaction? " 'Ceptin' you could pull her back anytime you wanted," Benjamin reminded him, having apparently found an acceptable objection.

The Prophet smiled benignly. "So long as you continue to want her, why would you give me reason to do that?"

Benjamin looked at him charily, as though uncertain of the proper reply but unsatisfied with the Prophet's question and its implied meaning. He dragged on the cigar and wreathed himself in smoke before replying. "Look, Your Divine Lordship, sir," he said with mock earnestness. "I feel like a man who's been took to a ritzy restaurant an' offered the seven-course meal. I know the check is gonna be a whopper, an' I figure I'm prob'ly gonna be pickin' it up."

The Prophet stretched across the desk to retrieve his lighter and took his time relighting his cigar. He decided that this man was poor material for a snow job, and so he spoke plainly. "The tab is pretty high. If you don't want to pick it up, then just promise me you'll keep your mouth shut and I'll find someone else to take care of things. The reason I'm giving you first crack at the assignment is that this is one instance when I believe that it would be beneficial to have someone around who is not a—true believer."

"You want someone cool. That it, man?"

The Prophet nodded.

"Sounds like somethin' heavy," Benjamin mused. "I don't know if I want to know about it."

"There is another reason why you might want to take part in it," the Prophet informed him. Benjamin raised his eyebrows inquisitively. "Sister Candace will perform this task for me," the Prophet said. "She will because I plan to tell her to do so." The Prophet could see from Benjamin's sudden quietness that he had the man in his pocket. He took a puff of his cigar and emitted his next words with a stream of blue smoke. "If she goes alone, or accompanied by someone else as fervid as she, there is no telling how things will turn out. But with some help from a practical gentleman like you, her chances of survival should be considerably greater. Don't you think?"

Benjamin's expression revealed that he, too, knew that he had been bested.

CHAPTER 38

So this was the big one, Benjamin thought as he drove the big car into town. And did he really want to do this? he asked. Beside him, pressed against the far door of the car, sat Candy, a form in the darkness except when someone's lights flashed across her face. Then he could see her eyes gleaming with the feverish excitement that he had seen the night they had run their previous errand for the Prophet. It gave him the willies. He had done a lot of crazy things in his time, and had consorted with people even nuttier, but for some reason the manner and feeling he detected in his lady love made him twitch inside.

What did she have, anyway? Why did he want her so much, and why did he care about what happened to her? It was the greatest paradox of all that he, who had considered himself too smart to get involved in anything this serious, should be driving this car out of concern and desire for a girl whom he had tried to rip off just weeks earlier. And perhaps the paradox was heightened by the fact that he had been drawn to her in the first place, and probably still was, by the very trait that scared him: her purity, her fanatical dedication to a cause.

He glanced at her as they entered the town, the streetlights illuminating her face, and saw that she was staring at something far beyond his range of vision. There was a smile on her lips, a look of subtle excitement. She moved, and he saw the light gleam on the worn surface of that damned gun. He had lived with her since that first night and had never known that she had kept the pistol. It was the kind of thing he would never have done even during his doper days. Hock the damned thing maybe, but not keep it. From the corner of his eye he saw her

217

stroke the barrel and receiver of the little automatic. The sight revived his nervousness and made him aware of a dim revulsion that had nagged at the corners of his consciousness since she had received her orders from the Prophet. There was something masturbatory about the way she stroked that pistol, an effect intensified by the way she laid it in her lap.

"Will you put that damned thing away?" he demanded. "What if some cop should stop us?"

She chuckled behind closed lips. "That would be his misfortune," she said, but she put away the gun, depositing it between the seat and the door.

Can't wait, he thought. She just can't wait to do the Prophet's bidding. On only the one other occasion had Benjamin seen her so excited. It was sexual, as though something she had been required to suppress for a long time were worming its way out by this devious and malignant route.

Finding out where the Chambers family lived wasn't very hard, though it necessitated some procedures Benjamin would have preferred to avoid. He stopped at a coffee shop, and then another, drinking coffee at the counter while Candy sat in the car, and struck up conversations with waitresses. He would casually mention the people who had come out of that strange farm. The Chamberses were a topic of conversation in that town, as would have been anyone or anything the least bit unusual. Benjamin tried to be inconspicuous, but he had the feeling that he might be remembered later. At least it could be recalled that someone had been in talking about the Chambers family, and that he had been tall and black. Benjamin's only hope was that the topic was discussed so much that this occasion wouldn't be recalled. One reason he had left Candy in the car was that the sight of a black man with a white chick would warrant notice in this hick burg.

The third coffee shop zeroed them in.

"Oh, yeah, that bunch," the waitress, a thin blonde with a goiter, said. "Sure I heard about 'em. You know the old man got a job near here? And they moved into an apartment down the street somewhere."

"You're puttin' me on," Benjamin said, sipping at his black coffee. That was something he was getting out of this deal anyway. He hadn't tasted coffee since joining the movement.

And at the Prophet's expense. He had given each of them a few dollars to enable them to carry out this night's work.

"No, really. It's down that way somewhere." She waved vaguely, giving him a convenient indication of the direction. "I heard some rumors that he's really upset about what happened to his old lady, and he blames the people out at that funny farm for all of it."

"What kind of crops they grow around here?" Benjamin asked, changing the subject to show a lack of interest in Chambers.

Candy sat in the car, appearing unaware of the passage of time. "Okay, I got a lead," Benjamin told her. She didn't reply, but he detected a fresh tension in her. Her right hand slid down between the car seat and the door to find and pet the gun.

The place was about what he had expected. An old, run-down cluster of frame buildings with weathered doors and sliding, pop-out windows. It was ideal for burglars. Benjamin was certain it was the right complex. He parked down the street and walked toward the apartments, stopping to look casually about before entering the grounds. He found the Chambers name on a label glued conveniently to a mailbox.

He returned to the car, feeling a sick nervousness in his stomach. He couldn't really believe he was going through with this. For what? This crazy woman next to him? He had never known himself before this night. It hadn't occurred to him that someone dwelt in his body who could do such a thing. He had killed once before, but that had been a spontaneous act of self-defense, and there had been no way it could be traced to him. He had nothing to gain by killing the Chamberses except to keep Candy from going off the deep end and to get into her pants, and he couldn't imagine why those things meant so much to him. She sat there as he started the car and pulled away from the curb, her eyes glistening with animal intensity. Her excitement gave Benjamin a sinking feeling, and he wasn't certain why.

He drove around the block one time, then pulled onto the apartment grounds with his lights off and killed the engine. When he turned to Candy she already had the gun in sight and was loading the magazine adeptly in the poor light.

"We can't shoot them here," he reminded her peevishly.

She nodded without looking at him, intent on counting out the nine shots the magazine would hold. "I know it. Unless we have to." She shoved a tenth cartridge up the spout and dropped the slide on it, then carefully set the safety and slid the magazine into the butt, making certain that it clicked into place. Then she looked up at him expectantly, as though surprised that he was still there.

Benjamin shrugged and opened the door on his side. He met her as he came around the back of the car. Together they approached the ground-floor apartment in which their quarry lived. An old credit card that the Prophet had given him served in lieu of a key. He had feared the place might have dead bolts but should have known better. He couldn't imagine why people even bothered to lock spring-latched doors.

Benjamin preceded Candy into the apartment, finding himself in a living room that ran the width of the place except for one bedroom at his right. There was a couch against the wall near the bedroom, and on it lay a somnolent form, so large it could only be Joseph Chambers. The opening of the door had been accomplished with such quiet and ease that the man hadn't even shifted or changed his breathing pattern. A blanket drooped from his massive belly, revealing the turned-down elastic of a pair of cotton briefs.

Benjamin stopped and turned, looking at Candy in the dim light from outside. Her eyes sparkled more avidly than before, and he was certain he could hear her breathing. She trembled like a woman sexually aroused. Looking at the sleeping man with gleeful hatred, she gripped the .22 automatic in her right hand until her knuckles appeared about to pop. Benjamin touched her on the shoulder and gestured to her to wait where she was. She looked at him resentfully but stood her ground.

Now give him your best, he told himself silently, snagging a wrench that he had thrust through his belt before leaving the car. It was a heavy wrench, straight from the tool kit in the Prophet's garage, untraceable. Benjamin hefted its unwholesome weight in his hand as he drew near the supine figure, thinking, You been away from it too long, man, that's your trouble.

He stood over the couch, looking down at the face of his victim, sweating as though the room weren't crisply chilly. He couldn't imagine what the trouble was. He had slugged people before, men and women, plenty of times. Only he had been strung out, or getting there, and the people wouldn't give him what he needed. He had thought of it as self-defense, or at least a necessity. Now he stood here, cold sober, about to sock this old man because a lunatic had told him to, and had promised him some ass from another lunatic.

And what did that make him, Benjamin, if not crazy? He was aware of Candy's eyes behind him, boring into his back, and he wondered whether she was thinking of using that little gun on him if he didn't get it done. Raising the wrench he steeled himself, started to strike, then realized that he hadn't given the swing as much power as he should. He raised his hand again and this time swung like he meant it, grunting with exertion.

Whether the grunt or just his presence, something woke Chambers at the last moment, and sleep-dulled eyes opened and stared, and gained just a scintilla of recognition before the wrench made contact with his skull, generating a dull pulpy sound that made Benjamin want to wretch. Chambers's head lolled to the side, the eyes closing, blood spurting from a long cut on his forehead. It continued to spurt in time to the man's pulse. Steeling himself afresh, Benjamin raised the wrench once more, ready to finish the job. A hand grasped his arm, almost wringing a cry of surprise from him. He jerked his arm free and spun about to face his assailant.

It was Candy.

The glint in her eye contained a measure of respect, as though he had surprised her by performing his task so well. At the same time she looked amused, possibly because he, who had been a street tough, had found it so difficult to clobber a sleeping old man. There was something magnetic, commanding about her look and manner, and Benjamin lowered his arm, working to regain control of his breathing. Her touch had put a scare into him. Despite himself he was relieved that she had prevented him from going through with it.

As he stood by she dropped to her haunches and examined the unconscious form on the couch. Her left hand reached forward, her fingers slipping over his skin lightly. The manner of it seemed almost affectionate. It gave Benjamin the whams to look at it. Finally she stood with the lithe energy of a jungle cat, leaning forward and rising to tiptoe. She whispered in his ear, "Tie him up."

Without waiting to see if he would comply she moved toward the bedroom, or what Benjamin supposed was the bedroom. He noticed that she held the pistol as though she knew how to use it and not in the bent-wrist manner of most women. He couldn't quite sort out his emotional reactions at the way she was taking charge of things. He felt relief at not having to make decisions in this curiously paralyzed state into which he had fallen. But he couldn't deny to himself that he felt disappointment in her for proving so adept at such doings, and in himself for not being strong enough to command.

He lashed Chambers's hands behind him with the blanket. The man was too far out of it to be aware of what was happening to him. There was no resistance, but just the limpness of a corpse. From the next room Benjamin heard murmurings and rustlings, and with belated concern he rushed in.

Candy had awakened one of the girls. In the dimness he couldn't tell at first which one she was. But he could see Candy standing there, her body rigid, the gun poked in the girl's face. It was a miracle that the girl hadn't screamed instinctively, but she just sat there, hugging the bedclothes to her bosom and staring into the muzzle of the little automatic. Candy hissed something that was unintelligible from where Benjamin stood in the doorway, and the girl nodded dumbly. Then, after a moment's hesitation and a false start, she lay down and rolled onto her stomach. Her sister hadn't stirred. Benjamin walked to that side of the bed so that he could slap a hand over the girl's mouth should she waken.

Candy stripped a pillowcase from the pillow under her victim's head and, thrusting the gun through the waistband of her skirt, began efficiently to tie the girl. Benjamin heard the girl sobbing mutedly into her pillow and felt another rush of conflicting emotions: sexual arousal and shame, pity and power.

Candy finished tying the girl, then picked up a pair of panties that had been tossed onto a chair and walked around to the same side of the bed as Benjamin. Crowding him aside she reached down and slammed her work-hardened hand and the panties over the sleeping girl's mouth. The girl erupted into action, but only for an instant. Her arms flailed and she kicked a couple of times and reached impulsively for the hand on her mouth. Then her eyes widened, and even in the dimness Benjamin could see them fasten, slightly crossed, on the gun. The slender white hands hung there for a moment, indecisive, and then lowered to her sides, the arms rigid as dry tree branches. Her eyes rolled to the side, either to avoid the sight of that black muzzle or because she had finally noticed the soft weeping of her sister. Her head rolled in that direction for a moment, but Candy grabbed a few strands of hair and yanked it back again, then pushed the wadded panties into her reluctant mouth.

Benjamin stood watching, almost retching himself, as Candy kept stuffing the cloth into her victim's mouth. Finally she got a gag response, but just brandished the gun and forced even more of the panties into her prey's throat. The girl on the bed raised her hands fitfully, involuntarily, then forced them to drop back into place as Candy reached down and took the blanket, yanking it away from her body. Then she pulled back the sheet as well, yanking at it until she freed it of the mattress.

"Tear this into strips," she ordered Benjamin. Automatically, he complied, ripping wide strips from the body of the sheet. He could feel the girls' body warmth in the cotton. When he had torn off the first strip Candy yanked it out of his hand, then turned and rapped the girl on the forehead with the muzzle of her pistol. "Roll over." After a moment the girl obeyed. Benjamin saw tears flash along her cheek as she turned away.

Candy set her gun on the floor next to the bed, where the girl couldn't have reached it even if she had known exactly where it was, and tied the strip of sheet around the girl's head, fastening the panty gag securely in place. Then she turned and grabbed the next strip. "Get a move on," she ordered Benjamin. "We have to get them back to the farm, and we haven't got all night."

He stared at her dully, feeling a surge of relief before he realized that the bit about taking them back to the farm was for the girls' benefit, to keep them docile. He felt sicker all the time, sick not only because of what he was doing but because Candy, the girl for whom he was doing it, was so good at this game, so natural and so casual. By the time he had torn off the next strip Candy had the girl's hands bound behind her and was picking up the gun. He followed her around the foot of the bed, ripping off some more cloth. In a moment Candy had gagged the other girl. His eyes were accustomed to the dark by this time, and he realized that the girl she had gagged first was Virginia, the girl who he had heard had given the Prophet so much trouble. The younger one.

Candy jammed the muzzle of the gun into Mary's spine, good and hard. "All right, get on your feet, you two," she commanded. "Fast!" The girls were struggling, their hands behind them, to rise from the bed. They were wearing pajamas, light-colored ones with short bottoms. Candy grabbed Mary's hair in her free hand, pulled her forward, and struck her left cheek with the barrel of the gun. The girl started to cry harder, and her sister, on the opposite side of the bed, glanced toward the other room as though fleetingly considering flight.

"Now I'm going to tell you bitches something," Candy said in a raspy, crazy-sounding voice. "The Prophet wants us to take you back to the farm so he can save your worthless fucking souls. But if you don't come along like good little girls, then he wants me to kill all three of you, you two and your old man." She raised the pistol to eye level, pointing it at the middle of Mary's face. "And you know I'll do it, too, don't you? No matter what happens to me!" The girl nodded rapidly, anxious to show her acquiescence, eager to please. "All right, then get moving," Candy said. "And stop when I say and go when I say, if you don't want your goddam heads blown open."

When they entered the living room the old man was just beginning to regain consciousness, which showed an awesome sturdiness considering the way Benjamin had clouted him. He looked blearily at the macabre entourage passing through the room, then started up quickly, wincing with sudden pain and falling back to the couch.

Before he could open his mouth Candy grabbed Virginia, clutching her about the chest, cupping one voluptuous young breast and pressing the pistol against her temple. "We're here to take you home," she told him. "You and your precious little girls. But if you make one false move, or try to attract any attention, you'll last just long enough to see both of them get their brain cells rearranged. You understand me, you fat turd?" He just lay there, staring at her. Benjamin glanced at Candy, saw her eyes glitter. "I think you understand," she said. "Now get on your feet."

This was the touchiest part, getting them out of the apartment and to the car, but it went like something lubricated. None of the prisoners did anything foolish, and no one came along to see the weird scene taking place. Benjamin went ahead to the car and opened the trunk as Candy directed him. It was a huge trunk, but he didn't think it would be possible to get all three of their prisoners into it. They managed, though, with the girls lying head to foot near the back of the car and the old man more or less wrapped around them, tucked under the spare tire. The lid caught on the second slam. Benjamin got in behind the wheel and started the engine. A moment later Candy slipped in beside him. He put the car in drive and began to creep toward the driveway.

"Where we goin'?" he asked, ceding to her the leadership she assumed and apparently rated.

She sat there, staring straight ahead and radiating excitement. "Out in the country," she said without looking at him, just staring as though she could already see the things that lay ahead. "Way out, where no one will hear us."

CHAPTER 39

There were hills within an hour's drive, with dishes and valleys between them. The sound of a shot might be lost in such a place. Benjamin headed in that direction, holding the car at an even fifty-five. From time to time, as the tires hummed along the asphalt, he imagined he could feel the vehicle sway slightly as the occupants of the trunk shifted and strained against their constricting environment. He even thought about the possibility of one of them working loose and perhaps opening the trunk lid from the inside, but he put it out of his mind. There was no way they could possibly work loose from Candy's expert binding job this quickly, and even if they did, and then found a way to open the trunk, it would be unlikely that he or she would attempt to dive out onto that highway while the car was traveling.

"That looks good," Candy said, pointing to a dirt road that jutted off at a right angle from the highway.

Benjamin removed his foot from the accelerator and tapped the power brake several times with his toe. The car slowed to fifteen miles per hour and he turned onto the side road, holding his speed.

"Douse the headlights," she said in a perfunctory voice, and Benjamin couldn't even work up any irritation at the manner in which she assumed the right to give him orders. It was such an obvious precaution that he couldn't imagine why he hadn't thought of it himself. He left the parking lights on just in case someone else might be coming from the other direction, or even from behind. The car bucked and swayed on the dirt road despite its expensive suspension system.

Candy chuckled, drawing a questioning look from him.

"Guess they're taking quite a bouncing around back there," she said, her eyes glinting in the moonlight.

"I guess," Benjamin agreed.

She chuckled again. "If they knew what's coming next, they'd relish every moment they can still feel anything." Then she turned and looked out the window at the barren ground they were passing.

A bit farther on they came to a branch road, even narrower and less level than the one they were already using. It seemed to head off to a niche between some foothills, and Benjamin knew beforehand that Candy was going to choose that place to do her work. She pointed to it, waving casually with the hand that held the gun, and Benjamin slowed further and turned.

In a few moments they were between hills, cut off from view on three sides, including the direction of the highway. Then Candy spotted a place behind an outcropping of one of the mounds and pointed to it. That would sequester them neatly, locking them off from sight on all four sides. Benjamin turned in there, crawling the car along until he was certain that they couldn't be seen by anyone more than a hundred yards in any direction, except atop one of the little hills. He set the brake and killed the engine.

"You can turn on the lights now," she said. "No one will see us."

It took him a moment to get her drift. Apparently she thought it would be more fun if she could see clearly what she was doing. Turning on the lights, he got out of the car as she slid out the other side. Carrying the keys with him, he walked to the trunk and opened it. They lay there, still neatly stacked and bound.

"Well, did we have a nice ride?" Candy asked. "This is where you folks get out, I'm afraid." Benjamin lifted Mary out of the car and tried to set her on her feet, but she staggered and fell on her hip. He started to lift her again, but Candy thumped the girl in the small of the back with one thickly shod foot. "Let her get up by herself," she ordered. "She ought to enjoy using her muscles and limbs while she still has them." Benjamin lifted out the other girl, who was a bit lighter, and who managed to keep her feet. Virginia stared up into his eyes with a searching, imploring expression that angered him. I can't help you, he wanted to yell at her. Meanwhile Mary was climbing laboriously to her feet, first working her knees under her.

Benjamin struggled with their father's bulk. He had worked up a sweat by the time he had him free of the trunk. The man weaved on his feet but managed to keep from falling.

Candy walked up to him, so close her breasts, through the thick dress and undergarments she wore, brushed against his bare chest. "Now, tubby," she said in a voice that squeaked with witchlike excitement and relish, "aren't you just a little sorry you were so naughty? I'll bet you'd like a chance to think things over, wouldn't you?" She reached up and tweaked his nose in a playful but probably painful manner. He pulled back his head indignantly and stared down at her in a helpless, baleful manner. "Move it, fatso," she ordered, gesturing toward the front of the car. He stood looking at her in a futile gesture of defiance. Candy stepped back, raising her pistol ceremoniously. She brought it around so that it pointed at the center of the man's face, paused for a bare instant, and then swung around to train it directly on Virginia's right cheek.

Joseph Chambers slumped slightly and began walking to the front of the car. The girls were both crying again, or perhaps screaming. It was difficult to tell because the sounds were muffled by their gags. Candy lowered her pistol and grasped Virginia's arm tightly, jerking her and then shoving her after her father. Mary followed automatically, without prompting. Like sheep, Benjamin thought with a touch of contempt. Their only chance, however slight, was to make a break for it. He had heard of people going to their deaths in this supine manner, but to experience it was something altogether different. Even when he had been mugging people he had never held such a dark, hopeless view of them as he did at this moment. To submit to one's own extinction seemed somehow less wholesome than the taking of someone else's life.

Candy shoved Virginia in front of the car, giving her a push that propelled her five yards from the headlights. The beams converged on her and her father, who took up his place beside his daughter as though to comfort her with his presence. Candy moved back and grasped Mary, who was hanging back, and shoved her roughly up with her father and sister so that they formed a ragged, pathetic line. Then Candy stood regarding them, weighing the pistol in her hand sensuously.

This, Benjamin thought, was her big moment at last, and she wanted to milk it for all its satisfaction.

The Chamberses, deprived of the interlocking warmth that had sustained them in the trunk, began to shiver as the night's cold bit into their flesh. The girls showed it first, giving way to little fits of shaking, while their nostrils hissed with their labored breathing. The old man held it off longer, though he must have been the coldest, standing there in nothing but his shorts. But when his massive frame did shake, it was something to behold.

Benjamin suspected he was exaggerating the shivers, using them to camouflage his attempts at breaking loose from his bonds. But he knew those knots would hold even against someone as powerful and frightened and angry as Chambers. They would hold at least as long as they had to.

Suddenly Candy raised the little pistol. She held the pistol in one hand, sighting down it like a target shooter, and her hand was awesomely steady. She clenched her left eye shut, using only her right. Chambers looked at her, the headlights playing on his face, and Benjamin could see him fighting back the terror, trying to go out with defiance. He very nearly made it.

The .22 automatic made a thin snapping sound in the night air, surprisingly, nerve-rackingly loud. It made Benjamin flinch. He knew there was no chance that anyone but the five of them would hear it, but that didn't keep him from reacting. It was so loud!

Chambers flinched too, but then he was still standing there, looking dazed. His knees buckled, but he managed to regain control of them. A stain appeared on the front of his shorts, and Benjamin could smell a faint whiff of urine.

The girls, who had been weeping silently, screamed into their gags. Virginia bent at the waist and stayed that way, as though trying to retch, while Mary dropped to her knees. She lowered her head, letting her long, silky hair fall and cover her face. She looked like someone praying, and perhaps she was.

Candy deliberately had missed that first shot. She wanted to see their reaction. And now she was almost doubled over with mirth, choking on it, gagging on the intensely comic nature of the tableau before her. Then she started to walk forward, still chortling.

Benjamin clutched her left arm, pulling her back a step. "Don't get too close," he warned her. "He can still kick."

She glanced back at him, her expression annoyed for a moment, and then sly. "That's right," she agreed. "He can, can't he." She brought the pistol up and fired, and this time Chambers yelled into his gag, a muffled groan of anguish as he dropped to the uneven ground. Landing on his knees, he screamed again and rolled to the side. His left knee was shattered. The bullet had struck just a little above it and possibly angled downward, turning it into a fistful of gravel. Even if they left him alive, he would never use that knee again.

"Now he's not going to do any kicking," she said in the arch voice of a little girl pleased with something she has done. Then she walked up close to the man. The pistol hung limp at her side. "Are you, old man?" she asked in a teasing, coquettish voice. "You're not going to kick anyone ever again, are you, turkey?"

The girls had stopped crying. They just gaped, stunned, at the woman who held their lives in her hand, as though this matter had gone beyond their capacity to feel or react. Their father lay there on his hip, apparently trying to relieve the pressure on his knee as much as possible. His face was contorted with pain now that the initial shock of the wound had subsided. He made no sound. Candy raised one heavily shod foot and brought it down quickly on the side of his shattered knee. Then, when she had it pinned and he didn't dare to pull away, she began to increase the pressure gradually. Even in the ambient light spilling over from the headlight beams it was obvious that he was draining, turning white with pain. When his eyes lolled back and he seemed about to lose consciousness she pulled back her foot, stepping just out of reach of his other leg.

Mary and Virginia were looking at anything but their father. Both of them were on their knees now, shivering from the cold of the night and the horror of the scene in which they found themselves.

Candy stepped to where Virginia knelt and, grasping her hair in one fist, twisted her head brutally toward the spot where her father lay wheezing like a winded horse. "Look, girls," she invited, and commanded. "Look at your daddy! Look at what I'm doing to your daddy, girls." Then she leaned down close to Virginia's face and hissed, "Because one of you is next!"

Releasing the girl, she stepped back and began moving back and forth in front of her victims in a movement that was almost a dance. "One of you is next," she chanted. "But I don't know which one yet. I don't know which one yet, but it doesn't matter." Dancing in close, she grasped Mary's chin and wrenched it up so hard the girl cried into her gag. Her sister whimpered in some sort of sympathetic response, as though she felt the wrench in her own spine. "It doesn't matter," Candy reiterated in that eerie chant. "It doesn't matter which one is next, because— You know why?" Rocking the girl's head back and forth in a syncopated rhythm, she answered her own question. "Because I'm going to get both of you before the night is done!" Her voice carried a note of gaiety, a travesty of a mother talking joyously to her infant. Laughing like a witch, Candy pushed the girl back, almost knocking her off her knees, and danced back again. Then, circling, she closed in on Chambers once more.

He lay there, covered in chilled sweat, looking up at her in fascination with this apparition. He seemed for the moment to have forgotten his pain and fear. Candy went down on one knee, holding the pistol pointed at his sternum. For a moment she was turned sideways to Benjamin, and he saw her face, contorted, manic, perhaps even demonic. She reached forward, hooking that slender, gentle-seeming hand under the elastic of Chambers's shorts. He drew back, wincing as he wrenched his shattered knee. Candy reached down in a casual, petulant manner and rapped the knee with the barrel of her gun. Chambers almost passed out, and the girls, who had apparently lost the ability to look away, gasped and shuddered.

"Be still, fat boy!" Candy barked. "Take what's coming to you like a little man." She yanked down the shorts, revealing Chambers's genitals, almost buried in his belly. Inserting her free hand into the mound of flesh, Candy took the organ and pulled it out, then stroked it gently. Chambers looked away, looked at something else, looked at nothing. "Aw, you got a limp weenie?" Candy asked teasingly. "Maybe Mama can get it to stand up, tubby. Mama can try, anyway, huh?" She continued to massage the flaccid penis, which remained lame.

"You know, this is what got you into all the trouble, isn't it?" she crooned, still stroking. "This is what got you where you are right now. If you hadn't had those evil, sinful daughters, you wouldn't have sinned yourself. And if you hadn't had this thing between your legs, then you wouldn't have had the daughters." Shifting the pistol, she pressed the muzzle against Chambers's penis, snugging it right into the man's belly so that it trained against the root of the organ. Benjamin stifled an involuntary lurch, a vestigial masculine urge to protect Chambers's endangered manhood. "Too bad it's impossible to go back and undo things," Candy continued. "Too bad Mama can't turn back the clock for you, isn't it, roly-poly man?"

She nudged the pistol in even tighter. Chambers seemed about to pass out, and his daughters were straining, their bodies taut, as though they would like to jump on Candy but were rooted in place. "But at least Mama can get rid of the offending part, can't she? Like it says in the Bible, 'If thine eye offends thee, pluck it out and cast it from thee.' Only it wasn't your eye that got you in trouble, was it, asshole!" The last words were raspy and acid, and the ending syllable was drowned out by the reports of the pistol, four rapid shots, slightly muffled by the flesh in which the muzzle was buried.

Chambers's eyes bugged with surprise, and a second later he screamed as the pain reached his numbed consciousness. Candy came to her feet in a graceful, supremely feminine motion, the pistol hanging at her side. Chambers thrashed on the ground, flopping like some huge, landed fish. Benjamin caught a bare glimpse of tattered flesh and spurting blood before looking away.

For once he was glad the Prophet didn't feed his people much. If he had had anything on his stomach other than the coffee he had drunk in the diners in town, he knew he'd be puking it up now. His stomach heaved in a futile attempt as Candy strode past him toward the door of the car. Benjamin leaned his knuckles on the hood and pressed them down against the metal with the weight of his torso. In a moment she was beside him. She had retrieved the partial box of ammunition and was extracting the magazine from the gun.

"Can't you get it over with?" he whispered and grunted, alternately gaining and losing the use of his vocal cords.

She paused in the midst of inserting a cartridge into the magazine, holding the little button down with her thumb, and smiled at him amusedly. "What's the matter, you big, strong street buck? Can't you take it?" She finished loading the nine cartridges into the magazine and slid it into the butt of the gun, then slipped off the safety. Before brushing past him she stopped and said in a voice too soft for the girls to hear, "They've earned this. All of it. Let's not cheat them."

Chambers had wrung out his life. He lay limp and incredibly white in the headlights, like some giant thing that had been washed ashore. The girls had sunk back, sitting on their feet like submissive geishas while their tormentor approached with protracted relish.

Candy stopped at a point before and between the two girls, making herself the apex of a triangle. Standing there, her back almost arched with the exultation of power, she examined her two victims. Then, apparently having made her decision, she wheeled slightly left and approached Mary.

The girl's body quickened slightly as Candy stopped in front of her, but she gave no other sign that she realized she had been selected to die next. Candy stopped in front of Mary, towering over the kneeling girl, a picture of dominance. She raised the gun and then brought it down, not gently, on Mary's head, the muzzle pressing straight down on a point just above the back of the girl's head. She stood like that for several seconds while Mary held almost preternaturally still, waiting for the shot she would never hear. Then Candy knelt in front of the girl, letting the muzzle of the pistol slip forward until it pressed upward against the subject's lowered forehead. Candy reached forward with her free hand and started to do something.

The angle of his vision was such that Benjamin couldn't tell just what she was doing at first. Then he saw that she was unbuttoning Mary's pajama top. Slowly, methodically, with clear savor, she worked upward from the bottom button, each time tugging down on the garment so that it fell open below the lowest button fastened. Mary huddled miserably, an occasional shiver her only response. Benjamin, who had beaten people who refused to yield their purses, was awed by Candy's cold ruthlessness. He even found himself hoping that Mary's shocked state had insulated her, stupefied her to such an extent that she was unaware of what was being done.

Candy finished opening the buttons and folded back the pajama top, draping the folds over Mary's shoulders. Mary still didn't show any sign of awareness but slumped, awaiting her fate. Candy fondled the girl's breasts for a moment, teasing one nipple and then the other.

Benjamin was too far away to tell whether they responded, but despite himself he felt excitement burgeoning inside him. His penis stood against his pants, stiffening to an almost painful degree.

"You really weren't as bad as the others, were you, dear?" Candy crooned. "All you did was what your father told you. You just left when he made you leave. You weren't nearly as bad as your evil sister over there. So I'll make it easier on you." She pressed the muzzle of the pistol directly between the girl's breasts, under the sternum, where the bullet would shatter the heart. She worked the muzzle as though moving it into some special niche. Then she paused for a moment and chuckled. "No," she said. "Not quite *that* easy."

Slowly she lowered the gun, slipping the muzzle down Mary's belly until it pressed against the pit of her stomach. The girl finally responded, looking at her torturer with an expression that combined vague shock and mild reproach. Candy reached up in a darting, serpentine motion and yanked the girl's gag down from her mouth, exposing a pink tongue and mother-of-pearl teeth. Then she yanked Mary's head forward and kissed her directly on the mouth. As though traumatized into a partial paralysis, Mary only stiffened slightly, her slim body seeming to freeze like a photograph for the last moment before, lips stilled pressed to the girl's, Candy fired the pistol.

The report was muffled and there was no visible flame because the muzzle was buried in Mary's flesh. In the glare of the headlights Benjamin clearly saw the slide kick back, saw the empty casing spin off to land in the dirt. And under the gun's muted blast he clearly heard a sound that wouldn't leave him for an instant during the days left to him: a dull, liquid thud, the sound of the hollow-point bullet burying itself in the helpless girl's flesh.

Mary jerked up straight, her tiny body rigid as rock. It was almost comical-looking in a macabre manner, as though she had been surprised by a particularly well-aimed goosing. Benjamin found himself fighting back an insane urge to giggle. Then he saw the raw wound, the oozing blood and protuberant organs before he could drag his eyes away. That was a mistake too, because he looked up at the girl's face, saw that last, heartsick glance at the world, that sad, reproving, somehow apologetic expression before Mary's body went limp, folding down gracefully over her knees as though she were salaaming. It was an amazingly graceful motion, leaving her back exposed as her breasts and the horrid wound were hidden from view. Her long hair lay thick on the ground before her.

Candy stroked it softly, with an affectionate and somehow sad gesture. "There," she sang softly, patting the dead girl on the head. "Now that wasn't so bad, was it, honey?"

It was the sound of soft, muffled sobbing that brought both Candy and Benjamin back. Benjamin had drifted into some sort of anesthesia, and Candy seemed lost in a reverie, as though the act of murder had calmed something turbulent in her.

The sight of her sister's death had brought Virginia back from the near coma into which she had fallen. Stung back to awareness and thus to vulnerability, she had grown more attractive to Candy. Her little frame seemed to roll with nausea, and Benjamin could tell that she was choking, possibly on her own vomit. He looked compulsively at Candy, saw her gradually emerge from her pensiveness, quickening like one who has awakened to remember that it is a special, long-awaited day. Finally she put her left hand on the ground before her and pulled her feet under her. She rose easily on legs strengthened by long hours in the Prophet's fields. In a long, languorous stride she approached the one remaining Chambers.

"Now, dear," she said sweetly, "we come to your turn." When Virginia lowered her head, Candy grasped her hair and yanked it back, forcing the girl to look up at her. "I was only fooling before. There was never any doubt which one of you girls would go first. I fully intended to keep you for dessert, Virginia. You deserved to see it all, to know what you brought on yourself and your family. But now it's your turn to die, little Virginia," she said, raising the gun and holding it up so that Virginia could see it. She didn't point it at her, but simply showed her the engine that would destroy her life. Virginia looked at it for a moment and then at her murderess. Her jaws worked, and garbled sounds came from her throat. She was trying to talk, to beg for her life. If the whispered rumors at the farm had been accurate, this was the girl who had refused the Prophet, rejected him flatly. If that was the case then the things that had happened to her since had certainly broken her spirit. Now she was groveling, obviously trying to plead for just one more minute of life.

"Sorry, dear," Candy said with an amused lilt to her voice. "I can't take off your gag. I'd be willing to let you beg for your life awhile, but of course you'd just start to scream. And if someone should hear you, then we'd be in trouble for just doing our duty." She pointed the pistol directly at Virginia's face for a moment, but by this time Benjamin had grown sufficiently accustomed to Candy's mode of operation to know she wasn't going to fire. Virginia stared at the pistol's bore, and he could almost smell the terror in her. Then the muzzle lowered and she looked up at her executioner with an expression of almost affectionate gratitude. In his mugging operations Benjamin had encountered something akin to that response. By some curious quirk of human nature, people often became attached, almost devoted, to those who hurt or misused them.

Candy seemed to swell with exultation. "I'll tell you what I will do for you, though, dear," she crooned softly to the girl. Virginia seemed enraptured, caught up in the ceremonious nature of her slaughter. I'll give you a chance. A little chance, but more than your father and sister had."

Benjamin readied himself to approach and take a hand in the situation. They couldn't risk the girl's escaping. She had seen them commit two murders, and legally Benjamin knew he was as guilty as Candy, though she had pulled the trigger both times, and had enjoyed it so much.

Candy hooked her wrists under the girl's arms, thrusting the pistol through Virginia's left armpit, and drew her to her feet. Virginia was shaky but she stood, looking into Candy's face searchingly. Candy stepped back a half pace and then, reaching forward, opened the front of the girl's pajama bottom. She pulled it down until it slid from its own weight into a puddle of cloth about Virginia's ankles. Virginia shivered but stood stock still, staring at Candy intently.

"Now," Candy said, "I'm going to let you run for it, dear. You can turn around and make a run for it when I tell you to. Uh-uh," she warned as Virginia tried to step out of the wadded pajamas. "Keep them like that. That's how you run. I'll count to ten before I open fire. Unless you try to leave the headlights. If you do that I'll start shooting right away, and I won't stop until you're dead. But if you run in a straight line, right down the middle of the lighted area, then you've got until I count ten. That's fair, isn't it? Well, isn't it, dear?" she repeated insistently. Reluctantly, still keeping her eyes fixed on Candy's face, the younger girl nodded. The motion caused her tears to flash in the illumination from the headlights. "Good. Since you agree to the rules, then you have no complaint coming, however it works out. Have you, dear?" She poked Virginia in the belly with the muzzle of the pistol to elicit another response. Virginia nodded again, then caught herself and shook her head, agreeing that she had no complaint. "Good. Now turn around."

Virginia turned awkwardly, twisting the pajama bottom more restrictingly about her ankles. She tried to move about a bit to loosen them, but before she could accomplish anything Candy shouted, "Go!" Virginia, her back to them now, froze for an instant before trying to run. It was a tragicomic, pathetic travesty of running. She couldn't have gone five good steps, even if Candy had kept her pledge, but even that had been a mockery.

"Twofoursixeightten!" Candy shouted, laughing gleefully, and, raising the pistol, fired it directly into Virginia's right buttock. She fired just as Virginia's right leg was in its rearmost position, driving the bullet into the soft, jiggly flesh. The cheek erupted in a red, ugly wound as the girl pulled in her fanny as though she had been switched. Candy was almost helpless with laughter, seeming to feel that what she had just done was the funniest thing imaginable. Virginia somehow managed to stay on her feet, though she couldn't run any longer. She managed a shuffling movement, angling off to one side in an apparent attempt to enter the protective darkness beyond the twin cone of the headlights. It was as pathetic as all the rest, of course. She couldn't even move fast enough to keep Candy from walking up beside her, had that been Candy's intention.

But Candy just took careful aim, holding the gun in both fists as she had probably seen the cops do on TV, and fired another shot. This one struck Virginia just above the crease of her left knee, sending her down in a heap, screaming into her gag.

Candy ambled up beside the writhing girl. "Crawl, fucker!" she commanded. "Goddam you, crawl!"

Virginia, as though still hypnotized by the game Candy had been playing with her, obeyed, trying for the darkness. Candy stood for a while, letting her move forward until Virginia's knees were even with the spot on which Candy stood. Then she took a casual step forward and aimed the pistol at the small of Virginia's back. She aimed very carefully, from a foot and a half, and fired. The gun cracked loudly and spat flame, gouging another hole in Virginia's body. Apparently Candy had missed the spine, at which she had been aiming. She took aim again as Virginia lay on the ground, no longer even trying to move, and compensated by shifting the gun a bit.

This time the shot was accompanied by a spasm of motion in the girl's legs, a violent kicking that lasted only a second. Then the legs went completely limp. "Go on, crawl, you little bitch!" Candy screamed, bending low over her victim. "You've still got your goddam arms! Crawl!" For an instant Benjamin thought Virginia was going to comply again. There was a desultory movement of her arms, a vague clawing motion in the dirt. But she was either unconscious or no longer interested in trying for her life. Candy kicked her hard in the side, trying to rouse her. She swore. But aside from a brief motor reflex there was no response. Finally Candy went down on her knees and grabbed Virginia's long blond hair in her fist, pulling her head back and looking at the girl's face. The eyelids fluttered uselessly for an instant, but there was nothing more. Benjamin wondered whether she was already dead. He thought he detected signs of breathing, but he wasn't certain. At any rate it didn't matter, because Candy pointed her pistol directly at the middle of the girl's face and fired until the magazine was empty.

CHAPTER 40

The day following the extermination of the Chambers family brought two events that displaced the Prophet's composure with fear and rage.

The first occurred before breakfast, at nine o'clock in the morning. He had lazed about in bed as was his usual procedure, this time with a new girl who had joined the movement three days earlier. She was a runaway of fifteen, very pretty once the dirt and grime had been rinsed away, and fairly skillful on the mattress. She was fetching his socks and underwear after toweling him down subsequent to their shower when the Prophet heard a discreet knock at his bedroom door. He snapped his fingers impatiently, pointing to the Pendleton robe hanging in his open closet, and the girl fetched it hastily.

"Come in," he grumbled, displeased at being disturbed.

It was Sister Penelope, and she seemed anxious, even distraught. "Forgive the intrusion, Lord," she said nervously.

"Yes, yes, what is it?" the Prophet demanded without looking at her.

"Two gentlemen want to see you," she explained.

"Converts?" He was sitting on the edge of his rumpled bed while the new girl knelt and pulled on his socks. When Sister Penelope didn't reply immediately, he looked up, sensing that there was more to her manner than simple anxiety at having disturbed him. She was looking from him to the girl. The Prophet tapped the little chick on the back of the head a bit harder than necessary and motioned toward the door when she looked up. Grabbing her dress and shoes she backed out hurriedly, obviously relieved at being released from his august

241

presence before she had committed some grave and inadvertent impropriety.

"All right, now what is it?" the Prophet demanded again, tugging at his socks angrily.

Sister Penelope scurried forward, knelt, and pulled the socks on for him. "The gentlemen are policemen," she explained, looking studiously at a sock that she was needlessly smoothing along his calf. She must have felt his leg stiffen because she looked up suddenly, with a reluctant impulse.

"And you let them in?" he asked, his voice heavy with ominous blame.

She fidgeted, remaining on her knees. "I didn't want to, Lord, but they threatened to return with a warrant, and I thought—"

"They were probably bluffing." His intestines were writhing like serpents held over a flame. He was glad that Chambers girl wasn't still around, running all over the house in her birthday suit. "Well, now they're in, I may as well talk to them. Tell them to wait in my library."

"Yes, Lord."

She seemed on the verge of tears, and that, at least, brought the Prophet some satisfaction. He bored into her with his eyes, deliberately aggravating her discomfiture. She backed to the door, still crouching. When she had it open, he cleared his throat as a signal to her to halt and heed him.

"Sister Penelope," the Prophet said softly enough so that she had to strain a bit to make out his words, "you may have served your purpose in this house. I shall consider the advisability of transferring you to more strenuous labors outdoors." She just stared at him for a moment, her makeup beginning to run. Then she nodded abruptly. "Now get out," he ordered.

The younger of the two men was tall and stringy, while his companion, a man in his forties, was half a head shorter and beefy. Both wore inexpensive-looking gray suits. The younger man made a concession to stylishness in the form of a red tie with a matching hankie in his breast pocket. They were looking about the room casually, which annoyed the Prophet. He took his place behind the desk, sitting while leaving them on their feet.

"What can I do for you gentlemen?" he asked abruptly. He could see them taking in his hand-tailored silk suit.

"This is Officer Blaine," the thick one said by way of introduction. "I'm Sergeant O'Hare." He flashed a badge, which the Prophet didn't spare a glance. "We'd like to ask you a few questions, Mr. Hartford." His voice was as thick as his body, unpleasant sounding, with a trace of some eastern accent. The Prophet nodded mutely. The two policemen looked at one another. "Mr. Hartford," Sergeant O'Hare asked, "do you know a woman named Peggy Boling?"

The Prophet didn't turn a hair. "Should I?" He was relieved that this was the subject of their inquiry, and not the Chambers family, whose fate he had not yet heard.

"That's the name she went by," the sergeant explained. "But legally she was named Peggy Hartford."

The Prophet hesitated a moment before replying. "It's quite obvious—Sergeant, is it?" O'Hare nodded. "It's quite obvious, Sergeant, that you are aware that I was once married to Miss Boling."

"You still are, so far as we can tell."

"Oh? I naturally assumed that she had taken care of that detail by this time."

"Have you seen her recently?" the sergeant asked.

The Prophet hesitated, decided they knew too much to be fooled by denials. "She contacted me a few weeks past. I went into town and met her. It seemed she wanted some money. I explained to her that I had none. I don't think she believed me, but there was nothing either of us could do about that, so I said good-bye. I haven't seen her since."

"You told her you were broke?" Officer Blaine asked, glancing around the room.

The Prophet smiled. "Don't be misled by my surroundings, Officer," he said. "All of this is the property of the Church of the All-Moving Spirit."

"We could run a check on your personal holdings, Mr. Hartford," he cautioned.

"And would find them quite extensive," the Prophet allowed. "But I don't consider any of that money to be mine. It has been entrusted to me by my followers. I could hardly give it away to anyone who asked for it, could I?"

"That's very convenient," Officer Blaine said with a little edge to his voice.

The Prophet looked at him blandly. "Yes, isn't it?"

"Do you read the papers, Mr. Hartford?" This from Sergeant O'Hare.

"This is a religious commune, Sergeant. We are not concerned with worldly matters. All that concerns us in this world occurs right here on our property."

"Along with the price of vegetables?" Officer Blaine asked quizzically, and received a glance of reproof from his superior.

"Then you don't know that your wife is dead?"

"No, I hadn't heard," the Prophet said, lowering his voice slightly. "I'm sorry. Not that she died. That is a trivial matter. I am sorry that she was unregenerate, and now must spend eternity atoning for her incorrigibility."

"Would you like to know how she died?" O'Hare asked a bit tightly.

"As I told you, death is a matter of little consequence to us. My wife was born dead, as all people are. It was her misfortune that she never chose to live."

"Well, murder is no trivial matter to us."

"If you're seeking the perpetrators of the act, I'm afraid I can't help you," the Prophet said, affecting boredom. "I certainly should have had no reason to commit such an act."

"Well, we won't take up any more of your time," Sergeant O'Hare said.

"That's fine." The Prophet rose and walked to the door, his one concession to worldly courtesy. In the doorway, O'Hare paused. The Prophet didn't like the man's eyes, which seemed to look past his face and into his skull.

"Just one thing, Mr. Hartford. Would you object to our having a look around the commune?"

"I certainly would object," the Prophet said, returning the man's stare. "My followers are not accustomed to the scrutiny of outsiders, and I do not want them disturbed in their devotions."

"We may have to get a search warrant, then."

"By all means do so, if you can persuade a judge that you have sufficient cause." The officers looked at him for a moment, apparently realizing, belatedly, that he would not be intimidated. A moment later they were gone, leaving the Prophet alone with his thoughts.

"Son of a bitch!" he roared at the thick oaken door. "Goddam it! That rotten, fucking cunt!" He stormed about his library furiously. That stupid bitch couldn't even get out of the country without getting herself killed. Finally he threw himself wearily into his swivel chair and leaned on his desk. He supposed that if he had given her the money she had wanted none of this would have happened. Alive, she would be less troublesome than she was dead. If the police couldn't find the people who had done this, and the Prophet doubted that they would, then they would probably come out here, armed with warrants, and snoop around the place until they found some sort of red herring, something to take the mind of the public off the murder. Something like a self-ordained prophet who got his jollies with underage girls. And the business about the Chambers family would come out, and Christ knew where *that* would lead! He should have given Peggy the goddam money.

"But why should I?" he demanded to the empty room. "It's my money, every penny, every mill. Mine by rights!" It had all been given to him by the boobs whose function it was to serve him.

If only Peggy had waited a few months to get herself snuffed. He'd have been in Switzerland by then, out of reach of these *fascists*!

Only now he couldn't stop thinking about the Chambers family, and the fact that he had delegated a small-time thug and a deluded girl to dispatch them. Impulsively, he punched a button that would summon Sister Penelope. She was in the room in seconds, looking as anxious as before. She had repaired her makeup.

"Send someone into town in one of the small cars," the Prophet directed her, "to buy me a local newspaper. Take the money out of petty cash."

"Yes, Lord," she said with a bobbing curtsy.

CHAPTER 41

The newspaper account was the thing that provided the Prophet with his second vexation of the day. Brother Benjamin was before him minutes after he read it.

"You stupid, empty-headed nigger!" the Prophet railed. "You incompetent!" Brother Benjamin stood dumbfounded through the first portion of this diatribe, too surprised to react. "And you had the temerity to demand a reward for the honor of working in my service!" the Prophet continued. "I can't believe you were possessed of such unmitigated brass, when you couldn't even do the job I assigned to you!"

"Now just a minute, Your Holiness," Benjamin said, his natural sarcasm finally awakened. "How was I supposed to know old man Chambers had another kid? You never told me, and I bet you never told Candy, neither."

"He worked in the fields every day!" the Prophet fulminated. "It was common knowledge!"

"It wasn't no common knowledge to me, 'cause how was I supposed to know, when that old man never talked about his boy, and the old lady never hardly talked about nothin' at all?"

"You can forget the excuses!" the Prophet roared, extending an arm across the desk and shaking a finger in his visitor's face.

Benjamin went cross-eyed in an almost comical fashion for a moment. Then suddenly his right hand sprang up and around in a fast swipe, knocking the Prophet's hand aside. Benjamin's face was as hard as gunmetal. "You keep your *finger* outa my *face*, you honky phony!" He leaned across the desk, planting both palms on the lustrous finish. "This wasn't none of my fault, an' it wasn't none of Candy's, neither! This was *your* fault, Your Infallible Perfection! It was *you* should've told us about this boy. Then we coulda took care o' things. We only knew about the old man an' his two goddam *cunts*, an' we *sure* took care of them all right."

He drew himself upright, still glaring at the Prophet, who was too shaken by this bold sally even to have become angry as yet. Benjamin turned away and walked in a little circle, completing it once and half again, to work off his rage. Glaring defiantly at the Prophet, he flipped open the humidor and took possession of a fat, expensive cigar. Lighting it with the Prophet's desk lighter, he sprawled in one of the chairs facing the desk. The Prophet continued to glower at him for a moment, realized that it was a fruitless exercise, and sank into his swivel chair.

"Now," Benjamin said in a voice that shook though it was softer than before, "we got to figure out what we're gonna do about this."

"I don't see—" the Prophet began.

"Shut up." Benjamin waved his cigar in an abrupt, imperative manner. He sat musing for a moment, letting the ash from the cigar drip to the carpet. "Those bodies ain't been found," he said finally. "All that kid knows is that his old man an' his sisters are missin'. Ain't no proof of no monkey business. Leastwise, nothin' that would stand up in court."

"Do you think—?" The Prophet was cut off by another wave of the cigar.

"That place was real well hid where me an' Candy did what we did," Benjamin said to the wall. Then his eyes focused sharply on the Prophet. "Couple of folks with shovels could go out there an' cover up those corpuses delicti, an' I'll bet they never would be found."

"Could you . . . ?" He let it trail off.

Benjamin was looking at him coldly. "You know I got to do it, 'cause my ass, and Candy's, is on the line more'n yours," he said. He pushed himself to his feet, aiming his cigar at the Prophet like a weapon. "Only I jus' want to say one thing, friend." He paused, waiting long enough for the Prophet to realize a response was expected.

"What?" he asked stupidly.

"I been around the streets a long time. I can vanish an' stay vanished for quite a while if I want. I can hold out a lot longer than you could. You dig?" The Prophet nodded. Benjamin leaned across the desk once more, farther this time, so that the Prophet could see the flecks of dust on his black face, smell the sweat of a day's labor. Benjamin's eyes bored into those of the Prophet. "I still want my reward, white man. You promised it to me, an' I earned it. Oh, Christ livin' Lord, did I earn it! An' you're gonna give it to me if you don't want this place crawlin' with cops. I can manage that, an' I can just vanish like smoke." The man's eyes seemed wild, as though they had seen things beyond human ken. For the first time the Prophet felt a touch of fear. This was no man to have around.

The Prophet raised his hands in a placatory gesture. "Now, Benjamin, no one has said anything about cheating you of your just reward. A bargain made is a debt unpaid, eh?" He chuckled, hoping he didn't sound too nervous. "You just do this one more thing, Benjamin. Just get rid of those bodies so they won't be found, and I promise you I'll order Candy to be whatever you wish. You know she will do as I say, don't you?" Benjamin nodded once, brusquely, and continued staring at him. "Well, I'll tell you what I'll do. You go on back to the fields now. You find Candy—your wife—and tell her to come in here to me. And I'll give her the word—but pending the completion of this one last task. Now, does that satisfy you?"

For a long moment Benjamin stood, staring down at his adversary. Slowly, he nodded. "Just don't try to back out later," he cautioned.

The Prophet's visage darkened momentarily, then softened with obvious effort. "There won't be any reason to do that, Benjamin," he purred soothingly. "You know I have no designs on the lady. After all, I have—" He caught himself just in time. "I have plenty of feminine companionship. Why should I begrudge a faithful helper the affections of one girl?"

"I don't know," Brother Benjamin said with measured caution. "But I got a feelin' you do."

This time at least there was no gun along, Benjamin thought. The headlights speared along in front of them, the engine droned, and the tires hummed incessantly on the asphalt, and the grisly chore came closer with each skipping, stuttering beat of his heart. But he could go through with it. He knew that, having gone through the previous night's experience, he could do anything.

On the periphery of his vision she sat, jammed against the right-hand door of the little car, her tiny body slumped a bit so that there was an empty space between the lazy back of the seat and the small of her back. She looked exhausted but still alert. From time to time she would glance in his direction and smile. The smile appeared soft in the dimness of the car's interior. Ever since she had gone to the mansion to see the Prophet that afternoon, she had been different toward Benjamin, though in the presence of the other followers the difference had been necessarily subtle. Benjamin decided that he would have to make it a point to see the Prophet again soon and make some sort of arrangements. He didn't care what the others—the suckers—did, but he intended to see to it that the Prophet kept his bargain, and to Benjamin that meant some place of their own, where he and Candy could be alone.

His pulse quickened at the thought, but he had no time to dwell on it, because the little dirt road was coming up fast. He slacked off on the gas and peered into the gloom to be certain he had the right place. His sense of direction had always been peerless, and he was gratified to find that it hadn't failed him this time. Slowing to a crawl and glancing in both directions, Benjamin pulled the car off the highway.

He turned off the headlights and crawled along the dirt road until he was safely out of sight of the highway, then turned them on again and accelerated slightly, bumping and swaying, holding to the wheel more tightly than necessary until his knuckles hurt. The car rounded the last turn and the lights fell across the landscape, casting lumpy distorted shadows behind the shapeless heaps that even he, with prior knowledge, didn't immediately recognize. His foot inadvertently let up on the gas pedal for a moment, and then he pressed down too hard, sending the car jolting across the bumpy ground. He made certain to park the car in such a way that the headlights would illuminate their work.

Two shovels were in the trunk, old ones from the farm with fine coats of dirt and rust. As they picked them up Candy's hand brushed Benjamin's lightly, bringing a quick glance from him. She gave him another smile and moved subtly closer. Even through the shapeless dress she wore, he sensed the nearness of her body, felt an excitement that seemed to communicate itself from her. Reflexively he moved toward her, placing his free hand on her waist. She yielded for a moment, then, with apparent reluctance, pulled away.

"We have to get this job done, Ben," she reminded him.

The way to go about it, he decided, was quickly, and with as little thinking as possible. He wished that he had something to take, something that would dull the edge of reality. Except that it would also keep him from enjoying Candy's closeness as they worked together, stripping the shorts from the old man's body. If the corpses had been clothed it would have been necessary to undress them, because naked bodies would be likely to yield sooner to the work of the earth's vermin, and because clothed bodies might be easier to identify. As it was they had only to pull the shorts from the man's ankles, where they were still wound, and toss them aside. The girls took only a bit more work. In a moment the two pairs of pajamas were heaped atop the father's shorts. The little pile of clothing seemed pathetic, and Benjamin avoided looking at them.

The digging began. The grave had to be deep enough to take the three bodies with some to spare, because they had decided that someone might bulldoze this property. The work went more swiftly than Benjamin expected, partly because Candy threw herself into it with the same fire as she expended on any job assigned her by the Prophet.

"That should do it," she said to him in a husky whisper. Her eyes flashed into his in a way that made his blood race. Benjamin thrust his shovel into the mound of dirt they had raised and then dragged the old man's body to the hole. He was heavier than Benjamin had expected, and the flesh had an unpleasant coldness to it, but Benjamin kept his mind on the reward he was earning.

The body fell into the grave with a thud. Little flakes of loose soil and pebbles dropped in behind it, making scratching sounds along the side of the hole. Candy had already gone to the nearer of the female bodies and was dragging it by the ankles, seemingly unconcerned about the nature of her burden. The slim body dropped in half atop the father's, assuming a grotesque, morbidly erotic position, the legs raised and spread, the patch of pubic hair exposed as though in ghoulish invitation.

Benjamin hiked to where the other girl lay. He made the mistake of looking at her. She lay on her belly, her head turned sharply to the side, revealing her profile. Her mouth was contorted from pressing against the ground, and the flesh of her nose was pushed to one side. Something had already been at her, animal or insect, particularly concentrating on the one eye that was visible. Benjamin wiped his hands on his pants, stalling, and then felt Candy's eyes boring into his back. Bending hastily he grasped the girl's ankles and dragged her toward the grave as quickly as he could. Every bump in the ground seemed to send shivers over the little body, fresh reminders of the nature of the thing he was moving.

Grunting, sweating in spite of the cold, he finally brought the frail corpse to the edge of the grave. The two forms already in it looked like white, nearly shapeless patches in the darkness. Benjamin stopped for a moment, regaining his breath, telling himself that it was ridiculous, that he couldn't possibly be out of breath from dragging this little weight such a short distance. He had dropped the girl's ankles, and went down on his knees to retrieve them. He shoved them out over the empty space and let go, but the body remained where it was, since the major portion of its weight rested on the ground. He worked the fingers of his left hand under one shoulder, the other under a flaccid hip, and shoved. Her hair swirled witchlike as she dropped into the grave with her father and sister. The car's headlights cast his shadow long, on the other side of the hole, and as he glanced up he saw Candy's shadow too, thin and giantesque, turning toward his own.

He looked up quickly, twisting toward her in reflexive panic. She had pulled up her long skirt, clear past her waist, and stood facing him. Her face seemed contorted into a fiendish smile, though that could have been the effect of the weird light. She came closer to him, clucking softly, little sounds that seemed travesties of love crooning.

"Come here, darling," she whispered. The sound was raspy, unnaturally loud in the fastness of the open field.

Benjamin wanted to draw away, but there was something

commanding about her, something perversely erotic. She came so close he could feel the warmth of her thighs, smell her, see the individual strands at the edge of the inverted triangle of her pubic hair.

"Isn't this what you wanted, Benjamin?" she crooned. "Isn't this what you've wanted all along, husband?" Her fingers tangled in his long, kinky hair and pulled his face forward with intense languor.

His face buried itself between her thighs, feeling the scratch of hair, the contrasting smoothness of feminine skin. Without his volition his hands circled her hips, cupping the fullness of her buttocks as they drew her closer, more tightly against him.

Her response was gradual. At first she seemed rigidly passive. Then, slowly, her body flowed against him. Wracking sighs moved through her, followed by gasps and tremors. Her legs spread more widely, inviting him with increased warmth and ardor. She cried out once, twice in little yipping sounds. Vaguely, Benjamin was aware that her right hand had left his head, but he was lost to the act in which they were engaged, nearly beyond thought or awareness. Only gradually did he become aware of the cold hardness of steel against his temple.

He froze, his eyes rolling up questioningly. He could see nothing but her flesh, blurred with closeness. In the last instant he tried to draw away, but the effort was as perfunctory as it was futile. He managed to pull back far enough to catch one last glimpse of her face in the light from the car, a face that had become a mask, trained down at him, grinning in some ecstasy incomprehensible to ordinary people. In the last second of his life his thoughts were strangely peaceful: an acknowledgment of her superiority, an internal recognition that she was stronger than he was, fitter and tougher. Then the tiny bullet punched through his skull, shattering bone and rupturing brain cells, terminating his life in a single, irretrievable instant.

Candy had backed him up to the edge of the grave so that he fell back, his body hanging on the edge, one arm dangling. Tucking the pistol back into the sash she wore under her dress, she tore off his shirt, which was worn thin with use, and then managed to work off his pants and shoes. Finally, puffing a bit with effort, she shoved the limp form unceremoniously into the hole. He dropped across the two girls.

"Good," she said softly, smiling to herself. "You should like that, you horny son of a bitch."

Working with feverish energy, she filled in the grave quickly, tamping down the dirt with the flat of the shovel and examining her handiwork with satisfaction.

"There," she crooned. "All nice and cozy, forevermore." Then, collecting the shovels and the clothing, she returned to the car and began the long drive back to the commune.

CHAPTER 42

Candy Sterling was up for work the next morning as though nothing had happened. She supposed the others in the hut were cognizant of the fact that her husband was gone, and perhaps curious as to his whereabouts. No one mentioned it. Talking was rare in the hut. The new people were still unfamiliar with the rules and routines of the place, and Candy thought she sensed in them a reliance on her for unspoken guidance. They seemed afraid to approach her directly, and Candy deliberately reinforced this reticence by her manner.

The air was already warm, indicating that it would be a scorching day. Candy led the others to the chow line, where they drew their cold breakfast, standing about while they ate it. Then it was time to go to work, and as people finished their meal and straggled into the field to begin the day's labor for the Prophet, Candy, as always, was one of the first.

She was gratified by the rule of silence. She worked steadily, picking the vegetables and stuffing them into a sack, lugging the full sack to the truck and returning to the field with an empty one, scarcely ever raising her head. Throughout the morning she relived the events of the previous night, relishing every incident as a delicacy.

For the moment the Prophet was feeling quite sanguine. The bodies were safely buried. And that intransigent spade had been eliminated. He had complete faith in Candy Sterling; almost as great as the faith she had in him.

As the day wore on, however, he became aware of nagging doubts that had been growing in him from the first. He tried to take his mind off it by playing around with the new girl, but his heart wasn't in it, and finally he sent her scurrying away with orders to summon Sister Candace to his presence.

The grubby little slut was there in six minutes, looking properly nervous. When he looked at her she flushed a deep pink under the layer of dirt that caked her skin. Her fingers, long and slender but cracked and red now, played with her long, shapeless skirt.

"I want you to tell me about last night's events," he said. When she looked a bit surprised and confused he rushed on, "Of course I know all about it, but I want you to tell me with your own lips. It will gain grace for you." He plucked an eight-inch cigar from the humidor beside his bed and toyed with the solid gold lighter.

Candy raised her eyes to his for a moment, and he saw in them a sparkle of excitement, laced with uncertainty. "It was all done as you commanded, Lord," she said, her voice broken with tension. "The bodies are buried safely. All the bodies." The Prophet felt a surge of relief at this news and, momentarily satisfied about the matter of the troublesome corpses, fastened her with a steely eye. "Did you have any trouble with Brother Benjamin?"

"Trouble, Lord? No trouble." She was studiously looking away from him. "I did as you commanded, encouraging him to think I would be his once the job was finished. And he believed it. He did everything just as you said he would."

"But you didn't actually allow him any liberties?" the Prophet asked, suddenly tense and stern.

She hesitated a moment, staring at the hem of her dress, or the thick, clumsy shoes she wore. "No, Lord. I couldn't do such a thing."

"It is very good that you didn't," the Prophet reminded her. "If you had I should have known it, and you would be damned. Your body is a vessel of slime, Sister Candace, hateful in the eyes of the All-Moving Spirit. And to yield to it, to serve it, would be the most depraved of acts."

"Yes, Lord."

She seemed confused, unsure, which was the way he liked to keep his minions. Her discomfort amused him, kept his mind, for the moment, off the matters that still concerned him.

"Do you think that this piece of good work redeems you

from your incompetent execution of my original orders?" he asked in a deliberately unctuous voice. She looked at him quickly, apparently frightened out of her wits. The Prophet felt a delightful surge of power. That was the best part of it, he thought. Not the money or the mansion, or all the ass he could handle. Those things were just the symbols of his power. It was refreshing to own people, to be able to terrify them with a word, a gesture, even by the simple fact of ignoring them. It was refreshing, and it was also arousing.

"I'm not certain I should keep someone around me who is so lax in carrying out tasks I assign," he said, savoring her reaction to each word. He could actually hear her breathing, see her fighting back sobs. "And another thing," he continued. "If I ever summon you into my presence again, clean yourself up. Do you have any idea how unappetizing you look at this moment?"

"I'm sorry, Lord." She was weeping openly, scrubbing the tears away in dirty streaks with the heel of one tiny hand. "I thought you wanted me right away. Sister Penelope said—"

"Don't blame Sister Penelope for your stupidity!" the Prophet snapped with genuine annoyance. He still hadn't lit his cigar, and now he threw it aside angrily. He returned the lighter to its place on the bedside table with an angry thump. "Now go in there and clean yourself up," he roared, indicating the bathroom door. "I won't be subjected to the smell of you!"

He had worked himself up into a minor dither. While the girl was showering he lit a cigar and lay back on his bed, allowing himself to wind down a bit. He was taking out his worries and frustrations on her, which was her function. Perhaps he should give some thought to the notion of getting rid of her as he had got rid of Benjamin. She was the only one left, aside from himself, who knew what had happened, and he could be perfectly safe with her out of the way.

The only problem was that if he didn't want to prolong the problem, he would have to do it personally, and he found that the thought left him strangely squeamish. Aside from that, it was only smart to keep himself away from the dirty work. He wished that fate would intervene in some way and eliminate her for him, but he didn't suppose it would be that easy.

"I'm sorry, Lord, but I only had the clothes I wore when I came in, and they're—"

He looked up and saw her standing naked in the doorway leading from his bathroom. He was surprised at how good she still looked after all the weeks in the fields. Her face and hands and the lower part of her arms were deeply tanned from the sun, but the rest of her remained as white as when he had first seen her. The contrast was rather exciting. Her blond hair hung past her shoulders without the bandana to hold it in place. It was sopping from the shower. It was as though she were emerging from her own bathroom, caught by surprise by a stranger in the house.

"Come here, child," he ordered in tones less stentorian than before but still firmly authoritarian. He could see a nervous tightness about her throat as she scurried to him. When she had come so close that her thighs touched the edge of the bed he jammed out his cigar in the big crystal ashtray next to the humidor and took her hand, pulling her forward casually. She sprawled across him, soft and warm, and for some reason the Prophet found himself inordinately aroused, as he had not been aroused by the fresher, sweeter morsels who peopled his house.

It was a swift coupling, efficient and unceremonious, leaving her breathless and limp. Afterward, because the Prophet felt good about it, he allowed her the luxury of lying next to him for a few minutes, in the crook of his arm. Then he ordered her to lay out a fresh towel and washcloth and adjust the shower for him.

As he lay listening to her scampering about the bathroom the Prophet rethought his intentions. It would be just as well to keep her around. He hadn't found a girl who could really turn him on recently, and for some reason she had got to him. Besides, from all that Brother Benjamin, rest his soul, had said, and from the Prophet's own highly developed instinct, she seemed to be his most fanatical follower.

And fanatics had their uses.

CHAPTER 43

After the disposal of the bodies, and the dispatch of the troublesome Benjamin, Candy had begun to feel rather complacent and virtuous. The encounter with the Prophet on the following day had taught her a lesson which she hoped she would not soon forget. After he had purified her blood she had donned the thick, shapeless clothing once again and returned to the field, where she had worked harder than ever, nearly fainting twice before quitting time. She drove herself through dizziness and pain, relishing the rawness of her hands and the ache of her calves and spine, allowing the sweat to run freely down her face and between her breasts, saturating the grimy dress. Pain was the only real pleasure, she decided, and filth the only true cleanliness, when they were endured in the name of the Prophet.

Despite the prohibition against talking without proper reason, and the general isolation from the outside, the commune was occasionally penetrated by rumors, particularly when new people came in. Candy, the hardest worker in the fields, moving through the rows of vegetables faster than the others, was most likely to hear these stories. It was hardly surprising, therefore, that with the advent of a new girl named Cathy, or Carla, or some such thing, who had been recruited in Los Angeles and put to work in town as a waitress just before joining the farm workers, Candy heard murmurings in the field about the Chambers boy.

Henry Chambers, according to the story, had been given shelter in a county facility for abandoned children. It had all been in the newspapers, the murmurs said. He never left this home except to go, under escort, to the sheriff's office, where he was questioned regarding the disappearance of his father and sisters.

The news filled Candy with an exciting dread. At first she feared, guiltily, that her concern was for her own safety, but after a moment, as she moved down the row plucking the vegetables and stuffing them into her sack, she felt reassured that her dread was for the Prophet. Certainly, if the police traced the extermination of those vermin to her, she would take the blame, but they might find some way to blame it on the Prophet, which would be insupportable.

She didn't know when the plan actually began to form in her mind. Probably from the very first moment that she heard the rumor about Henry Chambers. Likely it was there even before then in embryonic form. At any rate, once it had begun to take conscious form, she thought about nothing else through the dull, repetitive labors of the day or the quick, efficient fueling of her body at noon, or through the long afternoon that followed.

That night, as she lay in her bunk thinking about it, unable to sleep despite her weariness, she slid her hand under the blankets and felt the cold metal of the pistol. Her fingers traced the shape of the barrel with loving gentleness. This, she told herself, would be her chance to prove her devotion to the Prophet.

True devotion consisted not merely of obedience to specific orders. True devotion was voluntary action. This time the Prophet could honestly say that he hadn't given her a hint that he wanted her to take action. It would be her idea, and she would carry it out without his intervention.

She slept sporadically through the night, frequently waking to think again of her plan, to polish it in her mind, cultivate it, perfect it. She stroked the chilled metal of the pistol and smiled in the humid, rank darkness of the hut.

She worked through the next day with her usual vigor, buoyed by the anticipation of the night to come. She even managed to break her record for sacks of vegetables harvested.

That night she fell onto her bed with her shoes on. The others, if they noticed, said nothing. They were asleep before their heads came to rest, as usual. To be certain, Candy lay still for the better portion of an hour before rising. She tucked the pistol into the folds in the back of her dress, as she had done previously, carried the little box containing what was left of her ammunition in her left hand, and left the hut quietly. The couple who shared it slept heavily. With good luck she would be back before dawn, and they would never even realize that she had left.

The farm looked strange, almost lurid, in the moonlight. After the brilliant light of day there was an odd cast to the huts, the grounds, and the Prophet's house in this contrast of white light and black shadows. It was like an old photograph.

The garage was unlocked, as always, and the small car had the keys inside. Before starting the engine she fished out her pistol and loaded it full, even placing a cartridge in the chamber. Being careful to engage the safety, she deposited the gun in the folds of her dress once again and placed the ammunition box on the seat beside her.

Here I come, turkey, she thought with glee. Ready or not.

CHAPTER 44

Candy was rusty in her driving, which had never been all that good. Her sense of direction was less than unerring too, so she wasn't surprised when, the moment she left the farm, she got lost. She was surprised, however, when the cop turned up on her tail.

She supposed he had been put there to watch the place, and that he would stop her soon. She was right on both counts. She hadn't gone more than a mile when the red and blue lights filled her vehicle with their pulsing glow. She felt her heart sink, realizing that she would have to stop. She hadn't a jot of ID on her, and her appearance would invite suspicion, giving him just the excuse he needed to take her into custody. Technically the car was stolen, and there was no way she could explain that without worsening matters. If she wasn't prepared to take appropriate action right away, she would fail the Prophet again.

Pulling to the side of the road, she stopped the car, putting it in neutral and keeping the engine running. She set the brake, but then, as an afterthought, quietly released it. The police car pulled up behind her, its lights still flashing. In the side-view mirror she saw the door open, saw the burly officer step out and approach her car. Candy eased her pistol out from its place in her dress and slipped off the safety. She saw the cop unsnap his holster and felt a purely physical thrill of apprehension. He was within ten feet of her door. She rolled down the window.

With oily smoothness she thrust the little pistol out the window and fired. The sound of the gun was thin but surprisingly loud in the country night air. The cop reeled, grasping at the fleshy part of his left shoulder, but he didn't go down. Candy had never shot anyone before except helpless victims, and in her innocence of such matters she had grossly overestimated the destructive power of a .22 Long Rifle cartridge fired from a four-inch-barreled pistol.

Flustered, she pulled the gun back inside the car and jammed her foot on the accelerator before she even had it in gear. The car screeched, careening across the narrow road before she had control of it. Barely avoiding the ditch beside the pavement, she managed to aim the vehicle down the road just as the cop cleared his holster.

Some instinct prompted her to douse the lights just as he opened fire. The heavy revolver roared with incredible violence, and in the mirror she saw its flash, awesome in the night. Something slammed into the trunk deck so hard she felt the impact. The cop fired again, missing, and then managed to send a bullet through the rear window. It punched a webbed hole there and smacked the windshield, cracking that as well. It was his last shot, either because he had decided that more would be useless or because he had finally succumbed to the wound she had inflicted. The distance had opened to a considerable amount. She could still see the lights on his patrol car flashing distantly, and as she took the first turn she wondered whether it would have been more sensible to have backed up the car and run him over.

She found the city limits forty-five minutes later. Whether the cop had managed to radio in a description of the car she didn't know, but she didn't relish the notion of plodding around town afoot, so she decided to chance it. She also decided that they weren't going to take her alive.

Her luck turned good finally. She found the facility in which the Chambers boy was held in less than half an hour, looking it up in a telephone book in a service station phone booth. She parked the car two blocks away and hiked there after replacing the cartridge she had fired. There were still some cartridges in the box, so she took them along.

The place was surrounded by a Cyclone fence twelve feet high. Candy put away her gun, securing it carefully under the sash about her waist. But she couldn't find any way to secure the ammunition on her person so she thrust it through one of the openings in the fence. The place was almost totally dark, so she couldn't see the ammunition box once she let go of it.

Scaling the fence wasn't easy in her clumsy shoes, but it turned out to be less difficult than she had supposed. Her voluminous dress snagged on the top and tore when she let herself down the first few feet. It took several minutes to find the ammunition. She almost gave it up once, before remembering that she had signed for the box of cartridges. She didn't know whether there was any way to trace it to her, but it was worth some effort to eliminate the possibility. Finally she moved off toward a darkened hulk of a building on the other end of the grounds. She seemed to be on some sort of athletic field, stumbling over uneven ground.

It hadn't occurred to her to wonder how she would find the Chambers kid once she had got there. The building was long and low, with screened windows at even spaces. The windows were high enough off the ground so that even standing on tiptoe she had trouble seeing inside. There were beds in the rooms, two or three in each, and bodies in the beds, but it was impossible to make them out. She wasn't even certain, now that she thought of it, that she could recognize the Chambers boy if she saw him in daylight.

The foolishness of her errand dawned on her, and she considered turning back. The Prophet would be furious with her over what she had done, the damage to the car and the fact that she had shot a policeman, but there was no helping it now.

"Who's there?"

The voice wrung a startled gasp from Candy, bringing her around quickly. She raised the gun from acquired instinct. A dozen yards away a man's form, barely perceivable in the night, took a hesitant step toward her. Then a flashlight snapped on, the beam sliding up her bosom to shine full in her face. It glinted off the dark, worn metal of the pistol. "Jesus!" The man vanished through the door from which he had emerged.

For a moment Candy stood, bewildered, irresolute. Then she turned back to the athletic field and the fence over which she had entered the place. She seemed helpless, like a creature caught in an alien medium, unable to move quickly. Her shoes weighed ten pounds apiece.

She was halfway up the fence when she dropped the ammunition. In her haste she had forgotten that she was still holding the box in her hand. The gun was safely tucked away, but she heard the tiny cartridges spill as the box struck the ground. Then, as she continued to scramble for the top, she felt the gun slip from her sash. First it slipped far enough to hang up on the butt. Then, as she let go of the fence with one hand to make a grab for it, the gun dropped to the dark ground below. She stopped where she was, prepared to return to the ground and look for it, when a light fell on her.

"Hey! There!" a sharp, masculine voice called out, and another light struck her.

Candy froze like an animal at bay, confused, unsure. Then she remembered her earlier resolve not to be taken alive, not to be used against the Prophet. She let go of the fence, trying to push herself away. Her dress caught on the mesh, yanking up hard as she fell. It held for a moment. Candy hung by the thick wool skirt, thrashing wildly. Then the cloth tore with a loud popping sound, dumping her to the ground on one shoulder and the side of her head.

CHAPTER 45

The desk sergeant took an immediate dislike to the visitor. There was no reason for it that he could identify. The man looked to be in his thirties. He was well groomed and dressed in a very expensive-looking dark three-piece suit with a narrow stripe, and a shirt that looked like silk. His shoes glowed with well-bred softness as he approached the desk. He had the bearing of a man who is accustomed to being heeded.

There was just something that the desk sergeant had seen before, and had learned to identify without defining. There was a deep, restive look in the man's eyes, somewhere behind the normal attentiveness. The body seemed compressed like some contorted spring, though outwardly it was relaxed enough. The sergeant had seen a look not unlike that in men who had gone round the bend, and while the feeling he got from this chap wasn't precisely the same, it wasn't precisely different either.

"I should like to post bail," the man said in carefully enunciated tones.

The desk sergeant ran his fingertip along the edge of some papers he was holding, stalling to take in this man's aura just a bit longer before replying. "Bail for who, sir?" he asked finally.

The man hesitated, his lips pursing in cryptic displeasure, as though he wished to correct something but felt it would be imprudent. "Miss Sterling," he said finally.

The sergeant put down the papers and looked at the man in thinly disguised amazement. Of all the prisoners in the place, that girl was the last one he would have connected with this fellow. For a moment he wondered if she could be his daughter, decided the man was too young. "Mind telling me what your connection with her is, Mr. . . . ?"

"Hartford," the visitor replied a touch nervously. "I—I am her pastor."

The desk sergeant recalled having heard that a car found near the county facility in which the girl had been arrested had been traced to that bunch of crazies outside town. The car had been shot up, and it answered the description turned in by an officer who had been shot the night before out in that area, and who stated that he had returned fire and was certain he had hit the vehicle.

"Would you mind taking a seat, Mr. Hartford?" he offered, indicating the bench against the far wall. "It will take a few minutes to arrange matters." Hartford glanced around at the bench, looked at the sergeant as though he had been trapped in some manner, then nodded and strode to the opposite side of the room. The sergeant picked up the receiver on his intercom and punched the button for the brains division.

Five minutes later a tall, thin man with stooped shoulders, a nose that had been broken and set in a careless fashion, and an empty basket-weave holster riding his hip approached the bench on which Immanuel Hartford roosted.

"Mr. Hartford?" he asked in a voice that was surprisingly smooth and gentle, given his appearance. Manny rose. "Would you step into my office for a moment, sir?"

The office was small, equipped with a worn wooden desk, a four-drawer file on which rested a coffee-making machine with a half-filled pot, and a thinly padded wooden armchair facing the desk. The detective offered the chair and a Styrofoam cup of coffee to Manny, who accepted the former.

"My name is Lieutenant Baker, sir," the detective informed him. "The desk sergeant tells me that you are Candace Sterling's pastor?"

Manny nodded, wishing he had stayed on the farm. All this had seemed sensible at the time it had occurred to him, but that had been before he had seen these men with their blank, courteous expressions and penetrating eyes.

"Subsequent to Miss Sterling's arrest," the lieutenant said, "a car was found nearby which has since been traced to you, sir. A beige Pinto coupe." His expression seemed to invite reply.

"Yes, that car is mine. Registered to me, that is."

"Were you aware that Miss Sterling had taken the vehicle?"

"No!" He had said that too quickly, Manny realized. He was going to have to be more careful.

"Pardon me, Mr. Hartford, but are you connected with the religious commune north of here?"

"I founded it," Manny said, a note of pride creeping into his voice.

"And Miss Sterling is one of your—followers?"

"That's right, but—"

"Any idea where she could have gotten hold of a .22 automatic?"

Manny had expected something of the sort to be asked, but the swiftness of the question, the rapid change of subject, and the flatness of Baker's tone conspired to catch him by surprise. The lieutenant had a poker player's eyes, and they bored into Manny at the moment. He fought down an urge to fidget.

"You mean a pistol?" he asked innocently.

Baker nodded.

"Why, no. She must have had it when she came to us."

"There's no registration on the gun that we've been able to find. We're still checking Hawaii and Alaska. So we don't know how she came into possession of it."

"May I ask the full extent of the charges against Miss Sterling?"

"At the moment we have breaking and entering, illegal entry onto county property, and carrying a concealed weapon. Since she took that Pinto without your permission, I guess we can add grand theft auto."

"Oh, no," Manny said quickly. "The car—well, I consider it the property of the commune, and as Miss Sterling is a member—"

"Well, that's up to you."

"What would the bail come to?"

"We'll have to wait for a judge to decide that."

"Don't you have a schedule or something?"

Lieutenant Baker nodded.

"All the charges I just listed for you are on the schedule," he said. "But there is also the little matter of carrying a weapon into a county facility, which is a felony in this state. Not to mention assault with a deadly weapon." Manny sat staring at the man, stunned. "You see, a woman driving that car shot a deputy last night just a little while before Miss Sterling was apprehended. I'm afraid your car got shot up a bit."

"I can't believe Miss Sterling would do such a thing." Manny was aware of a sheen of sweat on his forehead.

"Well, that's up to the D.A. and a judge and jury. There's also the matter of the Chambers family."

Manny fought an urge to take out his handkerchief and mop his brow. "What possible connection could there be?" he asked, careful to keep his tone flat, his cadence measured. "The Chamberses left my commune weeks ago."

"And vanished without a trace not long after," Baker reminded him, those dead poker eyes still locked in. "And last night Miss Sterling broke into the county facility where Henry Chambers is kept. She had a gun on her, a gun which has definitely been identified as the one which fired the bullet into that officer's shoulder. Do you know of any animosity between her and the Chamberses?"

The man had the damnedest disconcerting habit of pulling questions out of left field, Manny thought; but at least this time he had been aware of it, and so better able to conceal his agitation. He pretended to ponder the matter while the agate eyes of the lieutenant trained on him.

"No, I can't think of any incidents," he said. "Of course, I can't know everything that goes on. You understand that I have over a hundred followers in my commune."

"It's good of you to take such an interest in Miss Sterling."

"I should be remiss if I did any less," Manny said with a modest smile. "Well, if I can't post bail for her, may I at least visit Miss Sterling?"

The lieutenant considered the request for a moment. Manny was certain he was going to demur, but finally he nodded. "Since you're her pastor, I don't suppose I can refuse her a religious visitation. But I'll have to limit you to fifteen minutes, Mr. Hartford."

"That should be ample," Manny said, and then blushed. "I mean, that will have to do. I merely want to comfort the poor girl, and to assure her of our prayers and support."

"Yeah, well, she's going to need both."

A matron brought her into the visiting room ten minutes later. She was wearing a gray dress apparently issued her by the authorities. She was clean and scrubbed, and her hair, freshly shampooed, hung to her shoulders. She was really a pretty woman, Manny decided. Even after all those weeks of drudgery in the fields she was beautiful. A shame she had got herself into this, and ruined everything not only for herself but for him as well.

Apparently they hadn't told her the identity of her visitor, because the moment she saw Manny she stopped and stared at him through the mesh screen as though stunned. The matron grasped her arm just above the elbow and urged her forward none too gently. Candy walked to the chair across from the one in which Manny sat, without glancing at her escort. The matron lowered herself into a chair next to the door. There were no other visitors, so as long as they kept their voices low they wouldn't be overheard.

"Sit down, dear," Manny said, and she pulled out the chair and perched on the edge of it as though she had expected to stand through the visit. She seemed nervous to find herself sitting in his presence. "You seem to have got yourself into trouble by going off on this alone," Manny said in a mildly reproving tone. She hung her head contritely. "You no doubt meant well, child," he continued. "But it was foolish and wicked of you to act without my direction." Tears began to spill from her wide blue eyes. "Now you could be the cause of trouble to the movement," he said, and she glanced up at him quickly, then lowered her gaze once again. The tears were flowing in earnest now. "What have you told them?" he asked, hoping that his tone wasn't too anxious. She didn't look up at him this time, nor did she reply except for a shrug. Her tiny body shook convulsively, and he had the impression that she didn't trust her voice. "You must answer me, Candy," he said firmly. She choked and made a distinct sobbing noise, glancing nervously at the matron, who was watching the scene with veiled intensity.

"I ha—ven't to—old them any—anything, Lord," she hiccuped, still staring at the worn surface of the table.

Manny felt a momentary burst of relief. "Well, you mustn't," he said. "And if they appoint you an attorney, you mustn't talk to him, either. It would be sinful to do so. Do you understand?" He injected enough firmness into his voice to give her a good scare.

She blanched so badly he thought he might have overdone it, but she suddenly looked at him, and there was something unreadable in her eyes. "No, I won't tell them anything," she said slowly. "Not anyone. You can count on me."

"Good. Good. Now listen to me. They suspect you of the Chambers thing as well." He had expected some reaction from her, but she just sat there staring at him. An uncanny calm seemed to have fallen over her, and she had stopped crying. The tears were drying, leaving her face streaked and her eyes red and swollen. "They have nothing to go on," he said, forcing himself to look into those suddenly stony eyes. "And I doubt that they will, since everything is— disposed of. But if they should come up with some kind of evidence, then you must—must—never intimate to them that I have any connection with any of it. You can see how evil that would be. Can't you?" His voice had risen just a bit, so that the matron sat up a bit more stiffly. Manny was aware of a touch of shrillness in his tone, and fought to control it. "Now, I am going to post bail for you, so you'll be out of here very soon," he assured her. "I offered to get you out today, but they tell me that I'll have to wait until after your hearing. The judge has to set bail, they said."

"That's all right," Candy said. From that unnatural calm she had moved to a subtle kind of agitation, as though she were waiting for some vague, horrid occurrence, and suspected that it had already happened. "I've been in jail before, Lord. It doesn't bother me."

"Yes, well, that's fine." Manny produced his solid gold pocket watch, checked the time, and replaced it in his vest pocket, carefully adjusting the chain across his midriff. "I'll attend your hearing," he promised, rising. "I see our time is up for now. But I'll be there, and I'll have you out and free that afternoon."

She hadn't risen, but sat looking up at him blankly. Her eyes unsettled him, reminding him of something he couldn't place at first. Then he realized that she looked rather like that lieutenant who had spoken to him earlier.

CHAPTER 46

He felt strength and confidence flowing into him as he entered the farm. It was like a transfusion. Even before he crossed the property line he could feel the difference, and as he drove down the lane, across the verdant, productive fields, it grew stronger with each revolution of the car's wheels. His people were out in the fields, working hard to enrich him. His slaves. Here he was safe, secure, powerful. It was a pity to have to leave it, but he would be a fool to stay around now. He supposed.

Pulling up in front of the mansion, he cut the engine and slid out. It was growing hot as midday approached, and he wanted to get into the air-conditioned house. One of his lackeys ran up to take the car into the garage for him, and he ignored the man, feeling his silk shirt wilt in the muggy air. A pity there was no way to air-condition the space between the car and the house. Perhaps he should have a connecting garage.

Sister Penelope was in the front room, supervising a couple of handmaidens, watching them with such obvious acuity that they seemed ridden with self-consciousness. She turned at the sound of the door, looked through the archway at him, and gave a little curtsy.

"Bring a cold drink into my library," he ordered curtly, and moved on without awaiting her acknowledgment.

By the time she made it into the library with the cooler he had spread out his papers and was poring over them avidly. Sister Penelope set the drink on the edge of his desk and began a quiet departure. Manny looked up and cleared his throat. When she turned, he just looked at her for a moment and she got the message, standing awaiting his pleasure. He clawed loose his tie and shrugged his coat back over his shoulders to let it slide down between his back and the chair. He examined his records closely, sipping the cooler from time to time.

Things weren't bad. It was well up in the millions now, almost all of it safely locked away in safe-deposit boxes or deposited in numbered accounts in Switzerland. It wasn't as much as he would have liked, not by half, but it would do. He could pull up stakes within a week, board a plane for Europe, and live a decently prosperous life. Sighing, he picked up the drink and leaned back, glancing finally at Sister Penelope.

She suddenly seemed incredibly alluring in her tiny skirt and spike-heeled shoes, standing there stiffly, waiting for him to tell her what he wanted or to give her leave. He scrutinized her until she began to fidget just a bit. Since the day he had leveled his cryptic threat at her she had been even more attentive to his needs, more eager to please, more anxious in his presence.

Lacing his fingers across his vest, Manny shoved his chair back from the desk with his feet. "Come here," he commanded in a quiet, laconic voice. She moved as though propelled by a hidden spring, coming around the desk and within reach. He took her wrist in his hand and pulled her forward, unzipping his fly with his free hand. In a moment she was astraddle, her shapely legs laced through the openings under the arms of the chair. He made it quick, wringing a cry of pleasure from her in seconds and finishing up for himself shortly after. She clung to him limply, her arms twined around his neck, her face against his. He slipped his hands over the roundness of her buttocks for a moment, then let them drop.

"Now get out," he ordered quietly.

He went into the adjoining bathroom and showered. When he returned to the library a fresh suit of clothing awaited him, draped over the back of the couch. After donning it, he returned to the desk and glanced at his papers some more, sipped his drink, which had become watery from the melting ice, and decided to brave the heat a bit.

He had come to love the stink of the shacks, and it was a treat to see the boobs working their hearts out for his betterment. He could feel their awareness of his presence, their nervousness at the nearness of divinity. As though he might open up the ground under their feet and drop them into perdition. He did an unaccustomed thing, going directly out into the field, pausing from time to time to look directly at one of his minions. They all reacted identically, cowering slightly, grinning in a sheepish manner as though he had caught them slacking off, increasing their pace. Awareness of him spread like a shock wave in all directions. It was palpable, their desperate hope that he wouldn't pick one of them for his individual scrutiny. Terrified that he might find them unworthy to break their backs for him.

He walked on through the field, ignoring them now, moving to the opposite edge of the plot, his back to the peasants. Still, he could sense their consciousness of him, almost smell their anxiety.

It was the power, he thought sadly. That was what it was all about: to own people, to do with them as he wished, to degrade them and to make them degrade themselves. That was the real prize. The money, any amount of money, could never substitute for the power. How could he give it up, having enjoyed it for so long? How could anyone expect him to give it up? Out there, with whatever amount of money, he would just be Manny Hartford, a little man among so many little men. Here, in this place, he wasn't Manny Hartford at all. He was the Prophet.

The solution to the predicament was simple, once he focused his full intellect on it. That girl. That stupid, insane girl. She had done so much for him, gone so far. Now she would just have to go a little further. She had killed for him.

Now she would have to die for him.

CHAPTER 47

Guilt was an old friend to Candy Sterling. She had lived with it all her life, most of the time unaware of its hovering presence. As a Christian she had been attracted to the recognition of guilt, and the doctrine of its universality. It was the serene forgiveness that had driven her away, and that flaw had not been present in the worship of the Prophet. For the first time her natural proclivity for guilt had been encouraged totally, and she had responded with pathetic gratitude, even more so than her fellow worshipers. The Prophet's ruthlessness, and the strength she saw in his cruelty, had drawn her to him irresistibly, had made her an ecstatic slave. Like most people at the commune she had seen him as omniscient and omnipotent. To obey him was the only virtue, and the only hope of salvation. To doubt him would be intolerable.

And so the doubts she had been suffering for the past days were the worst trial of her life, and brought an insecurity and a species of guilt that she couldn't bear.

It had begun when he had demanded to know whether she had allowed Benjamin any sexual privileges on the night of his demise. She had lied reflexively, fearful of his wrath, but when he had reminded her that had she granted Benjamin liberties he would have known of it, she had felt a tinge of confusion and doubt, which she had hastily buried. The fact that he had not known instantly of her transgression was more horrifying than any punishment he might have visited upon her for it, and so she had had to forget it.

But it was harder to forget his performance in the county jail's visiting room. It had never entered Candy's mind to betray him. She would have undergone torture without bringing his name into the matter. That she would take the full blame for all the deeds she had performed in his name was taken for granted. The fear he had shown, the signs of weakness, had shocked her. And she had been able to think of nothing else since that day.

The hearing was short. The judge heard the charges and set the bail at twenty thousand dollars. The Prophet, who sat in the rear of the courtroom, came forward with some cashier's checks, offering to post the bail. The matron who had brought Candy in from her cell escorted her back to the jail, where she was given her clothing. She had had no other belongings except for the pistol, which had been confiscated as evidence, so she only had to sign for the bulky dress and shoes. When she had changed back into those garments she was told by a brusque officer that she was free to go. She found her way to the street and then to the front of the courthouse. After waiting for a moment she went inside.

The Prophet was waiting in front of the courtroom. Spotting her, he moved to her side quickly. "My car is outside," he informed her, smiling in a charming manner that gave Candy an unsettled feeling.

"Yes, Lord," she murmured, lowering her gaze and going with him obediently.

He was silent until they were out of town. Then, looking at her with an engaging smile, he reached across the width of the car and squeezed her knee.

Candy felt a sudden, reflexive urge to draw away, but she caught it in time and smiled at him.

"I've been thinking," he said, "that it's time I changed my personnel about a bit. Sister Penelope has been chief hand-maiden far too long. She's come to take the position for granted." Candy looked at him, wondering if he was actually going to say what she expected. "How would you like the job?" he asked. There was a subtle air of nervousness about him, as though he were carrying through on bluff.

Candy felt a stab of panic. She couldn't be right! It sounded as though he were bribing her, placating her! "Whatever you think, Lord," she murmured.

"Yes, well, I think you'd be excellent for the position. You have proved yourself to be very devoted to my welfare."

"Thank you, Lord."

The praise made her uncomfortable. She told herself that it was all her imagination, that she was a wicked girl to harbor such doubts about the Prophet and his motives, but the doubts persisted. She had expected nothing better than to go back to her hut and work for him in the fields until her trial and her stint in prison.

As usual she felt out of place in the big house in her baggy, dirty clothes. The routine of the jail had included regular showers, which had finally rid her of the caked-in dirt that had seemed to be a permanent part of her anatomy after weeks in the fields. The Prophet led her to the library and then summoned Sister Penelope. She materialized in seconds, a bit breathless, as though she had run from another level of the house, and nervous as though she had an inkling of what was about to happen. When she saw Candy her agitation waxed manifestly stronger. She smiled ingratiatingly at the Prophet, who faced her from halfway across the big room.

"I have decided," he said without preamble, "that you are to work for the cause in a different capacity in future." He paused, apparently waiting for his words to take their effect. Sister Penelope seemed to wither slightly, to shrink within herself. The Prophet seemed simultaneously to expand, as though puffing up from something he had drained from her spirit.

He glanced dartingly in Candy's direction, and she realized suddenly that this was partly for her benefit, that she was supposed to be enjoying her moment of triumph. Instead she felt pity and contempt for Penelope. She wasn't certain just what she felt for the Prophet. Her attitude toward him seemed to have taken residence behind some sort of wall, obscured even from her.

"You have grown lax in your duties," the Prophet continued.

For the first time Candy seemed to detect something false and vain in his tone, as though he were in love with the sound of his own voice, and particularly with its effect on others. The more Sister Penelope shrank and quivered, the more he seemed to inflate.

"You will take Sister Candace's place in the fields," he said, his voice growing almost stentorian. "And in her quarters.

Sister Candace, who has proved herself my most devoted disciple, will take your place here in the house. Is that clear?"

Sister Penelope mumbled something in broken, muffled tones. She had lowered her head, but Candy was certain she saw the gleam of tears. She felt disgust for the girl, though she wasn't certain why.

"Answer!" the Prophet bellowed, taking a step closer to Penelope.

She stepped back reflexively, raised her gaze to meet his for an instant. "Y—yes, Lord," she stammered.

"Take Sister Candace to the servants' quarters and find some garb fitting to her station," the Prophet commanded. "And some garb fitting to yours."

CHAPTER 48

In the following week Candy accustomed herself to her new post. It was easy work after the drudgery of the field, entailing no physical exertion at all. As the chief handmaiden she was expected to supervise the chores of the other girls, not to join in them. She found herself prey to a vague anxiety. Her back had grown accustomed to stooping, her hands to toiling constantly. It was as though her muscles and nerves had learned, had taken on a life and preferences of their own. She paced about the house, issuing curt orders and acrimonious criticisms until the girls learned to fear her tread even more than they had that of Sister Penelope.

Candy couldn't even feel any satisfaction at having displaced the girl who had lorded it over her with such relish. She had thought of Sister Penelope as a symbol of her guilt, an engine of the Prophet's purgation. She had never liked the girl, had even resented her, but to see her brought low, and herself, so clearly unworthy, moved into her place, was fearful.

Most awe-inspiring of all was the Prophet's sudden attentiveness. He called her into his presence often, on various pretexts or on occasion without rationale, talked to her of inconsequentials, and frequently purified her blood. She felt a new, creeping guilt because his actions seemed so transparently designed to secure her loyalty, loyalty which he should have taken for granted. This was a species of guilt new to her, one which she couldn't handle since it led her ineluctably to the suspicion that he wasn't what he was supposed to be, and what she had serenely assumed that he was.

Concentrating on her job, becoming outwardly even more fanatical in her adherence to the doctrine of the Prophet's divinity, Candy tried to bury her doubts, telling herself that she was even more wicked than she had suspected, else why would she harbor suspicions against her Lord and Savior? The one thing she had never been was a doubter.

There was no attempt to secure counsel for her, much less prepare a defense. Candy assumed that once the time came for the trial the Prophet would simply have her plead guilty and take her rap. Until one day more than two weeks after her release on bail, she had no slight suspicion of his actual intentions.

On that morning he had driven himself into town, an uncommon occurrence, and had seemed rather nervous upon his return. When he called her into his library, Candy felt her misgivings wax stronger than ever. She didn't like facing him because it rendered her doubts more difficult to inter. Entering the library, she gave him the customary curtsy. He was standing at the bar, pouring himself a double-and-a-half shot of bourbon. He spun about at her entrance as though taken by surprise by a potential enemy. The whiskey sloshed over the rim of his glass and ran down in little droplets onto his fingers. He smiled a bit sheepishly, she thought, and transferred the glass to his other hand so that he could lick his fingers. Then he took a careful sip of the bourbon and advanced on her. For some reason Candy felt a powerful urge to draw back at his approach, but it manifested itself in nothing more than a mild sway of her body. His arm circled her shoulders and he kissed her on the mouth. She could taste the whiskey on his breath. It was a pleasant flavor, but somehow it brought home to her his humanity. She had never thought about that before, taking his divinity for granted even when he lay atop her, grunting with pleasure, his eyeballs bulging and that vein in his forehead distended, as she had seen so many times. Ringing her tiny waist with his arm, he led her toward the couch. She followed, managing to hide her reluctance.

"You've been doing an excellent job here, Candy," he said before taking another swig of liquor.

"Thank you, Lord." Something deep in Candy, some sense she could not have explained even to herself, warned her. The Prophet's manner was subtly unctuous, evasively placatory. It made her stomach knot up, not only because it was out of the character he had forged for himself, and which all of them, especially Candace Sterling, had accepted as incontrovertibly accurate, but for some other, more immediately ominous reason that she couldn't define. It was like the times, early in her career as a hooker, when she had cruised a cop and known it after the first seconds. Now, as then, her own compulsive nature carried her forward against the counsel of her glands.

"I've been thinking," he continued, looking studiously ahead, his brow creased in a consciously ordered frown, "about those little jobs you did for me." Sinking to the couch, he drew her down beside him.

Candy could feel his thigh against her own, and for the first time felt no tingle of excitement. The knot in her stomach had tautened to the point of genuine pain.

"It isn't likely that anyone will find the—residue of that work," he said, placing his drink on the end table. The whiskey had run down the side of the glass, and would leave a ring there, she thought. But he seemed unaware, as he usually was of such things. There were others around to take care of such matters.

With a curious inner start Candy became aware of a waxing resentment of this man, and she wondered how long it had been growing in her. The awareness of it gave her a desperate sinking feeling.

"No, not likely," he repeated. "But possible. And neither of us would want that to happen, eh, Candy?" He paused long enough for her to realize that he intended her to reply.

"No, Lord," she said.

With a smile meant to be reassuring he laid a hand on her bare thigh, squeezing the flesh lightly. Candy felt just a tinge of conditioned arousal at the touch of his hand, but the heaviness in her stomach didn't recede a bit.

"I don't think it would be wise to move—things—at present," he continued. "But one never knows when it might prove advisable to do so." Pausing, he took a sip of his drink. There seemed to be a little catch in his voice, as though he were extremely nervous. Candy wanted to flee from him and from her feelings, but she sat rooted to the couch, fascinated as she was terrified. His hand slid up her thigh, raising the hem of her skirt.

"Yes, Lord, it might prove so," she said, glancing at him from the corner of her eye.

"And we don't know that you will be here when that time comes," he said.

"No. We don't."

"I think it might be prudent, therefore, if you showed me where those items are stored."

"I—Yes, Lord," she said, lowering her gaze. She felt that the realization of what he intended was on the perimeter of her mind now, and that if she allowed herself to focus on it she would know. But she didn't want to know.

"Tonight," he said, "when the other girls are asleep, you and I shall drive to that place, so you can show me the exact spot."

"There will be a girl—"

"I've thought of that," he said. "You will relieve the night maiden yourself and send her to her cot. That way no one need know that you and I have left the house, let alone the grounds." His hand slid her skirt up farther, exposing her genitals. Leaning toward her, he pushed her back and to the side until she came to rest in a reclining position. She felt his hand slide between their bodies and knew that he was unzipping his fly. He paused then, and Candy felt a tension in his body. She couldn't see his face, which was averted. His hand moved in a slow, repetitive motion. She wasn't certain of what he was doing, but she had an idea. The hand grasped her crotch, manipulating her. There seemed an air of desperation in his actions. For just an instant she felt his organ lying against her, flaccid and helpless. Then he drew away, adjusting himself. He slid to the end of the couch, staring straight ahead, studiously avoiding her eyes. His body was rigid as he picked up his whiskey and tossed it off in one gulp.

Candy, who had lain without moving through all of this, rose, brushing her skirt into order. Taking the empty glass from his hand, she moved to the bar, refilled it, and returned to him. "I'll return to my duties now," she said in a low, succinct voice. "With your consent, Lord."

CHAPTER 49

Candy encountered no trouble in leading the Prophet directly to the spot of the executions. Throughout her life she had been plagued by a sense of direction so bad as to amount to bewilderment, but tonight for some reason her mind was possessed of a Kodachrome clarity. Without missing a turn, without any of the musing that usually accompanied such a chore, she gave him directions in a clear, concise tone, even calling on him to slow the car a quarter mile before they were to turn off onto the dirt road. She checked the odometer out of curiosity and found that it was exactly a quarter of a mile. That elicited a smile of self-approval.

He eased the car down the bumpy dirt road, climbing over each hillock and carefully driving through the ruts and clefts. Unlike Brother Benjamin, he didn't turn off the headlights. Candy couldn't decide whether that was foolish or courageously defiant. Perhaps, a residue of her former piety advised, it was simple confidence in his invincibility.

"There," she said, pointing to the side, past his nose. He hit the brakes a bit too hard, throwing her against the dash, then smiled apologetically and turned down the pathway she had shown him. With mounting excitement Candy saw the open space surrounded by the little swelling of the ground, the spot, now somewhat grown over with weeds, where she had buried Benjamin and the Chamberses. It brought back those two nights, the intense, even painful arousal she had felt during the act of killing, the stark terror the old man and his two daughters had shown, the look of dumb surprise mingled with the beginning of horror on Benjamin's face just before she had blown his brains all over the place.

The Prophet pulled to a stop and set the brake. Laying his hand comfortably on her knee, he smiled. Since that afternoon, when he had seemed so unsettlingly nervous, a cold calm seemed to have settled on him. "I'll want you to show me the exact spot, of course," he told her, opening his door before she could reply.

Candy slid out on her side, leaving the door open so that the dome light cast a weird glow over the scene. She walked the few yards from the car to the burial place with difficulty, her spike-heeled shoes threatening to turn an ankle with each step. The cold of the night bit into her bare thighs as she stopped in the middle of the obscure mound and turned to face him. He stood two yards distant, looking almost ridiculously inappropriate in his expensive suit.

What a sight we must be, Candy thought—she in her blue cocktail waitress's uniform, as it had always seemed to her, and he in his custom-tailored suit.

"Is this the exact place?" he asked, taking a tentative step toward her.

She stood facing him, neither totally conscious nor completely unaware of the expression of defiance on her face. "Yes, Lord," she replied, an almost vampish lilt to her voice. "I'm standing right over the corpses."

"All right."

The words were superfluous, just something to take the ringing out of the night air. Candy felt the excitement flooding through her, making her legs tingle and her skin rise in gooseflesh to a greater degree than the cold had already done. He came another step closer, this time with greater resolution. It only made him look more imperfectly human in her eyes, because in him there should be no need for courage or determination. She was his property. She had decided that months back. An expression she had heard somewhere once jumped into her mind: the moment of truth.

This was where she found out once and for all whether he was what he had claimed to be, whether he was worth all the things she had done in his name, all the things she had learned about herself. When he was just three feet away his hand slipped behind him, dipping into the hip pocket of his pants.

The little gun was nickel plated and gleamed in the moonlight as he drew it and brought it to bear.

He's going to do it, she thought with a flood of gratitude and a touch of her old worshipfulness. He's strong enough to do it. Just as the narrow muzzle came into sight she fell to her knees, relishing the roughness of the ground, the gouging of a pebble into her left knee. Making it easier for him, and to show her acceptance of his will, Candy lowered her head, looking at the toes of his deeply polished shoes. Her hair dropped around her face, obscuring the sight. As from a distance she heard a pair of dull clicks as he cocked the hammer. Closing her eyes, she waited for him to do it.

She waited for what seemed ages, waited for the blast of the little gun, the destruction she had accepted at his hands. Finally she raised her head, brushing back her hair.

He stood there as before, his body arched back slightly as though he were unconsciously pulling away from the act he had ordained for himself. The pistol was pointed roughly in the direction of her face, though it trembled so wildly that half the time it seemed that were it to fire it would miss her by a foot. She saw, as she had not previously observed, that the gun had not one but two muzzles.

She shifted her attention back to the Prophet, who stood there, both hands clamped about the grip of the pistol, his face bathed in sweat. As she stared up at him, little noises began to issue from his throat. Whimpering sounds that wracked his entire body. They disgusted Candy. The fright she had felt before at signs of weakness in him were curiously absent now. With easy, lissome grace, Candy rose to her feet.

She didn't even have to help herself up with her hand, or stumble or gasp. It was as though her body had become light and buoyant suddenly, or her muscles stronger without her consciousness. She faced the little man before her. The ground on which she stood was slightly higher than that on which he stood, and so she looked down into his eyes, which seemed to plead with her to make it easy for him.

"Can't you do it?" she asked softly, gently. "It's easy. It's really so easy. Here." Reaching out one slender, graceful hand, Candy lifted the pistol from his grasp. She brought it up level with her face, looked into the inscrutable, unblinking muzzles. Easy, she thought. It was always so easy. Then she turned the pistol around and fired it twice into his midriff.

The expression on his face was shocked, but gently so, as though he had half expected this; admonitory but apologetic, as though he realized how and why and when he had given up the right to command her; and relieved, as though she had exorcised something that had haunted him for a long time.

Candy fell to a crouching position, stroking his hair gently for a moment. His eyes had glazed, and she closed them with her thumb and finger as she had seen it done in old movies on TV. Then, laying his gun next to him, she rose and looked down at him one more time before starting toward the car, and town. She had intended to end her own life with his, but the gun was a derringer, holding only two cartridges. Typical of him, she decided. Inept and inconclusive. As though he could diminish his guilt by purchasing a less competent weapon. It was possible that he had extra ammunition on him, but she didn't want to touch him again, or to disturb his body. And besides, it didn't seem worth the trouble.